Have you ever played chess with someone really good? Perhaps with that cute guy at camp after lights-out? The game seems easy, but chess experts formulate their strategy dozens of moves in advance. You might feel manipulated when the game is done. Blindsided. Like you're the biggest idiot ever.

A certain someone does that to four pretty girls in Rosewood—again and again.

Once upon a time, there was a girl whose mind was like a never-ending chess game. Even when she seemed beaten, she always had a plan. Everyone was her adversary—especially the people who adored her most. All she wanted was her pieces to be the only ones left on the board at the end of the game.

And she wouldn't stop until she'd won.

BOOKS BY SARA SHEPARD

Pretty Little Liars
Flawless
Perfect
Unbelievable
Wicked
Killer
Heartless
Wanted
Twisted
Ruthless
Stunning
Burned
Crushed
Deadly
Toxic
Vicious
Pretty Little Secrets
Ali's Pretty Little Lies

The Perfectionists
The Good Girls

The Lying Game
Never Have I Ever
Two Truths and a Lie
Hide and Seek
Cross My Heart, Hope to Die
Seven Minutes in Heaven
The First Lie (a digital original novella)
True Lies (a digital original novella)

For Adults

The Heiresses
Everything We Ever Wanted
The Visibles

Toxic

A PRETTY LITTLE LIARS NOVEL

SARA SHEPARD

HARPER TEEN

An Imprint of HarperCollinsPublishers

alloy**entertainment**
Produced by Alloy Entertainment
1700 Broadway, New York, NY 10019

Library of Congress Control Number: 2014934802

ISBN 978-0-06-228702-1

Typography by Liz Dresner

15 16 17 18 19 CG/RRDH 10 9 8 7 6 5 4 3 2 1
❖
First paperback edition, 2015

To Volvo

If you poison us, do we not die?
And if you wrong us, shall we not revenge?

—WILLIAM SHAKESPEARE

YOUR MOVE, ALI

Have you ever played chess with someone really good? Perhaps with your cousin on a rainy afternoon? Or with that cute guy at camp after lights-out? The game seems easy, but chess experts formulate their strategy dozens of moves in advance. That way, they can hit you with sneak attacks, leaving you thinking, *What just happened?* You might feel manipulated when the game is done. Blindsided. Like you're the biggest idiot ever.

A certain someone does that to four pretty girls in Rosewood—again and again.

Once upon a time, there was a girl whose mind was like a never-ending chess game. Even when she seemed beaten, she always had a plan. Everyone was her adversary—especially the people who adored her most. All she wanted was her pieces to be the only ones left on the board at the end of the game.

And she wouldn't stop until she'd won.

* * *

One week after the fire in the Poconos that almost killed her, Alison DiLaurentis sat with her boyfriend, Nicholas Maxwell, on the floor of an empty town house in Rosewood, Pennsylvania, a suburban Philadelphia town in which she'd spent several years of her life. The room was dark, and the only items in it were a mattress, ratty flannel blankets, an old TV someone had abandoned, and food Nick had shoplifted from the nearby Wawa mini-mart. The air smelled dusty and sour, which reminded Ali of The Preserve at Addison-Stevens, the mental hospital in which she'd been trapped for years. Still, it would do for a while. It just felt good to be free.

"Turn it up," she said, gesturing toward the television.

Nick adjusted the dial. They were stealing electricity and cable from the main transformer in the complex—for a rich kid, Nick was great at ripping off The Man. The screen showed a live feed of police officers searching through a pile of rubble at Ali's family's vacation home in the Pocono Mountains. Ali knew full well what they were looking for: *her.* Or, more specifically, her bones.

"We're still searching," the chief of police said to an interviewer. "There was no way Ms. DiLaurentis survived that blast."

Ali snickered. *Idiots.*

Nick looked at her worriedly. "Are you okay?" He took her hand. "We can watch something else if you want."

Ali pulled the hoodie Nick had stolen from Target over her head, still self-conscious about the oozing burns on her face. They would heal—Nick had arranged for a nurse to come once a day—but she would never be as pretty as she once was. "Don't change it," she demanded. "I don't want any more surprises."

She'd already been surprised enough. Her foolproof plan of incinerating her sister's old friends, along with Melissa Hastings and Ian Thomas's body, inside her family's mountain house and then slipping into the night, never to be seen again, had backfired. Spencer Hastings, Emily Fields, Aria Montgomery, and Hanna Marin had escaped the house virtually unharmed. Somehow the cops had found the letter Ali had slipped under their door—it was in the grass outside the house. The letter confessed *everything*—that she wasn't Courtney, her twin, but the *real* Ali, a girl falsely imprisoned in a mental hospital. That she'd killed Courtney on the night of her seventh-grade graduation. That she'd killed Ian Thomas and Jenna Cavanaugh. And that she'd duped the girls into trusting her, and that she was going to kill them, too.

As luck would have it, the reporter on TV, a waxy-looking idiot with ugly fuchsia lipstick, was rehashing what the news was calling the Dark DiLaurentis Secrets—everything in that letter. "If she *had* lived, Miss DiLaurentis would be going to prison for the rest of her life for all the crimes she'd committed," she said gravely.

Nick bit his thumbnail. "I wish that letter hadn't been so definitive."

Ali rolled her eyes. "I told you to write all of that. Quit

worrying." Nick had been the one to write the letter to the girls, not Ali. She'd begged him to, saying he was better with words *and* could imitate her handwriting. Nick was always a sucker for flattery. His writing it was a key piece of a plan she'd hoped she would never have to put in place, one she didn't even like thinking about.

She peered at Nick now, and he stared back hungrily. Even in her ugly state—she also had a broken nose and horrid bruises, and she was missing a back tooth—there was such love and devotion in his eyes. She thought about the day she'd met him at The Preserve. It wasn't long after her sister made the fateful switch a few days into their sixth-grade year, sending Ali to the new mental hospital in her place. Ali had been at her first group therapy session, sitting in a circle with bona fide mental freaks.

"I shouldn't be here," she'd complained to the therapist, a tool named Dr. Brock. "I'm Alison, not Courtney. My sister tricked me, and now she's living my life."

Dr. Brock looked at her with his sad, dopey eyes. "Your doctors at the Radley said you had trouble with this. But you're Courtney. And it's *okay* to be Courtney. Hopefully we can work through that together."

Ali had stewed for the rest of the hour. After the session ended, someone touched her hand. "I know you're telling the truth," said a soft voice behind her. "I'm on your side."

Nick Maxwell had been staring at her fervently. Ali had noticed him at meals; he was a few years older, with wavy hair and strong shoulders. Every girl had a crush on him. Ali had also heard that he was in the hospital for borderline personality disorder. She'd been so bored during one-on-one therapy sessions that she'd read parts of the *Diagnostic and Statistical Manual of Mental Disorders* in her therapist's office; borderline-personality people were impulsive and reckless and extremely insecure.

Well, well, well. Ali *thrived* on insecurity. Maybe Nick was a good guy to have on her side.

And so she'd brought him into her fold. They planned everything, making sure not to be seen together too much so no one could connect them after everything went down. They developed a bond so deep and powerful, Nick compared it to Romeo and Juliet's. Ali thought it was cute that he had a mushy side.

Now she owed Nick so much. If it hadn't been for him, she wouldn't have been able to take down Ian and Jenna. She wouldn't have been able to stalk her sister's old best friends, slipping into the role as A. If Nick hadn't rescued her in the Poconos, she might have perished in that explosion—or the police would have caught her. Ali wouldn't have a roof over her head now. This town house was one of the many properties that Nick's family owned around the country, and she and Nick had chosen it because it had been unoccupied for months. Most of the other town houses were in foreclosure; others hadn't sold yet. Whole days had gone by when they didn't see a single car drive past.

There were new images on the TV screen. First was a video she'd seen quite a few times of her parents at the Philadelphia International Airport, running away as reporters hounded them. "Have you been in touch with your daughter?" the reporters cried. "Did you have any sense she was a murderer?" Ali's father turned around and stared into the camera lens, his eyes vacant. "Please leave us alone," he said in a tired voice. "We're as horrified by this situation as everyone else. Now we just want some peace."

Assholes, Ali thought. She hated her family almost as much as she hated her sister's friends.

Then, speak of the devil, those bitches popped up. It was a press conference. Spencer stood straight and proud in front of a microphone. Emily had her hands in her pockets. Hanna held hands with her boyfriend, Mike Montgomery. And Aria was sticking close to Noel Kahn as though they were stuck together by Velcro.

Noel. Ali stared at him hard. For a long time, Noel had shared her secret. Not anymore.

She turned to Nick, her hatred flaring hot. "We have to get them back."

He flinched. *"Really?"*

Ali lowered her shoulders. "Did you think I was going to let them get *away* with this?"

Nick looked panicked. "But you almost *died* last week. Is it really worth it? I mean, I have an untraceable bank account. We can use it to escape anywhere we want. You'll heal, we'll relax, and maybe, after a while, revenge won't matter so much anymore."

"It will *always* matter," Ali said tightly, her eyes blazing. She inched closer to Nick. "You said you'd do anything for me," she growled. "Were you lying?"

A frightened look passed across Nick's face. "Fine. What do you want to do?"

Ali turned back to the press conference. Spencer had started speaking. "We're all looking just to move past this and get on with our lives," she said in a loud, clear voice. "There are more important things in the world for the press to focus on instead of us. We mourn for Courtney DiLaurentis and her family. We even mourn for Alison; may she rest in peace."

Ali rolled her eyes. "They are *so* lame."

"What are you going to do now?" a reporter bellowed to the girls.

Emily Fields came to the microphone next. She looked sick, like she was going to throw up. "We've been given the opportunity to travel to Jamaica for spring break," she said shakily. "I think it's a good thing for us to get out of Rosewood for a little while."

Nick sniffed. "*I* wouldn't mind going to Jamaica."

Something clicked. "Can you get us passports?" Ali asked.

Nick's eyebrows made a V. "Probably. *Why?*"

Ali grabbed his hands, an idea forming in her mind. "No one will be looking for us there. We get to get out of here, just like you want. *And* we get those girls, just like *I* want."

"How?" Nick asked warily.

"I'm not sure yet. But I'll figure it out."

Nick looked uncertain. "You aren't letting those girls see you. There are cops in other countries. They can still turn you in."

"Then I find someone who will impersonate me."

"Who's going to do that?"

Ali's eyes darted back and forth as she pondered the options. A light snapped on. *"Tabitha."*

Tabitha Clark was another patient at The Preserve, a sweet, tormented little slip of a blonde who idolized Ali and was a genius at imitating Ali's voice and gestures. She looked even more like an Ali clone than Iris Taylor, who'd been Ali's roommate. Even better, Tabitha had burns on her arms from a fire. The girls would see those, make the Poconos connection, and lose their minds.

"She's out of The Preserve," Ali said, leaping to her feet. "She'll do anything for me. Get in touch with her. Tell her it's all expenses paid. Make it out like it's a fun little holiday. Will you?"

Nick pinched the bridge of his nose. "Okay." He gave her a warning look. "But you have to promise that after Jamaica, we move on to the Bahamas. Or maybe Fiji. We disappear . . . *for real.*"

"Of course." Ali drew him into her arms. *"Thank* you. You're the best boyfriend ever."

Nick kissed the tip of her nose. Then he scowled and clamped a hand around her wrists. "After Jamaica, you're going to be my prisoner," he said in a deep, grumbling voice. "I won't have to share you with anyone. No family. No friends. You'll be my captive . . . *forever*."

"I'm at your mercy," Ali said in a fake, high-pitched drawl. But inside, she laughed. As *if* Nick would ever control her.

Ali *was* at Nick's mercy, though—it was his money and cunning know-how that got the tickets and fake passports to Jamaica. But she also knew Nick would stick by her if Jamaica didn't go according to plan. And when things *did* go wrong and they had to regroup, lay the groundwork for framing the girls, and get them on even *bigger* secrets than ones they'd ever kept, he helped every step of the way. When she and Nick had to return to Rosewood instead of escaping to other Caribbean islands and plant Nick in key roles in each of the girls' lives to orchestrate their downfalls, he'd done it so willingly and devotedly. Ali put Nick through trial after trial, positioning him as a drug dealer, a bartender, even dragging him to Iceland and forcing him to woo Aria and steal a painting. And Nick—sweet, sensitive, borderline-personality Nick—complied again and again, so dutiful, so loving. Her perfect little soldier.

We'll leave after they're in jail, Ali convinced him. And then, later: *We'll leave after they die. And if they don't die, well, we'll both go down together.*

But even that was a white lie. Deep down, Ali had been laying another set of tracks, a just-in-case plan Nick didn't know about. It started with that letter he'd written to the girls for her, and it ended with the video of him killing Tabitha alone. There were other things, too. Things she'd done when Nick wasn't looking, using pliers and wincing in pain, using a leaky pen and her imagination. Last-ditch-effort things, only in play if she was pushed to her most desperate limits.

The only thing that mattered was that those bitches died.

Only then would she be done.

1

HANNA'S BIG BREAK

On a warm Monday morning in mid-June, Hanna Marin walked into Poole's, an old-fashioned ice-cream parlor in downtown Rosewood. The inside hadn't changed since Hanna had been here last—the same penny candy under the glass, black-and-white checkerboard floor, wrought-iron stools and tables, and long, marbled counter. The owners even offered the same flavors of ice cream, including the Phillies Fundae, a sundae in honor of the Philadelphia Phillies baseball team. Just breathing in the heavenly scent of homemade waffle cones and cookies-and-cream ice cream made Hanna's empty stomach growl.

Her old friends Aria Montgomery, Spencer Hastings, and Emily Fields were in a back booth underneath a large poster of a 1950s-styled girl daintily eating a banana split. It had been two weeks since Hanna had seen them, but she and the others had received a note from Emily asking if they could talk today. It was pretty obvious what Emily wanted to talk about. Hanna wasn't sure, though, if she was ready.

"Hey, Han." Spencer slid over to make room. The others said hi, too.

Hanna threw her leather satchel on the seat and sat down. For a moment, silence hung over them. Spencer sipped a cup of the parlor's famous fresh-brewed coffee, her blond hair falling in her face. Aria picked at a bowl of sherbet. Emily peeled off a wrapper of a Charleston Chew.

"So," Hanna finally said, "what's *new*?"

Everyone chuckled awkwardly. Hanna hoped *nothing* was new with them. The last few months had been a whirlwind of activity—and hell. First, a diabolical text-messager who called herself A had returned, tormenting each of them with their secrets. After all *that*, A had framed them in the murder of Tabitha Clark, a girl they'd gotten in an altercation with while in Jamaica on spring break of their junior year. The police had false evidence showing all four of them beating Tabitha to death.

It was clear who was behind it: Alison DiLaurentis, their old best friend's twin sister. Two weeks ago, the girls traced Ali to an old, abandoned house in Rosewood. But Ali and her boyfriend, Nick Maxwell, had trapped the girls in the basement and pumped in noxious, suffocating gas. The police had saved everyone just in time, and Nick had been arrested.

But Ali? She'd slipped away, unseen. Without a trace.

Aria looked at Spencer. "Did you have a good vacation?"

Spencer shrugged. Her family had gone to their house in Longboat Key, Florida, for two weeks, and she'd just gotten back. "I beat Amelia at tennis." She looked at Hanna. "How was Cabo with your mom?"

"Not too bad," Hanna murmured. Unexpectedly, her mom had swooped in after Hanna was released from the hospital and announced that the two of them were going to Mexico. "And I'm not bringing work," Ashley Marin had even added—a huge shocker, as her mom practically conducted conference calls in the shower. They'd spent the week tanning, drinking virgin margaritas, and rating hot surfers. It'd been actually kind of . . . *fun*.

Aria pouted. "I'm jealous you guys got to go somewhere. I was stuck here all this time."

Emily raised a finger. "I was stuck here, too. Thinking about Ali." She lowered her eyes.

Hanna shuddered at Ali's name . . . but it was inevitable. They were bound to get around to her soon enough.

"I can't stop thinking about her," Emily admitted. "How was there *no* trace of her in that house?" Forensic teams had swept the crime scene after pulling the girls and Nick out, and though they had found tons of *pictures* of Ali—Nick had set it up like an Ali shrine—they didn't uncover a single fingerprint. The cops were back to thinking Ali had died in the Poconos.

"Well, we know what we saw," Hanna mumbled, that night still haunting her. Ali had looked so . . . *crazed*. She'd raised a gun to Emily's head. The gun had gone off . . . but the next thing Hanna remembered, Hanna and the others were lying in hospital beds. Alive. What had happened in between?

Aria cleared her throat. "Has anyone heard how Iris is doing?"

All the girls shook their heads. Iris Taylor had been Ali's roommate at The Preserve, though she'd recently spent some time with Emily, giving her clues about what Ali had been like and who she'd been involved with. After helping Emily, Iris had been kidnapped by Nick and Ali, and the FBI had found her half-dead in the woods. Iris was recuperating now at a local hospital.

"What about this?" Emily said, pushing that day's edition of the *Philadelphia Sentinel* to the middle of the table. Nick, clad in an orange prison jumpsuit, stared out from the front page. MAXWELL CLAIMS HE WORKED ALONE, read the headline.

"He's on trial for killing Tabitha," Emily paraphrased. "And get this: Police found a late-model Acura sedan parked in the woods behind that shack. Nick's fingerprints were all over it."

Spencer's eyes lit up. "There was an Acura keychain at my stepfather's model home after it was trashed. That explains *that*, anyway."

Hanna pulled the paper toward her. "What does Nick say about Ali?"

"He's insisting that Ali died in the fire in the Poconos," Emily said. "And he denies that Ali had anything to do with killing Tabitha, or stalking us, or being there that night in that house."

"So he's taking the blame for everything?" Hanna made a face. "What crazy person would do that?"

"Well, he *was* a patient at The Preserve," Spencer reminded her. "Maybe he's under Ali's spell."

Aria rolled her eyes. "How could *anyone* be under her spell?"

An uncomfortable look crossed Spencer's face. She brought out her cell phone and placed it in the center of the table. "Nick's not the only one."

Hanna looked at the screen. THE ALI CATS, said a banner at the top. A WEBSITE DEDICATED TO THE SUPPORT OF ALISON DILAURENTIS. ALISON IS A STRONG, DETERMINED, MISUNDERSTOOD YOUNG WOMAN, AND WE HOPE THAT SOMEDAY THE WORLD WILL KNOW THE TRUE HER. HEAR US ROAR, ALI!

Aria's eyes widened. "What *is* this?"

"A fan club," Spencer explained hoarsely. "I found it about a week ago. I was *hoping* it would go away, though."

"'A strong, determined, misunderstood young woman'?" Emily made a face. "And 'someday the world will know the true her'? Do they think she's alive?"

Spencer shook her head. "It seems like more of an in-memory-of thing. There are posts about parties where everyone dresses like Ali and—get this—*reenacts* the Poconos fire scene. Except they have Ali get out alive. Some of them write fan fiction about what Ali did next. They're actually *selling* it on Amazon."

Hanna shuddered. "That's gross."

Aria folded her paper napkin into smaller and smaller triangles. "Maybe we should contact one of them. Maybe they *do* know something."

Spencer sniffed. "I tried that. But they all go by code names. And anyway, why do you think they'd tell us?"

"These people could be *dangerous*," Emily said worriedly. Aria looked at the newspaper again. "I wish we could get Nick to admit he's lying."

"How?" Hanna folded her hands. "It's not like we can go to the prison and just force it out of him."

"Maybe there's a way to trick him into confessing," Emily suggested. "Or—"

"*Or* we could let this go," Spencer interrupted.

Everyone fell silent. Hanna gawked. "Are you serious?" Spencer had always been at the front of the let's-find-Ali crusade. She'd suggested they have a situation room to try to figure out who Ali's helper was. She hadn't wanted to drop the idea of sniffing Ali out even after the girls were arrested.

Spencer fiddled with her silver Tiffany keychain. "This has ruined almost two years of our lives. I'm just . . . done, you know? And I haven't received any new A notes. Have you guys?"

Emily muttered no; so did Aria. Hanna reluctantly shook her head, too. She kept expecting a new note to ping into her in-box, though. "That doesn't mean we should give up," she said weakly. "Ali's *out there*."

"But how useful is Ali without Nick by her side?" Spencer pressed. "She's probably hanging by a thread."

"An Ali Cat might help her," Emily reminded.

"I suppose that's true." Spencer turned her phone over in her hands. "But they sound like crackpots, don't they?" She balled up her napkin. "It sucks that Ali's walking free. It sucks that Nick took all the blame, but hey, if he wants to rot in jail, that's his choice. But *we* need to live our lives." She looked at Hanna. "Speaking of which. Doesn't summer school start today?"

Hanna nodded. Rosewood Day had dropped her and the others after they were charged with murder, but now the girls were allowed to graduate if they completed their course requirements. The Fashion Institute of Technology, the college that had accepted her, even said it would hold a place for her in the fall as long as her final grades were acceptable. The other girls had been given similar offers—except for Aria, who had chosen to take a gap year. "I have history in a half hour." She looked at the others. "When do you guys start?"

"I have to repeat chemistry, but it starts tomorrow," Emily answered.

"All I have to do is submit my AP Art portfolio and take my finals," Aria said. "Most of my classes wound down before we were kicked out of school."

"Same," Spencer said. Then she stood. "Well, come on, Han. You shouldn't be late."

The other girls stood, too, giving one another tight

hugs. They exited into the bright day, promising to call one another later. And then, just like that, the meeting was over, and Hanna was alone on the street. She wasn't sure what to think about everything they'd discussed. As much as she wanted to take Spencer up on just letting Ali go, it was terrifying to think Ali was out there . . . roaming free. Plotting. Scheming.

A high-pitched screech of a semitruck sounded from around the corner. Laughter echoed from an alleyway. Suddenly, goose bumps rose on Hanna's arms, and she got that old, nagging feeling that someone was watching.

There's no one here, she told herself determinedly.

She shaded her eyes and started the few blocks to Rosewood Day Prep, a sprawling compound of stone and brick buildings that had once belonged to a railroad baron. It was amazing how different the place looked now that it was summer. The regal blue-and-white Rosewood Day flag, complete with the Rosewood Day crest, was absent from the flagpole. The marble fountain in front of the gym was dry. The swings and the climbing dome on the Lower School's playground weren't full of screaming little kids, and no ubiquitous yellow school buses lined the curbs.

Hanna pushed open the main door to the Upper School. The halls were deserted, and the floors looked like they hadn't been swept since the regular school year let out. Every poster advertising class elections, upcoming dances, or charity drives had been removed from the walls, leaving behind faded spots of painted concrete. No between-classes classical music blared from the PA system. Some of the lockers were wide open and empty like dark, gaping caves. Hanna pressed one door lightly; it squeaked spookily on its hinges.

A shadow shifted at the end of the hall, and Hanna froze. Then a deep laugh spiraled from another direction. She turned just in time to see a figure slipping, ghostlike, up the stairs. Her heart began to pound. *Stay calm. You are being paranoid.*

She tiptoed to the history wing and peered into her classroom. The air smelled like sweat, and only the back rows were occupied. A boy wearing a dingy Phillies cap traced a pattern into the wooden desk with the pointy end of a key. A girl with dreadlocks was facedown, snoring. A kid in the corner with vacant eyes was reading what looked like *Playboy*.

Then she heard a cough and whirled around. A boy with bad posture and a knitted cap whom she didn't recognize was standing way too close. There was a weird smirk on his face.

"H-hello?" she sputtered, heart lurching again. "Can I help you?"

The boy lazily smiled. "You're Hanna Marin." He pointed at her. "I *know* you."

Then he slid past her and entered the classroom.

Her phone began to ring, causing Hanna to shriek and press her body against the lockers. But it was just Mike

Montgomery, her boyfriend. "Are you in school yet?" he asked.

Hanna made an *uh-huh* sound, still feeling her pulse rocket at her temples. "It's a little like *Night of the Living Dead*, though. Who *are* all these kids? I've never seen them before."

"It was the same way when I took driver's ed last summer. They keep summer school kids hidden in the utility closet during the year. I wish I could come down there and keep you safe. Maybe I should take the first bus back."

Hanna chuckled shakily. Ever since she'd told Mike that Ali was back on the scene, he'd become her de facto bodyguard. The other day, before he'd left for soccer camp in New Hampshire, she'd squealed at a spider on her front porch, and Mike had swooped in like a superhero. He'd also been hypervigilant whenever she received a text, checking her expression for worry or fear. He'd asked her a million times if he really should go to camp for the whole month. *You might need me* had been his excuse.

"You're not getting on a bus," Hanna demanded now, watching as a few more people brushed past. And okay, they all were wearing ugly shoes and weren't usually kids *she* hung around with, but they didn't look quite as zombielike. "I can handle a few weirdos."

Then she hung up. Seconds later, her phone pinged again. *Good luck on your first day of school!* her mom wrote. *Let's get dinner tonight to celebrate!*

Hanna smiled. For years, she'd leaned on her dad, but

that had changed once and for all the day she was arrested for Tabitha's murder and her dad told her that associating with her was "wrecking his political campaign." Amazingly, her mom had taken the reins, and she was actually trying really hard to be present. Last night, they'd even gone to Otter, Hanna's favorite boutique, for a "back to summer school" outfit—the striped minidress and dove-gray ankle boots Hanna was wearing today.

Sounds good, she texted back. Then she walked into the classroom, her heels clicking noisily, her auburn hair bouncing on her shoulders. The sun streamed through the long windows so prettily that she suddenly felt a contented sense of well-being. So what if she had to repeat history class with a bunch of D-listers? At least she'd get to graduate. The press and the town didn't hate her anymore, or think she was a murderer. And she still had her friends, an amazing boyfriend, and now, for the first time ever, a mom who actually cared. Maybe they *should* let this Ali stuff go and just enjoy their lives.

The only seats left were in the front row, so Hanna plopped down, arranged her dress around her, and waited for the teacher to arrive. Her phone rang again. The call was from an area code she didn't recognize, which always set her on edge.

"Hanna Marin?" blared a voice once Hanna said a tentative hello. "My name is Felicia Silver. I'm the executive producer of *Burn It Down*. It's the true story about your terrible ordeal with Alison DiLaurentis."

Hanna suppressed a groan. That sounded like another

Pretty Little Killer, the made-for-TV movie that docu-
mented Hanna and the others' *first* struggle with Ali. God,
that movie was awful. Every part of it: the sets, the script,
the frumpy girl who had been cast as Hanna. For a while,
it had been on every week. Hanna used to have to endure
kids quoting scenes in the locker room and at lunch. Did
the world really need *another* movie about her life?

"I know what you're thinking—that made-for-TV thing
was crap." Felicia chomped on gum as she talked. "But
this one is going to be different. In theaters. With serious
actors and a great script. *And* we're filming right here in
Rosewood, so we're going to get the ambience just right."

"Huh," Hanna said, surprised. She hadn't seen any
film trucks or equipment.

"Anyway, the reason I'm calling is because of *you*,
Hanna," Felicia said. "I've seen you in the commercials
with your father. The camera loves you."

Hanna blushed. Before her father disowned her, they'd
filmed some campaign ads together, including a "Don't
Drink and Drive" public service announcement. Hanna
didn't want to brag, but she thought she'd nailed it, too.

"I want to offer you a part in the movie," Felicia went
on. "It would be *amazing* publicity for us—and a fun
experience for you, we hope. We were thinking of you as
Naomi Zeigler—someone small but still crucial. She has a
big role in the cruise ship scenes."

Uh, yeah, Hanna almost blurted—she'd *lived* those
scenes. But then she realized what Felicia had offered.

"You want me to have an actual speaking role?"

"That's right. Here's your chance to show the world that you've put that nonsense behind you, and now you're a fabulous actress. What do you say?"

Hanna's mind whirled. She wanted to tell Felicia that maybe they *hadn't* put the nonsense behind them . . . but Felicia would probably think she was nuts. *Should* she do it? Spencer had always been the drama girl, starring in every school play, memorizing Ibsen monologues just for the hell of it, and always wanting to do improv exercises during sleepovers. But it *was* tempting. Would this movie have a red-carpet premiere in Hollywood? Would she get to *go*?

Still, she wasn't sure. "I don't know," she said slowly. "I'll have to think about it."

"Actually, we have to know now," Felicia said, suddenly sounding impatient. "C'mon, Hanna. It'll be an amazing experience. Hank Ross is directing. And guess who's playing you! Hailey Blake!"

Hanna's mouth dropped open. Hailey Blake was a beautiful, glittering, überfamous young starlet who'd been a presence in Hanna's consciousness for years, starting with her starring role as Quintana in *Abracadabra*, Hanna's favorite Disney show. After that, she'd gone on to do a slew of cool teen movies. Most recently, she'd hosted the Teen Choice Awards and shared a kiss onstage with her cohost, the sexy guy from *Bitten*, a hot vampire movie. And if this movie was good enough for *Hailey* . . .

"I guess I can give it a try," she heard herself say.

"Fabulous!" Felicia crowed. "I'll email you the details."

Hanna hung up, still in a daze. She was going to be in a movie . . . *with Hailey Blake.* A *real* movie, with a red-carpet premiere. Red-carpet premieres also meant film festivals in Sundance and Cannes, didn't they? And all that meant interviews with Ryan Seacrest and all those people on E! Maybe she could do a guest spot on *Fashion Police*! She *and* Hailey, together!

All at once, her future unfurled before her, bright and glittering. For the first time, something actually *positive* might come out of the A nightmare.

2

TORTURED ARTIST

Aria Montgomery steered her family's rattling, sputtering, rusty Subaru into a parking space in Old Hollis, an artsy neighborhood resplendent with uneven sidewalks, shabby-chic Victorian houses, and out-of-control gardens (some of which yielded nothing but marijuana plants). The sun streamed across the leafy street in bright, broad stripes. A child's bicycle was tipped over one lawn, and across the street was an abandoned lemonade stand with a sign that said ALL ORGANIC INGREDIENTS!

"Hey!" Aria's mom, Ella, crowed as Aria walked through the door of the Olde Hollis Gallery, where she'd worked since the family moved back from Iceland two years ago. Ella's dark hair was pulled into a messy bun, and she wore a long, gauzy skirt and a ribbed tank top that showed off her toned arms. Bracelets jangled on her wrist, and huge turquoise earrings swung from her earlobes. She hugged Aria tight, giving off a strong scent of patchouli oil. Ella had really been into hugging lately. She'd been into giving long, meaningful looks, too. Aria had a feeling her latest attack by A had really thrown her mom for a loop.

"Want to help me set up this show?" Ella asked, gesturing at a bunch of paintings tipped against the walls around the room. The artist, an old, hairy-eared guy named Franklin Hodgewell, had shown at the gallery a zillion times before, and his works of eastern Pennsylvania landscapes, flocks of geese, and Amish buggies were tried-and-true big sellers. "I mean, only if you want to," Ella added quickly. "If you have something else to do, that's okay, too."

"Nope, I can help." Aria picked up a painting of a barn and placed it on a hook. "I can help with the cocktail party, too, if you want."

"If *you* want," Ella said tentatively, giving her a long look.

Since Nick's attack, Aria had spent almost every minute at the gallery. There were legitimate reasons. One, she *did* have a job here, though her hours were only part-time. Two, it felt good to be near her strong, stable, comforting mom. And three, she didn't have anything better to do.

She knew her mom thought it was weird. And she knew the question Ella was dying to ask: What *was* Aria going to do with herself this summer . . . and next year? Her friends had applied to colleges, and if they completed their course credits, they would still be able to matriculate in the fall. Aria had planned to take a gap year and travel through Europe, but now the idea of going to a foreign country alone sounded daunting. Maybe that was because the *last* time she'd gone abroad, back to Iceland, she'd been embroiled in an international art scandal *and* she'd met Nick, Ali's crazy boyfriend, disguised as a sexy vigilante named Olaf.

She'd halfheartedly considered signing up for an artist retreat in Oregon, but the application deadline was last week. Then she'd toyed with the idea of taking art classes at the University of the Arts in Philly, but the first day had come and gone.

She felt . . . stuck. And freaked. It seemed like whenever Aria shut her eyes, Ali's face shimmered into her mind. She'd looked so creepy the last time they saw her, like a hollowed-out corpse. The image haunted her so completely that, in hopes of expunging it from her brain, she'd painted Ali's likeness on a huge canvas in the back of the gallery. She'd painted *two* versions of Ali, actually: one of the most recent Ali, the girl she saw in the basement of that dilapidated building next to Hanna's father's office; the second a portrait of the old Ali, the unattainable, überpopular girl from the beginning of sixth grade. Aria had used an old sketch of Ali she'd drawn the day Ali tore down the Time Capsule poster outside Rosewood Day and announced that she was going to get a piece of the Time Capsule flag. It was from before the twin switch happened. Before Courtney DiLaurentis approached the four of them at the charity drive and asked them to be her besties.

Once she'd finished helping Ella, Aria stepped into the back room and dared to examine both Ali paintings more closely. Usually, she had trouble with portraits—she'd painted a ton of Noel Kahn, her maybe-ex-boyfriend, and none of them quite captured his essence. But Ali's *Ali-ness* had flowed from Aria's brush, every feature chilling and precise. Just by looking at the canvases, she could almost smell Ali's rotting breath and felt a shiver when she examined her wide, furious eyes. When Aria turned and peered at sixth-grade Ali, the girl's condescending smirk made her feel as small and insignificant as that day Aria had sat alone on the wall at Rosewood Day sketching her.

She backed out of the room and shut the door. Spending too much time with Ali's *portraits* even freaked her out.

She looked around the main gallery space for something to do, but it wasn't her shift, and the two assistants on duty, Bernie and Sierra, were bored themselves. Suddenly, a figure out the window caught her eye. Her heart leapt into her throat.

Noel.

"Be back in a sec," she muttered to her mom, darting out the door.

Noel was halfway up the block by the time Aria hit the sidewalk. "Hey!" she called out. "Noel?"

He turned around. The bruises on his face from when Ali and Nick had trapped him in a storage shed behind Rosewood Day on prom night had healed, and his dark hair had grown out a little, curling below his ears. When he saw Aria, though, his expression became guarded.

Heartbreak filled her. When they were together, Noel had always been so happy to see her, even if she interrupted him in the middle of lacrosse practice. He'd always run toward her, his arms outstretched. Did Aria *want* him to do that now? No. Yes. *No.* She'd been the one who'd told Noel they couldn't be together—he'd lied to her for years about knowing the truth about Ali and even visiting her at The Preserve. But lately, she'd begun to second-guess that decision. Everyone made mistakes. Maybe she could forgive Noel.

And *God*, did she miss him.

"H-hey," Aria said nervously as she approached. "Thanks for the text." She had sent Noel a few texts lately, just saying hi, hoping to broach a conversation. Finally, Noel had written back, a simple *hi*. Maybe it was a sign.

Noel's brow crinkled for a moment. "Oh. Right. No problem."

An aching silence followed. Aria pretended to be interested in a bumper sticker on the back of a passing Honda Civic. "What are you doing in this neighborhood, anyway?" she asked finally. *Say you came to see me*, she willed.

Noel shuffled his feet. "I'm taking an English class at Hollis so I can skip the course requirement next year. A bunch of kids are taking it. Mason, Riley Wolfe . . ."

Aria started to giggle. "Remember the time you told me you thought Riley looked like a leprechaun?"

Noel looked pained. "Um, I should get going."

Aria grabbed at him. "Wait!" she bleated, hating how desperate she sounded. "Um, maybe we could have coffee soon or something? Or there's that fund-raiser at the country club—maybe we could go together?" A bunch of society ladies in Rosewood were throwing a party to benefit Rosewood's disadvantaged and troubled youths, and the whole town was invited. It was kind of ironic, as wealthy, privileged Rosewood really didn't *have* many disadvantaged or troubled youths. Ali had kind of been a one-off.

Noel shifted. "I'm busy that night."

"Oh!" Aria cringed at how chirpy her voice came out. "Well, maybe a movie sometime?"

He kept his eyes on the pavement. "Actually, I think I just need some space right now, Aria. I'm sorry."

Aria blinked. "Sure. Okay." A feeling of hurt surged through her chest. She thought about when she'd seen Noel in the hospital after her attack. *I believe you*, he'd said, referring to them seeing Ali. *I'll always believe you.* He'd seemed so loving and concerned. But that was two weeks ago. It was as if he'd forgotten it happened.

"Well, see ya," was all she could manage now.

"See ya." Noel waved. A few paces away, he pulled out his phone and tapped on the screen.

She counted to ten, but Noel didn't turn around. Her throat itched, and she could feel that the tears were imminent. The bells that Jim, the gallery owner, had purchased on a trip to India jingled as she stepped back inside.

Ella lowered the canvas in her hands. "Aria?" Her voice cracked. "Was that Noel? Are you okay?"

"I just . . ." Aria put her head down and stomped past her. The humiliation was probably clear on her face, but she did *not* want to talk about it.

She disappeared into the back room, shut the door, and locked it, then let the tears fall. She glared at the Ali paintings through blurred vision. This was all her fault. Everything was her fault.

She grabbed the sixth-grade Ali one, enraged by her taunting expression. *You'll always be under my thumb*, Ali seemed to tease. With jerky, hurried movements, Aria rammed the thing onto an easel and grabbed her oil paints from the windowsill. She squirted some black paint on a wooden palette and made broad, obsidian slashes with her fattest brush, covering Ali's shiny hair, her flawless skin, and that hateful smile. She painted and painted until the entire canvas was black except for one small triangle around Ali's eye. A single blue eyeball stared out at Aria. But even *that* was too Ali. Too much.

So Aria painted over it, too.

3

THE WRITE STUFF

Monday night, a valet in a white shirt and red pants extended his hand as Spencer Hastings climbed out of her stepfather's Range Rover. "Welcome to the Four Seasons, miss," he said in a smooth voice. "Do you need help with anything?"

Spencer smiled. She *loved* luxury hotels. "I'm fine," she said, turning to watch as her mother; her stepfather, Mr. Pennythistle; her fifteen-year-old stepsister, Amelia; her older sister, Melissa; and Melissa's boyfriend, Darren Wilden, climbed out of the car next. They looked like a Brooks Brothers advertisement, the men in dark suits, the ladies in tasteful black cocktail dresses—even Amelia, who usually dressed like an American Girl doll.

The family headed toward the grand ballroom, where they were attending a fete honoring the Fifty Most Prominent Philadelphians. Mr. Pennythistle was on the list because his homebuilding company had put up so many new developments in the suburbs. Spencer wasn't a fan of her stepfather's cookie-cutter, Stepford Wife–esque housing plans, but it was awesome to see his name on a large plaque and in *Philadelphia* magazine. And after the hellish few months she'd had, a fancy party with dancing and drinks might take her mind off things.

"Cocktail?" a waitress holding a tray of martinis said to the group.

Spencer glanced at her mother. Mrs. Hastings nodded. "Only one."

Spencer grinned and grabbed a glass from the tray. To her delight, Mr. Pennythistle shook his head before Amelia could ask.

Then Spencer turned to Melissa, about to ask her if she'd like a drink, too. Melissa was scowling at something on her cell phone.

"What is it?" Spencer asked, moving closer.

Melissa's face creased with worry. "It's an article talking about how there are numerous fake As all over the country."

Darren scowled. "I told you to stop reading that stuff."

Melissa swished him away, squinting at the little screen. "It says here that a group of girls in Ohio got so many A notes that one of them *killed* the girl who was doing it."

"Ugh." Spencer leaned over to look, too. There was a sidebar about the Ali Cats, Ali's psycho fan club. MEMBERS OF THE ALI CATS HAVE BEEN HOLDING CANDLELIGHT VIGILS IN VARIOUS LOCATIONS, PRAYING THAT ALISON DILAURENTIS IS STILL ALIVE. "THE MEDIA HAS SPUN THIS STORY ONLY ONE WAY, JUST LIKE

THEY ALWAYS DO," SAID A WOMAN WHO ASKED TO REMAIN ANON-
YMOUS. "BUT ALISON IS A BRAVE, UNIQUE INDIVIDUAL WHO IS A
VICTIM OF STIGMA, PREJUDICE, AND INTOLERANCE. SHAME ON ALL
THOSE WHO CANNOT SEE THAT."

An oily feeling filled her. *A victim of prejudice and intolerance? What was that lady smoking?*

It was so frustrating. Spencer had told her friends she
wanted to let Ali go—before this mess, she'd been accepted
to Princeton, and she'd recently heard from the Princeton
admissions committee that there was a good chance she
could still attend as long as she aced her final exams. But
forgetting Ali was easier said than done; Ali kept popping up. And those Ali Cats—it was insane. How could
they worship someone who had *murdered* practically half
of Rosewood?

As soon as Spencer had discovered the Ali Cats, she'd
felt an itch to retaliate. Taking them down didn't seem
like an option—they had a right to form whatever weirdo
group they wanted. Instead, she'd created a website for
other people who'd been bullied, a safe forum for kids
to share their experiences and feelings. So far, it had gotten pretty decent traction; she had almost two thousand
"likes" on the blog's Facebook link. Every heartbreaking
new bullying response she received on Facebook, Twitter,
or email just reaffirmed how necessary a site like this was.
There were *so many* people who'd suffered from bullying,
some at much worse a cost than Spencer. Maybe putting
these stories out there would stop it from happening,

somehow. Or at least slow it down.

"I wish people would find something else to obsess over," Melissa said angrily, slipping her phone back into her purse.

Spencer nodded. She wanted to talk to her sister about Ali still being alive, but so far, Melissa hadn't seemed open to the conversation. Spencer could understand. Melissa was probably sick of thinking about it, too.

Then Melissa's eyes lit up. "Oh my God, there's Kim from Wharton! We have to say hi!"

She clutched Darren's hand, and they flitted off into the crowd. Spencer gazed around the room once more. Someone giggled behind her, and she suddenly felt an eerie prickle on the skin of her arms. This place was so crowded, and there was barely any security. It seemed like a perfect place for Ali to hide.

Stop thinking about her, Spencer scolded silently, smoothing down her hair and taking another sip of the martini. She drifted toward the bar. Only one barstool was free, and Spencer settled into it and grabbed a handful of mixed nuts from a small bowl. She gazed at her reflection in the long mirror behind the bar. Her blond hair shone, her blue eyes were bright, and her skin was a golden color from the week she'd spent in Florida. But it was pretty much wasted here— everyone was over forty. Besides, Spencer didn't want to get mixed up in another relationship. All guys ever gave her were trouble and heartbreak.

"Excuse me, are you Spencer Hastings?"

Spencer turned and stared into the eyes of a young woman in a gray pin-striped suit and brown pumps. "Yes, but I've forgotten your name," she said, figuring the woman was one of Mr. Pennythistle's business associates. He had a rotating cast of businesspeople over for cocktails.

"That's because I haven't told you yet." The woman smiled. "It's Alyssa Bloom." She set her glass of white wine on the counter. "My goodness, my dear. You've been through so much."

"Oh, well, you know." Spencer felt her cheeks redden.

"How does it feel for everything to actually be *over*?" Alyssa Bloom said. "You must be so thrilled, I would think."

Spencer bit her lip. *It's not over*, she wanted to say.

Ms. Bloom took a tiny sip of her wine. "I'm assuming you've heard about the Alison groupies? What do they call themselves again?"

"The Ali Cats," Spencer groaned automatically.

"And the copycat As all over the country?" The woman sniffed. "It's dreadful. It's not the lesson people should be learning."

Spencer nodded. "No one should have to go through what I did," she admitted. It was the response she often gave the kids who wrote to her blog with their stories.

The look in the woman's eyes indicated she wanted Spencer to say more. But suddenly, Spencer felt paranoid. Who was this Alyssa Bloom? Lately, Spencer had received a lot of calls from insidious, gotcha-journalism types who tried to lure her into a conversation just to get her to say something stupid.

"I'm sorry, what is it you do?" Spencer blurted.

Ms. Bloom reached into her jacket pocket and handed her a card. Spencer stared down at it. *Alyssa Bloom*, it said. *Editor. HarperCollins Publishing, New York.*

Spencer was speechless for a few beats. "You work in publishing?"

Ms. Bloom smiled. "That's right."

"Meaning you publish books?" Spencer wanted to smack herself for sounding so idiotic. "I'm sorry," she back-tracked. "It's just that I've never spoken to an editor before. And actually, I've always seen myself as an author." She'd thought that ever since she came up with a book series idea with Courtney years ago. It was about field hockey–playing fairies who shape-shifted into supermodels, and Spencer and Courtney had written almost half of the first novel. Well, *Spencer* had written it. Courtney had directed from the sidelines.

Ms. Bloom leaned into one hip. "Well, if you have any ideas, I'd love to hear them. I'd love to talk about your blog sometime, too."

Spencer's eyes widened. "You've heard of my blog?"

Ms. Bloom nodded. "Sure. Bullying's a hot topic, and you've started something very interesting." Then her phone rang, and she shot Spencer a tight smile. "Sorry. I've got to take this." She pointed to the card in Spencer's hand. "Call me sometime. Nice to meet you."

Then the editor whirled away, her phone pressed to her ear. Spencer's mind started to race. Princeton would *have* to let her in if she wrote a book. Even Melissa hadn't done that.

"Can I get you something?"

The bartender was smiling at her from behind the counter. Spencer felt her spirits lift even higher. All at once, everything felt so shiny and new. Possible. *Amazing*.

"You can get me another martini." She slid her empty glass toward him. What the hell? She'd just gotten a business card from an editor of a huge publishing house.

That was totally a reason to celebrate.

4

ORANGE IS THE NEW ROMANTIC

On Tuesday morning, Emily Fields sat at a high table in a Rosewood Day chemistry classroom. A periodic table hung on the wall, along with a poster describing the electron arrangements of various basic molecules. Bunsen burners were lined up in a glass cabinet, and the drawers along the back held flasks, beakers, and other lab equipment. The teacher, a frizzy-haired woman named Ms. Payton whom Emily had never met before—she suspected Rosewood Day's regular staff wouldn't set foot in the place during the summer—stood at the board, turning a silver ring on her finger around and around. All the students except for Emily were talking, texting, or rooting through their bags, and one girl was even sitting on the windowsill, an entire Chick-fil-A meal spread out on her lap.

"Now, if you look at the next item on the syllabus," Ms. Payton said in a wavering voice, adjusting the wire-rimmed glasses on her nose, "it talks about lab work. It's going to be very important in this class, at least thirty percent of your grade, so I suggest you take it seriously."

Several boys from the JV crew team snorted. Vera, Emily's lab partner, whose military jacket was faded and ripped but had a tiny tag on the back that said DOLCE & GABBANA, looked at the teacher with stoned eyes. Hanna had warned Emily about how freaky summer school was— "I didn't recognize, like, *anyone*," she'd said dramatically.

Emily didn't think it was *that* bad. Hanna was right about two things, though. One, Rosewood Day *did* seem eerie without its normal hustle and bustle. Emily had never noticed how creaky the doors were, or that there were so many long, ominous shadows around corners, or that so many of the overhead lights flickered. And two, no one particularly cared about passing the class.

Don't you realize how lucky we are to get to graduate? Emily wanted to yell at her classmates. But maybe you didn't appreciate that sort of thing until it was taken away.

Then Vera tapped Emily's arm. "*Hey*. What was it like to almost, like, *die?*"

Emily looked away. Sometimes she forgot that her classmates knew everything about her. "Um . . ."

"I remember Alison," Vera went on. "She told me I looked like a troll." She curled and uncurled her fists. "But hey, at least she's dead, right?"

Emily didn't know what to say. It was always a shock that her classmates remembered Ali, too—Emily had spent so much time obsessing over her it sometimes felt as if Ali were a figment of her imagination, unknown and unknowable to everyone else. But actually, her classmates had known *both* Alis: Courtney, their old friend, and the sociopathic *real* Ali, who'd tried to kill them twice.

And who was definitely still alive.

"So here are your books," Ms. Payton said, handing a stack to the front row and asking them to pass them back. "Would someone like to read the introduction page for the class?"

A bunch of kids snickered, and Ms. Payton looked like she was going to cry. *Poor thing*, Emily thought. Didn't she know that the reading-aloud thing stopped in elementary school?

Feeling a surge of sympathy, she raised her hand. "I'll do it."

She turned to the first page and started to read in a loud, strong voice. Rosewood Day had given her a gift by allowing her back here, and the least she could do was pay it forward.

Even if it meant everyone in the class was now laughing at her, too.

A few hours later, Emily pulled into her family's driveway, cut the engine of her parents' Volvo station wagon, and ducked under the garage door, which was halfway open, probably in need of repair again. The garage door opened into the den, which smelled like potpourri. The first thing Emily saw was her mother sitting on the couch, a blanket wrapped around her legs and a knitting project in her lap.

The TV flashed blue against her face. It was a show on HGTV about custom building a pimped-out doghouse.

Mrs. Fields turned and saw her. Emily froze and considered scurrying away. But then her mother smiled. "How was your first day back?" she asked weakly.

Emily slowly relaxed. Her mom's acceptance and friendliness was still unexpected: Two weeks ago, her parents hadn't been speaking to her. Emily hadn't even been allowed to visit her mom in the hospital room when she had a mild heart attack.

Crazy how fast things could change.

"It was fine," Emily said, sitting on the striped loveseat. "So, um, do you need anything?" The cardiologist had advised Mrs. Fields to take it easy for the next few weeks. Emily's sisters, Carolyn and Beth, had been here, helping out, but they had both left for summer programs at their respective colleges yesterday.

"Maybe some ginger ale." Mrs. Fields blew her a kiss. "Thanks, honey."

"Sure," Emily said, rising and padding into the kitchen.

Her smile dropped as soon as she turned her back. *Déjà vu*, she thought. Emily had lost count of all the times her family had disowned her and then, after a tragedy, welcomed her back with open arms. After Nick's attack, when she opened her eyes in the hospital and saw her whole family standing there, she'd almost burst out laughing. Could they really go through this *again*? But her father had leaned down and said in a heartfelt voice, "We will never let you go, honey." Her siblings had hugged her tight, all of them crying. And her mother had said, "We love you so much."

Emily was grateful that they'd come around again, of course. But she also felt jaded. Would something else happen to make them drop her once more? Should she bother to get attached? And Emily didn't dare bring up that she believed Ali was still alive—her family would think she was nuts.

It was sad not having her family as her touchstone anymore. Something huge was missing from her life, a hole she needed to fill. But she didn't know what *would* satisfy her. Finding Ali? Definitely. But she had a feeling that wasn't entirely it.

"Oh, I forgot to tell you," Mrs. Fields's voice floated in from the den. "There's mail for you on the kitchen table. Who do you know from the Ulster Correctional Facility?"

Emily almost dropped the ginger ale she'd taken from the fridge. She walked over to the table, which was covered in a creaseless, chicken-print tablecloth. The daily mail was tucked under the chicken-shaped napkin holder. There was a white, wrinkled, square envelope with Emily's name right on top. Sure enough, the stamp on it said ULSTER CORRECTIONAL FACILITY in smeared letters.

Her mind scattered in several different directions. She sure did know someone at the Ulster Correctional Facility. Only, that person wasn't speaking to her . . . *was* she? Emily squinted at the handwriting on the envelope.

Could it be? Emily had a postcard upstairs of the Bermuda international airport with the same loopy *E*s and spiky *F*s. *We'll find each other someday*, the love of her life, Jordan Richards, had written.

This couldn't be from Jordan. There was no way.

Jordan's presence swooped back to her. Her long, dark hair and soulful green eyes. Her bow-shaped lips, the way she smelled like tangerines, the eyelet dress she'd worn when Emily first saw her on the deck of the cruise ship. It'd felt so good to kiss her and hold her, and it had been so easy to talk to Jordan about her life, her worries, her fears. But Jordan had a checkered past: She had been wanted by the FBI because she stole cars, boats, and even an airplane in her former, bad-girl life. A had called the police on Jordan, but Jordan escaped the FBI at the last moment. Emily had reached out to Jordan afterward, desperate to maintain a connection, but somehow her Twitter messages had tipped the police off to Jordan's hiding place in Florida. The worst part was that Jordan blamed her arrest on Emily's foolishness. But Emily knew that A–*Ali*–had tipped the cops off to those Twitter messages. Ali was behind everything.

Emily had never loved someone like she loved Jordan, not even the girl she'd thought of as Ali. But because of Jordan's troubling past, Emily hadn't shared their relationship with many people. Her friends knew, obviously, and so did Iris, Ali's old roommate from The Preserve. But there was no way she could tell her parents. They wouldn't understand.

Her fingers shook as she opened the envelope. *It's a joke*, she told herself. Someone else had contacted her, pretending to be Jordan. Maybe it was from Ali herself. She unfolded a piece of lined paper.

Dear Emily,

I'm writing to you from prison. It's taken me a while to work through my feelings, but I've watched your horrible ordeal on TV. My lawyer has told me about it, too. I feel awful for what you've gone through. I also understand why you were so desperate to leave and why you reached out even when you knew it was dangerous. I forgive you for those tweets, and I know now you never meant to hurt me. I would love for you to visit me here if you're up for it. We have a lot to talk about. But I understand if you've moved on.

Much love,

Jordan

Emily read the letter three times before it sank in. It was Jordan's handwriting. Jordan's tone. Jordan's *everything*. Emily's nose felt peppery and hot. She fumbled for her cell phone in her pocket and dialed the number Jordan had written at the bottom of the piece of paper for the Ulster Correctional Facility. When a tired-sounding woman answered, Emily spoke in a shaky, quiet voice so her mother wouldn't hear. "I'd like to schedule a visit."

She gave Jordan's name. Sure enough, Jordan had

listed Emily as one of the guests she was willing to see. Emily was so overcome with emotion she almost couldn't speak. It was incredible: Ten minutes ago, there hadn't even been a possibility that Jordan would ever be back in her life. *This* felt like the fulfillment she needed.

She hung up, her smile stretching from ear to ear. But when her phone beeped again, she flinched, alarmed by the timing. ONE NEW TEXT MESSAGE, said the screen.

Emily's heart started to pound. Was Ali lurking outside the window, listening? But the backyard was silent and still. Nothing moved in the cornfields; there wasn't even traffic on the road.

She looked at her phone. ALERT FROM VERIZON WIRELESS: YOU HAVE USED 90% OF YOUR MOBILE DATA FOR THE MONTH.

Emily set her phone down and ran her hands down the length of her face. Maybe, just maybe, the others were right: Ali *wasn't* watching.

And maybe Emily should try to live her life, like they'd said. She should try to be free.

5

A STAR IS BORN

"You have amazing skin."

Hanna closed her eyes as a makeup artist named Trixie brushed blush over her cheeks. "Thank you," she murmured.

"And really pretty eyes, too," Trixie added, her breath smelling like violet candies.

Hanna giggled. "Do you work on commission or something?"

"Nah." There was a sharp *click* sound as Trixie closed a compact. "I just tell it like it is."

It was Wednesday, and Hanna was sitting in the very same soundstage in West Rosewood where she and her father had filmed the drunk-driving PSA. Now the place was bustling with different interior sets, a million lights, cables, and microphones, and tons of writers, directors, and crew members. It was day three of *Burn It Down* production, and they were filming a scene where Spencer and Aria received a creepy postcard from New A about

Jamaica. Hanna's big scene as Naomi Zeigler was coming up soon.

The director, a portly man named Hank Ross who was apparently *the* guy in the movie business—Hanna hadn't seen his latest conspiracy thriller, but she was definitely going to check it out—stood. "Cut!" he yelled. "I think we got it!"

Hanna watched on a video screen as Amanda, the girl who played Spencer, and Bridget, the girl who played Aria, relaxed. Hanna agreed with the director: The girls had nailed it, perfectly embodying her best friends' personalities and mannerisms and expertly conveying how *scary* the situation with Ali had been without resorting to camp or melodrama. All the actresses in this movie were awesome, in fact. The woman who played Spencer's mom had even won a Golden Globe.

Then Hank noticed Hanna behind him and gave her a big smile. "Doing okay?"

"Great." Hanna smiled, adjusting her short blond wig. It was styled to look exactly like Naomi's pixie cut, and it actually looked amazing on Hanna. That wasn't the only amazing thing. When Hanna had arrived on the set, Hank had given her a script of a few lines, stuck a camera in her face, and asked her to "be natural." If it had been a test, Hanna knew she'd aced it when she saw Hank's toothy grin after she said her lines. "Yep, the camera loves you," he'd said generously.

Then she'd been shown her trailer—her *own* movie-star

trailer, complete with a small bed for naps, a vanity with three types of flattering lighting options, and a refrigerator for the two coconut waters she'd brought after reading in *Us Weekly* that Angelina Jolie drank coconut water, too. A production assistant had whisked her off to wardrobe, where a talkative costume designer put her in a fabulous patchwork dress and studded booties. The outfit was way too cool for the real Naomi, but Hanna looked so good she wasn't going to quibble.

She'd barely had time to memorize her lines for the first scene—a quick one where she and Jared Diaz, the admittedly gorgeous boy who played Mike, gave each other suspicious looks across the cruise deck. But she'd sailed through that, too. Maybe it was easy to get into Naomi's character since she'd known her for so long.

Or maybe it was because she was a natural and her next stop was definitely Hollywood.

Hank slid off his chair and went to talk to the actresses on the other side of the wall. Hanna reached for her fringed leather bag hanging from the back of one of the chairs and removed her cell phone, eager to send some updates. First, she checked Twitter: Two hundred people had retweeted her post about how awesome the craft services spread was. Her stepsister, Kate, reposted the tweet with a series of exclamation points. The *real* Naomi Zeigler, whom Hanna had made sure had seen the news that she was playing her part in the movie, replied *dislike* in all caps.

Hanna composed a new text to Spencer, Aria, and

Emily. *You guys really should be down here,* she wrote. *You could so score a part.*

Spencer replied after a beat. *I don't think I'm ready to reenact my worst nightmare,* she wrote. *But I'm glad you're having a good time. Break a leg!*

Aria sent a congratulatory note as well, and Emily said there was no way she was getting in front of a camera—she'd break out in hives. *But hey, did I tell you Jordan wrote me from prison?* Emily added at the end of her text. *I'm going to visit her in a few days!*

Hanna grinned. She was glad Emily had something amazing going on in her life, too. They all deserved good things.

She wrote Mike next. *A star is born!*

He pinged back an answer. *Are there any hot girls there? Take pics!*

Hanna snickered and looked around. There were tons of hot girls in the cast, on the crew, and even in catering. Suddenly, she clapped eyes with the only person in the cast she hadn't met yet. Her long, dark hair was unmistakable. It was Hailey Blake. *The* Hailey Blake.

Hailey's eyes widened when she saw Hanna across the room. "Oh my God. Oh my *God*," she said, pushing her stylists aside and rushing over. "It's you! Hanna Marin!"

Hanna tried to answer, but Hailey grabbed her hands and rushed on. "I have been dying to meet you all day, but I had this *thing* this morning that I couldn't get out of." She rolled her eyes and mouthed the word *overslept*.

"Anyway, it is so awesome that you're here! Are you loving it? Has everyone been nice to you? If anyone's mean, I'll kick their ass."

Hanna's mouth fell open. Hailey's public persona was a sugary-sweet girl next door, but in person, she was whip-thin, her dark hair was cut in funky layers, and she wore a pair of over-the-thigh boots Hanna could never pull off without looking slutty. And what was this about ass-kicking?

Hailey turned to one of Hank's assistants, a pale, vampire-esque guy named Daniel. "Hey. Does Hanna have a few minutes to hang before our next scene?"

"Well, I'm still working on her." Trixie rushed forward with her makeup kit. "I needed to get a different blush color." She held up a compact full of pink powder.

Hailey sniffed. "That new color is hideous. She looks fantastic already." She linked elbows with Hanna. "Come on."

Daniel gave Hanna a strange look. "I'd be careful, if I were you," he said, his sunken eyes wide.

"Oh, *please*." Hailey rolled her eyes and yanked Hanna around the set. "I swear everyone who works with Hank has a vagina," she whispered loudly to Hanna before they were out of earshot. Hanna glanced apologetically back at Daniel, hoping he didn't think *she'd* said it.

They crossed the soundstage, climbed a set of stairs, and walked down a narrow hallway that overlooked a few cruise ship sets. Halfway down the hall, Hailey opened a door with her name on the front. Inside was a room with furry pink wallpaper, a couch in the shape of pursed red lips, a mini-fridge, a SoulCycle spinning bike, and a bookcase filled with trashy magazines. Hanna glanced at a vanity, where pictures of three different guys were arranged. Each one was cuter than the last. She was pretty sure she'd seen one of them in the latest Jake Gyllenhaal blockbuster.

Hailey noticed her looking. "My three boyfriends. Adorable, aren't they?"

Hanna frowned. "You're dating them all at the same time?"

"Uh, *yeah*," Hailey said. She dug out a pack of Parliaments from a corduroy pouch atop the fridge. Lighting one up, she flopped onto the lip-shaped couch and exhaled blue smoke. Then she extended the pack to Hanna. "Want one?"

Hanna hesitated, not having smoked since she was best friends with Mona Vanderwaal. She took one but didn't light it.

Then Hailey's phone bleated the ominous, two-note theme from *Jaws*. "Ugh, sorry," she said, looking at the screen. "What do you want *now*, Mom?" she screamed into the phone. She paused, then sighed. "I *told* you they were lying about that. Who are you going to believe, me or him?"

Hanna started for the door, figuring Hailey wanted privacy, but Hailey signaled her back, making a winding-up gesture that she'd be off soon. "You are being *such* a bitch today," she yelled into the phone. "Your shrink needs to up your meds."

Then she hung up and smiled at Hanna. "Sorry about that!"

Hanna gaped. "Was that really your mom?"

Hailey shrugged. "She *so* isn't in my corner sometimes."

Hanna blinked hard. If only she had the balls to talk to her father like that.

Hailey took another drag of the cigarette. "So. Hanna Marin. I've watched all your interviews."

Hanna felt her cheeks grow red. "You *have*?"

Hailey shrugged. "I had to figure out who you are since I'm playing you." She leaned forward. "You are the most poised of the group. Definitely the coolest. I feel so lucky to play you."

Hanna lowered her eyes. She certainly hadn't *felt* cool or poised in the past few months—in the past two *years*, actually. "I'm the one who should feel lucky. It's a dream that *you're* playing *me*."

"You really think so?" Hailey clutched her hand to her chest. "You are so, *so* sweet!"

Hanna was about to say that Hailey probably heard that stuff all the time—she'd won a zillion People's Choice Awards, after all. But Hailey leapt off the couch and moved closer to Hanna, suddenly pumped with even more enthusiasm. "We should really get to know each other. Maybe you could show me around Rosewood? Or wait, we're not that far from NYC, are we?" She squeezed Hanna's hands hard. "I can get us into any club in Manhattan. Tons of bouncers owe me favors."

"Okay," Hanna said breathily, trying to imagine the jealous looks on everyone's faces when she walked into a club with *the* Hailey Blake.

"We should take Jared, too." Hailey looked excited. "He's hot, don't you think? And *so* nice. I could totally fix the two of you up."

It took Hanna a moment to realize she was talking about Jared Diaz, the boy who played Mike. "Um, I already have a boyfriend," she said, laughing. "The *real* Mike."

All at once, someone exhaled behind them. Hailey's door was open now, and Daniel, the director's assistant, stood in the dressing room. Hanna nearly yelped. There was something definitely creepy about his almost translucent skin and thin lips, and the way he'd slipped soundlessly into Hailey's room. Hanna wondered how someone like him could have gotten such a plum job.

"Ladies?" he said, his eyes narrowing at the swirling smoke. "We actually need you downstairs for the cruise scene."

Hailey's face soured. "Already? My contract *specifically* states downtime. I'm calling my agent to complain." She reached for her phone, then rolled her eyes and let it drop. "Oh, whatever. I'll let you slide this once."

She stubbed out her cigarette on the floor. Daniel led them down the stairs, and Hailey squeezed Hanna's hand. "Always remember, *you're* the talent," she whispered. "Don't let them push you around. They're supposed to cater to you."

Hanna couldn't help but giggle.

Hank was waiting for them at the bottom of the stairs. "About *time*," he said, glowering at Hailey. "Marissa wants to get you in a different outfit. She's been looking for you for a while."

"I *told* Daniel I was in my dressing room," Hailey snapped. "It's not my fault he doesn't give you messages."

Hank ignored this, turning to Hanna. "You're in the crowd, honey," he said in a much gentler voice. He pointed across the room to what looked exactly like the deck of the Eco Cruise complete with the brass railings, a tiki bar in the corner, and purple plush booths along the walls. There was even a reggae band absently plucking their instruments.

Hanna said good-bye to Hailey, who still looked pissed off, and sat down at a nearby table with Penelope Riggs, the girl playing Riley. Hanna's only instructions for this scene were to make it look like she and Riley were having a conversation and to shoot Hailey-as-Hanna daggers every so often. In moments, Hailey reappeared in a beachy sundress that looked precisely like something Hanna would wear. She stood within earshot of Hanna, and Hanna could hear Hailey repeating a bunch of *muh-muh-muh* vocal exercises under her breath. *What a pro*, Hanna thought. Maybe she should do vocal exercises, too.

Hank disappeared behind the wall of cameras. "And, action!" he yelled out, and the cameraman moved in on Hailey. The band started to play. Hanna turned to Penelope and pantomimed a conversation in a low voice, but her attention was really on Hailey across the room. She wanted to see how Hailey played her in this scene.

"You're not going to believe this, Hanna," Bridget-as-Aria said as she ran up to Hailey, her eyes wide and her mannerisms perfectly Aria-like. She clutched Hailey's hands. "Graham, my partner for the scavenger hunt? He was *Tabitha's boyfriend.*"

"Oh my *God*," Hailey said exaggeratedly, her mouth dropping open. "You have to get rid of him!"

Hanna tried not to twitch. Why was Hailey using that weird Valley Girl voice? *Her* voice didn't sound like that, did it?

"I can't just get rid of him," Bridget argued. "What if he suspects something is up? Maybe I should just tell him the truth."

"No *way*," Hailey said, popping out a hip. "Like, Aria, that is the *last* thing you should do."

Then she made vigorous chomping movements, like she was really chewing hard on a huge wad of gum. Hanna felt queasy. She didn't even *chew* gum.

"Cut!" Hank cried a few moments later, reappearing on the set. Hanna figured he was going to give Hailey some advice on playing Hanna—she kind of needed it. But instead, Hank walked over to the band, speaking in a low voice to the lead singer.

Hailey turned and glided to Hanna's table, her eyes shining. "So?" she chirped. "Don't I make an ah-mazing you?"

She looked so pleased with herself. And though Hanna was kind of offended at, well, *everything* Hailey had just done, she couldn't imagine saying so.

So Hanna smiled brightly. "You were great," she said in a small voice.

"Okay, everyone, places!" Hank interrupted, running back to his post. "We're going again!"

The cameras rolled once more. The band launched into the opening bars of "Three Little Birds," and the partygoers milled around happily. Hanna pretended to talk to Penelope, all the while keeping her eye on Hailey as she did the scene *exactly the same way*, gum-snapping and all. A horrible feeling welled in the pit of Hanna's stomach. If Hailey kept this up, Hanna would be the laughingstock of Rosewood—and FIT—once this movie came out. People would do hip-popping, gum-chewing, Valley Girl Hanna impressions. What if they actually thought she was *like* that?

She turned her head to idly look around the rest of the set, hoping for some distraction. Suddenly, a flash of blond hair shot through the back of the room. Hanna did a double take. There was another streak of blond. Hanna's heart started to pound. There was something about the person's movements that filled her with jitters.

She half-rose to her feet. The girl playing Riley gave her a strange look. "What are you doing?"

"Cut!" Hank yelled again. Everyone broke character. Hanna thought he was going to reprimand her, but he went over to Bridget. Seizing the opportunity, Hanna shot off the chair and pushed through the crowd. She had to see who that blonde was.

She had to weave around a lot of kids, fake palm trees, bistro tables, a large statue of a scuba diver, and several huge potted plants to get to the back. Then she peered around into the sea of extras. None of them was Ali. Spots formed in front of Hanna's eyes. Had she imagined it?

But one of the exit doors was easing shut. Hanna rushed for it, nearly tripping over a light cable. She almost had her hand on the knob when someone grabbed her arm. She whirled around, her heart thudding hard.

It was Jared, the guy playing Mike. "Hanna, right?" His eyes shifted back and forth. "Everything okay?"

Hanna looked at the door. "I—I need to go outside for a sec."

Jared shook his head. "Not through that door. An alarm will sound. Hank will freak."

Hanna glanced at the door again. EMERGENCY EXIT, read big, bright letters above it. "But someone just went through here, though, and nothing happened," she protested weakly. Her head was suddenly swimming.

Jared patted Hanna's arm and guided her away from the door. "Take a deep breath, okay? I've worked on a lot of films, and first days can definitely be hairy. I've seen people with way more experience panic much worse than you."

"But I'm not . . ." Hanna trailed off. She *wasn't* panicking. She'd been perfectly calm and centered before Ali appeared in the crowd.

Only, *had* it been Ali? How could someone go through an emergency exit without setting off the alarm?

You imagined it, she told herself as fake-Mike escorted her back to the scene. But she peeked behind her one more time to be sure Ali wasn't there.

She wasn't, of course. But Hanna still had the eerie sense she was close. Watching.

6

AND NOW, INTRODUCING
ROSEWOOD'S LATEST PRODIGY . . .

Aria sat in her father's airy den, listlessly pulling apart a stick of Monterey Jack string cheese. Byron flitted around the room, doing his annual reorganizing of the bookshelves, a ritual in which he pulled all his tomes off the wall and arranged them in a new way that was understandable only to him. His new baby, Lola, cooed happily from a jungle-themed jumping apparatus in the corner, a tinny version of "Head, Shoulders, Knees, and Toes" tinkling through the tiny speakers.

Byron's wife, Meredith, flipped through channels. Finally, she settled on a celebrity exposé on Bravo, which was utterly *un*Meredith—Aria had always thought she'd be the type of person who hated reality TV. She turned to Aria and smiled brightly. "I heard your friend Hanna is going to be in a movie!"

"Uh-huh," Aria mumbled, hoping that Meredith wouldn't ask the obvious follow-up question—why *she* wasn't in the movie, too. Aria was happy that Hanna felt comfortable enough to act in the film—*one* of them should get to capitalize off this nightmare. But Aria was a behind-the-scenes kind of girl—when she and her friends were younger, she used to direct artsy movies, usually making Courtney-as-Ali the star. And anyway, she'd had enough time in front of a camera with all those torturous Ali interviews.

When the show broke for commercials, Meredith flipped the channel again, this time landing on a local newscast. Aria tuned out—now that their Ali struggle was old news, the reporters were back to talking about pica-yune stuff like squabbles at town hall or whether to put a new GAP on this corner or that corner. But then Meredith exclaimed brightly, "Oh! How nice!"

"Huh?" Aria turned around. On the screen was a ban-ner that read ROSEWOOD RALLIES FOR YOUTHS. Then came a shot of the outside of the Rosewood Country Club; Aria used to spend a lot of time there because Spencer's dad was a member.

A woman with light blond hair held back in a black headband popped up on the screen. The name *Sharon Winters* appeared under her face. "We've had a lot of trag-edy happen in this town, but it's time to turn it into some-thing positive," she said. "Next Friday, we're throwing a fund-raiser for all the disadvantaged and troubled youth in Rosewood and its surrounding areas. My hope is that everyone comes out and supports the cause."

Meredith looked at Aria excitedly. "Didn't you get an invite for this?"

"Maybe," Aria mumbled, staring at the string cheese in her hands.

Byron stopped to look at the screen. "Hmm. Perhaps we should all go."

"Are you kidding?" Aria cried. Her dad usually hated big parties.

Byron shrugged. "They should throw you a party after all you've been through. And you can take Noel."

He smiled at her dopily. Aria looked at the floor. "Noel's busy that night," she muttered, thinking about their conversation outside the gallery the other day.

Her phone buzzed, and Hanna's name appeared on the screen. Aria squinted at the text. *I just saw Ali.*

Aria's blood ran cold. She shot up and walked out of the room, dialing Hanna's number.

Hanna picked up right away. "What are you talking about?" Aria whispered.

"I know it sounds crazy," Hanna whispered back. "But she's on the set—she was in a crowd scene I was in. I looked across the room and saw this blond head . . . and I had this sense. It was her."

Aria sank into the window seat in the living room. "But you're not *sure*."

"Well, no, but . . ."

Aria jumped up nervously and started pacing around.

"Let's try to think about this logically. Could Ali actually get onto a movie set? Isn't there lots of security?"

"Yeah . . ." Hanna sounded uncertain. "But she's a master at sneaking in and out."

"But why would she risk mixing with people who might recognize her? And she'd be on camera."

"True," Hanna said. She exhaled loudly. "Okay. Maybe it was my imagination. I mean, that has to be it, right? Ali wouldn't be that stupid."

"She wouldn't," Aria assured her.

But when she hung up, she wandered into the kitchen and stared blankly out the stained-glass window over the sink. Past the flat expanse of grass was a long, gradual slope leading to thick, dark woods. Ali had set fire to those woods the year before, nearly killing Aria and the others and decimating Spencer's family's barn. What if Hanna was right? What if Ali *was* somewhere close, ready to torment them again?

She stared at her phone, figuring it was the perfect time to receive a text from A. On cue, her phone bleated. The device fell from her hands and clattered to the wood floor. A 610 number flashed on the screen.

It took Aria a moment to realize it was her mom at the gallery. "Aria?" Ella said when Aria answered. "Are you sitting down?"

"Yeah . . . ," Aria said uncertainly, her heart starting to thud all over again as she sat at the breakfast table. Maybe *Ella* had seen Ali?

"You aren't going to believe this"—Ella's voice swooped—"but we got a call from a very wealthy New York collector today. Mr. John Carruthers."

"Wait, *the* John Carruthers?" Aria asked. There'd been a profile of him in *Art Now* magazine—he'd recently bought two Picassos at auction because his wife wanted one for each of their kids' rooms. He was *the* collector every artist and gallery owner wanted to woo.

"Yep," Ella chirped. "His assistant called and had me describe the paintings we had. I almost fell out of my chair. *Then* he asked me to send a few pictures. He hung up, but he called back a little while later saying Mr. Carruthers was interested in purchasing one. And guess what? It's one of *yours*."

"W-what?" Aria shot to her feet. "You're kidding!"

"Nope!" Ella screamed. "Honey, you've been discovered!"

Aria shook her head. "I can't believe it," she murmured.

"Well, you should," Ella insisted. "You've been so prolific in the past few weeks, and your work is fantastic. Apparently, Mr. Carruthers thinks you're luminous and a huge talent to watch. And, honey, that's not all. You know what he bought the painting for? A *hundred thousand dollars*."

Aria's mind went blank. She tried to picture that figure in a bank account, but she felt as if her head might explode.

"That's . . . *amazing*," she finally managed to say. Then she cleared her throat. "W-which painting did he buy? One of the dark abstract pieces? One of the portraits of Noel?"

Ella coughed awkwardly. "Actually, no. It was the portrait of Alison. That big one in the corner."

Aria flinched. It wasn't even her best work, the brushstrokes crude, Ali's face so creepy. Ella had sent a photo of *that*? And someone had bought it? What if he bought it *only* because it was of Ali—and because she was a Pretty Little Liar?

Then again, maybe she shouldn't look a gift horse in the mouth. A hundred thousand dollars was a hundred thousand dollars. "Well, that's great," she murmured to her mom, trying to sound unruffled.

"Listen, I have to get off the line—Jim's back, and he's over the moon," Ella said, suddenly sounding rushed. "I think he's going to give me a promotion!" she added in a whisper. "But I'll call you back with all the payment details. I'm so proud of you, honey. This is going to change your life."

Then Ella was gone. Aria held the phone in her hands, her mind whirring fast. Then she stood and slid the door to the porch open, stepped out, and leaned against the cool glass, taking heaving breaths. The fresh air felt invigorating.

She let what Ella told her sink in. Her first sale. For a painting of *Ali*.

Aria looked at her phone again. After a beat, she called up her photo gallery, then flipped through the pictures she'd taken of her recent paintings. She stopped on the portrait of Ali. The girl on the canvas was skin and bones, her cheeks hollowed, her hair dulled, her eyes wide and crazy. Then, as Aria stared, Ali seemed to . . . *move*. One corner of her lip rose in a smirk. Her eyes narrowed a tad.

Aria dropped the phone once more. What the hell?

The device landed faceup, Ali's picture still on the screen. Aria looked at it again, but it looked like a snapshot on a cell phone. She grabbed the phone, exited out of the photo, and stabbed at the DELETE button.

Good riddance. Thank God Ella was packaging that portrait up and sending it far, far away. Aria couldn't bear the idea of that face haunting her any longer.

7

THE BULLIED . . . OR THE BULLY?

Spencer was finishing dinner with her mother, Mr. Pennythistle, and Amelia. Chinese takeout boxes sat around them, but, typical of Spencer's mom, they were eating on fine china from Mrs. Hastings's great-grandmother and using porcelain chopsticks from a specialty shop in Shanghai. Spencer's mom had dressed for dinner, too, changing out of the jeans and plaid shirt she'd worn at the family's stables and into a crisp off-white linen dress and shiny black Tory Burch flats.

"So being selected for the orchestra trip is *really* prestigious." Amelia adjusted the tortoiseshell headband that held back her tight curls. Even though it was summer vacation, she, too, was dressed up in a crisp white shirt and a gray pleated skirt that didn't look much different from her St. Agnes uniform. "The orchestra director told me I should be really proud," she added, looking around expectantly.

"That's great, honey." Mr. Pennythistle smiled warmly.

So did Spencer's mom.

But Spencer resisted rolling her eyes. Every time Amelia opened her mouth, it was to brag. Yesterday at dinner, she'd boasted for a while about how good a *sleeper* she was.

Suddenly, she couldn't deal with one more boastful thing out of Amelia's mouth. "May I be excused?" she asked, placing her chopsticks in her soy sauce–stained bowl.

"Yes, but only after we talk about the Rosewood Rallies event," Mrs. Hastings said.

Spencer fell back into her chair and wrinkled her nose. "We're actually going?" Why did she need another event to remind her of Ali? Wasn't the point to get *over* it?

Mrs. Hastings nodded firmly. "You're an honored guest. And actually, I've volunteered to help out." She clicked her chopsticks together. "You girls can bring a date, if you like. It should be fun."

Spencer felt her cheeks flush. *A date.* Her mind shuffled through her long list of failed romances from the past year. Andrew Campbell had pulled away from her shortly after the Poconos fire, probably because he didn't want to be associated with someone surrounded by so much drama. And Chase, another Ali detective Spencer had met online, had dropped Spencer when his life was in danger.

Every boy she'd gotten close to had run away screaming . . . and it was all Ali's fault. Spencer *wanted* to be with someone . . . but she also felt as if it could never happen.

"I'll go if it means that much to you," she told her

mother, picking up her dishes. "But I'm not going to enjoy it."

She carried everything to the stainless steel sink in the kitchen. As she was rinsing off the chopsticks, she sensed a presence behind her and turned. Amelia stood by the fridge. Spencer cringed, anticipating a nasty remark.

But Amelia moved forward almost shyly. "Um, I meant to tell you. A friend directed me to your new blog. It's kind of . . . awesome."

Spencer's mind froze. "You really think so?" she blurted.

"Of course." Amelia placed her bowl on the counter. "I think it's really great that you gave all those people a voice." And then, with a smile, she turned and pranced back into the dining room.

Spencer stood still. She was so dazed she didn't realize she'd left the tap running until the water flowed over her dirty bowl.

Huh.

Then she climbed the stairs to her bedroom and sat down at her computer, bringing up the blog. It was astonishing, actually, that Amelia even *knew* about the blog . . . but then again, it had recently garnered quite a following, even showing up on the very first page on a Google search for *bullying.*

She scrolled through her email. Today's crop of stories made her own experiences with Ali pale in comparison. There were tales of kids being verbally and physically attacked by whole gangs of enemies. Kids were made fun of for their sexuality, like Emily had been, or for their race or religion. A girl wrote in telling a story about how her best friend committed suicide, unable to take the jeers from her classmates any longer. *I miss her every day*, the email said. *And I'm not even sure the kids who were mean to her understood what they did.* Spencer thought of Emily there, too—how they'd saved her from taking her life off the covered bridge. If they hadn't gotten there in time, she might have gone through with it.

She checked the website stats. To her astonishment, the blog had gotten eight thousand hits in the past twenty-four hours.

Halfway down the list, she opened an email from Greg Messner from Wilmington, Delaware. Greg hadn't been bullied himself, the letter said, but he'd witnessed other people being picked on and had stood by, doing nothing. Eventually, his passivity began to haunt him, he said. He should have stood up for what was right, yet he'd been too scared that the bully would turn on him. *Your site is inspirational*, he said, *and I want you to know that not just kids who were bullied are reading it. Everyone can use it as a tool to understand what bullying feels like.*

Spencer sat back. It was an interesting perspective. Years ago, she and her friends had stood idly by as Ali tormented kids, too. Sometimes, Spencer had even actively participated. She remembered laughing at Mona's askew glasses or Chassey Bledsoe's ubiquitous Razor scooter. She'd helped write teasing missives on the sidewalk outside Mona's house and, one time, filled her locker with tampons with their tips painted bright red.

She started to write a response. *Dear Greg, Thank you for your letter. Like you, I was passive around bullies, too. In fact, there have been many times I've wondered if what happened to me is karma. We all make mistakes. I'm just glad the site is helping people.*

She sent it off. Within a half a minute, Greg replied. *Hey, Spencer, Thank you so much for writing back to me. Don't kid yourself: You're awesome. The best thing you can do is admit your mistakes and try your best to help others. You are truly an inspiration.*

Tingles ran up her spine. It was such a nice thing to say. But then she set her jaw. No more boys. No falling for someone on the internet. No freaking way.

She continued to scroll down the list of stories, taking time to read each one. Then she got to one written by someone who called himself DominickPhilly. Not *him* again.

You think you're so awesome, but you're not, the message read. *You're nothing but a poser, and pretty soon, people are going to figure you out.*

Her head started to pound. DominickPhilly had sent her messages practically since she'd set up the blog. He'd said that the site was pathetic. That Spencer didn't know what she was talking about. That she used her fake bullying story as a stepping-stone to fame, and that she didn't know what *real* pain was. In this latest message, he'd included a thumbnail photograph of himself. Spencer clicked on it, leaning in close to look at his square, angry face. If his profile details were to be believed, he lived in the city of Philadelphia, and he was her age. Why did he hate her so much? Why was he trolling this site? He hadn't included a tale of being bullied. Maybe *he* was a bully.

Pots and pans clanged in the kitchen, followed by the soft sounds of the family's two Labradoodles, Rufus and Beatrice, drinking water from their metal bowls. The sun had sunk lower in the sky, and everyone's front lights had snapped on, casting a warm golden glow along the circle. Spencer stared out the window at the neighborhood she loved and hated. Her gaze drifted to Ali's old bedroom next door. For a split second, she thought she saw Ali standing there, smirking at her.

She blinked hard. There *was* someone at the window. Someone blond.

But then she looked again. The window wasn't even lit. The St. Germains, who had lived there for almost two years now, were on vacation in the Outer Banks. Of course Ali wasn't there. *You're supposed to forget about her*, Spencer thought.

Beep.

It was her computer. Spencer turned away from the window and moved the mouse to wake up the screen. There was a new email for the bully site from someone called BTH087. *Please Read*, read the subject line.

She opened the email, grateful it wasn't from DominickPhilly. A new bullying tale was written in swirly pink font, each sentence on a separate line like a poem. For whatever reason, the author had bolded the first letter of every sentence. Still a little freaked out, Spencer began to read.

I want to tell you my story.

All my life, I have been persecuted, and

My heart breaks every day.

Why people are after me, I don't know, because

Anyone will tell you I am a nice person.

Try to get to know me is all I ask.

Can you do that? But no. You won't.

Help me, please!

It's getting too much to handle!

No one seems to listen, though.

Get over it, everyone says.

Yet they're sometimes the ones tormenting me.

On and on it goes.

Until one day, when I've had enough.

—And then it's over.

Spencer felt even more uneasy when she got to the end. Something about the message struck her as strange, maybe even cryptic. She looked at the signature at the very bottom of the email. It wasn't from BTH087. Instead, it said *Maxine Preptwill.*

Her stomach dropped. That was the alias Ali and Noel

Kahn used to contact each other when Ali was at The Preserve.

No, she thought, backing away from the computer. It was a coincidence. Maybe someone else *did* know about that stupid Ali-Noel code name.

She looked at the bolded letters at the beginning of each line again. *Was* it a code? She wrote each one on a separate sheet of paper. They began to make a message. *I am . . .*

She kept writing, then sat back to look at the whole statement. She clapped a hand over her mouth to suppress a scream.

I am watching you. —A

8

BREATHLESS

On Friday, Emily sat in the chemistry classroom, fanning herself with a notebook. Rosewood Day must have forgotten to turn on the AC, because the room felt sticky and closed and smelled like feet. Several kids had already walked out, complaining about the heat. Others were asleep at their desks. Flies buzzed noisily around Ms. Payton's head.

A long swim would be wonderful. Emily needed to keep up with swimming anyway, in case UNC wanted her for the team next year. But her parents didn't belong to a summer club. Last year, she'd swum on a summer team at the YMCA, but that was miles from here. If only she could use the Rosewood Day pool. It was right down the hall.

Dear Jordan, I'm thrilled to be in summer school, don't get me wrong. But this room couldn't smell any more like BO. And I swear someone has the worst gas ever. Help!

She'd been writing letters to Jordan in her head ever

since she heard from her on Tuesday. Not that she'd even written them down, but knowing that there was someone out there she could talk to, someone who might listen to every stupid little thing she had to say, lifted her spirits. *A few more days until I see you in New York*, she thought, smiling to herself.

As Ms. Payton languidly drew diagrams of ions on the board, Emily's phone buzzed in her pocket. She pulled it out and peeked at the screen.

Need to talk, Spencer had texted. *I think Ali sent me a message through my bullying site last night.*

Emily looked around, almost as if Ali would be standing at the door, glaring at her. Hanna seeing Ali in a crowd on a movie set was one thing—they chalked that up to Hanna being confused and overwhelmed. But Spencer wasn't one to cry wolf.

Emily texted Spencer back for details. Spencer explained what had happened. *I tried to trace the IP address to see who sent the note, but the details were hidden. I looked into the email it was sent from too, but it's an alias.* A fourth text said the alias was so protected she couldn't get any details there, either.

So someone is really trying to hide their identity, Emily typed back, growing more and more nervous. Ali and Nick had configured all their past A messages to reroute back to their own phones, making it look like *they* had sent them to themselves. Maybe Ali was doing it again.

We should take the note to someone who knows more about

computers, Emily typed, her fingers flying. *We need to take this bitch down.*

She waited for Spencer to respond, but her friend didn't address Emily's comment, saying she had to go.

Emily slid her phone back into her pocket, feeling antsy. Maybe Ali *was* planning something. But what? Was there anyone they could report this to? Would anyone help them?

Dear Jordan, I think Ali's back. And I don't know what to do or how to find her.

She pulled her phone from her pocket and typed *Ali Cats* into Google. Several fan sites appeared, and she read the new posts. One girl whose screen name was TabbyCatLover had listed intimate Ali details, like her eye color, her estimated weight, her favorite clothing brands, movies she used to like. Another poster had written an itinerary of what Ali's life must have been like inside The Preserve, down to what sorts of meds Ali had taken. *She's tougher than all of us combined*, the poster wrote at the end.

Emily couldn't read any more—it wasn't like any of the posts gave hints about Ali being alive or where she was. How could people *support* such a maniac?

The rest of the class passed in a sweaty blur, and soon enough, Ms. Payton was dismissing them. Emily stepped into the steamy hallway, then glanced to her left toward the natatorium. The door looked unlocked. *Could* she swim a few laps?

A half minute later, she was at her car, grabbing the

bag of swim stuff she always kept in the backseat. She padded back into the school, cut through the girls' locker room, and peeked into the natatorium. Blue water lapped against the sides. Every lane was empty, and the water looked glassy and smooth and *cold*. All the lights in the natatorium were still on, and even the digital time clock on the wall was working.

She tried the door handle. It turned easily.

She dropped her bag on a bench in the locker room and began to change into her swimsuit. During the school year, the locker room walls were filled with motivational posters, newspaper clippings, and pictures of the team, but now that had all been stripped away. The only poster still up was one for the Rosewood Rallies charity event next week. Emily's parents had RSVP'd; her mom thought it was particularly important to go because she thought doing good in the community would help the whole family heal. If only it were that easy.

Emily pulled the swimsuit straps onto her shoulders. A faucet dripped at the sink, the noise echoing through the empty space. Sudden movement flickered across the room, but when Emily turned, all she saw was her reflection in the long mirror on the wall.

Dear Jordan, I've become a huge baby. I'm afraid of my reflection.

Emily slung her towel over her arm, slipped on her flip-flops, and strode into the pool area. The radio the team listened to during practice sat on its usual step on the bleachers, which relaxed her a little. She switched it on to the regular rock station her old coach, Lauren, used to play, and a Red Hot Chili Peppers song sounded through the room. It made everything feel a little more normal.

Then she stuck a toe in the water. Just as she'd expected, it felt cool and refreshing. She pulled her cap over her head, fixed her Swedish goggles to her eyes, and dove in. *Ahhh.*

Dear Jordan, she thought as she swam smooth, even strokes, *I love swimming so much. And I know I should be excited that UNC might keep me on the team for next year, but I don't know what I want anymore. I feel like a jerk for even saying that, though. It's my chance to get away. And I am dying to get away.*

She swam a hundred yards, then two hundred, flipping compactly at the wall and pushing off in a streamlined shape. Emily suddenly remembered Jordan running her thin, delicate hands over her strong shoulders during those blissful days on the cruise ship. "You're like a sexy mermaid," Jordan had whispered in her ear, her breath warm on Emily's neck.

What would it be like to see Jordan again? Where would things go from there? Could she actually date someone in prison?

A loud clap of thunder sounded above. Emily stopped and peered through the skylights. The sky had turned very dark. Rain began to pelt the glass. She treaded water, wondering if she should get out. She listened for more thunder, but couldn't hear anything over the rain.

She put her head down and decided to swim a little longer, but after a few laps, the room had darkened even more. The bright spots of sunlight had vanished. And then, suddenly, there was a *snap* . . . and the overhead lights dimmed and then went dark.

Emily touched the wall and looked around. The digital clock had lost power, and so had the radio. It was so dark on the pool deck that she could barely see the bleachers a few feet away.

She almost didn't see the figure standing above her.

Then Emily jolted and gasped. It was a girl. She was wearing a dark zip-up hoodie, dark jeans, and sneakers that were getting wet from the lapping water in the gutter. She was standing right above Emily, leaning with her hands on her thighs. Just staring.

Before Emily could say a word, lightning flashed through the sky, illuminating the girl's face. Her mouth was open, revealing a few missing teeth. Her eyes were wide and crazed. She leaned farther into the lane, her features so close. Emily smelled the faintest tinge of vanilla soap on her skin.

A scream froze in her throat. *Ali.*

"Oh my God," Emily cried, paddling backward. But Ali reached out and grabbed her before she could get far, pulling Emily back to the wall with surprising strength.

"Hello, Emily," Ali said in an eerie, craggy voice, pausing to cackle. "Did you really think I'd leave for good?"

Her smile stretched wider. "I haven't visited your friends, but I just *had* to see you. You're my favorite!"

Emily tried to wriggle out of Ali's grip, but Ali was holding her hard by the shoulders. "Please," Emily said in barely more than a whisper. "Please let me go."

Ali pursed her lips. "First tell me you love me."

"What?" Emily sputtered.

"Say you still love me!" Ali demanded.

"N-no!" Emily cried, astonished. There was no way she could lie about that.

Ali's eyes widened. A dangerous look crossed her face. "Okay, then. You asked for it."

And then she pushed Emily under.

Water rushed into Emily's lungs. She kicked hard, groping for the surface, but Ali wouldn't let her up, her nails pressing into Emily's right temple and the left side of her neck. It was a perfect plan, Emily realized. No one was in here. The room was so big no one could hear her scream. Much later, maybe even tomorrow, a janitor would find Emily in the pool, dead, and figure she'd drowned.

She struggled and kicked, clawing for Ali's hands and using her feet to push off the wall. But Ali kept holding her down. Emily's throat caught, and her lungs began to burn. "Please!" she screamed under the water, the word exploding out of her like a keening wail.

She could hear Ali laughing on the surface. Ali's nails dug even deeper into Emily's head, pressing her toward the bottom of the pool. Spots began to form in front of Emily's eyes. She opened her mouth again, letting in more water. One more scream escaped from her mouth, her addled, oxygen-starved brain hardly registering the sound.

But suddenly she felt Ali's grip release. The blurry figure over her receded, growing smaller and smaller above her.

Emily shot to the top, gasping for air. She gripped the sides of the wall hard and coughed up water. Her head still pounding, she pushed to the deck and gazed around. The door to the girls' locker room swung shut. Emily ran for it, her limbs heavy, her lungs tight.

She crashed into the locker room. "Ali!" she screamed, groping past sinks and the showers and slipping on the tiled floor. A black-hooded shape rushed for the door to the hallway.

Ali. Emily barreled forward, catching her by her sleeve. Ali kicked and bucked, her hands outstretched for the doorknob. Finally, she swung around and glared at Emily, her features twisted and furious and unbearably ugly. She opened her mouth and sank her teeth into Emily's arm.

Emily let out a yelp and released her grip. With a laugh, Ali slipped free. Emily reached to grab her again, but suddenly, all she was holding was Ali's hooded sweatshirt, the zipper undone, both sides flapping free.

Emily lunged for the door, but Ali had slammed it behind her so forcefully that it swung inward, cracking Emily on the head. Emily staggered back, seeing stars. It took her a few seconds to regroup. Then she rushed into the hall.

There was no one there. No sound of footsteps, either. No wet footprints leading in a direction, even.

Emily stared right and left, feeling like she was going crazy. Ali had vanished into thin air.

Water dripped off her fingertips, making puddles on the ground. She ran her hands down the length of her face, suddenly realizing she was still in her bathing suit and swim cap. Then she noticed how freezing she was. She inspected the sides of her neck, wincing at the tender spots where Ali had squeezed. She took a step to the left, and then to the right, and then sank down to the ground, horribly dizzy.

Ali had escaped. *Again*. But she'd sent a message, all right. Loud and clear. And next time, Emily wasn't sure if Ali would let her live.

9

SHE'S BAA-ACK. . . .

Hanna stood in the middle of an empty soundstage, studying her Naomi lines, which a production assistant had printed out and highlighted for her earlier that day. Hank, *Burn It Down*'s director, had dismissed the cast and crew for the day because filming during a lightning storm was dangerous, but Hanna had decided to hang back for a while to practice. She wanted to be perfect for her next big scene. Even though Hank had told her she was doing a great job, she still felt like a little bit of a fraud. She was acting opposite people who had so much experience . . . and her only claims to fame were doing a PSA and being tormented by Ali. "And *that's* why we're not friends anymore, Hanna Marin," she said into the still, quiet room, among the idle cameras, equipment, and lights. She glared at an imaginary Hailey opposite her. In this scene, she, as Naomi, found out about Hanna's almost killing her cousin in a car accident. "Because you're *crazy*. And you're a liar. And there's only so much a girl can take."

Then she imagined Hailey's response. Would Hailey use that ditzy voice again? Snap that imaginary gum? Earlier, Hailey had performed yet another scene as Hanna, and it was just as dreadful as the other day. To Hanna's relief, Hank had sprung up and said, "Hailey, I don't know if you have the character right. Why don't you do some thinking on it, and we'll reschedule your scenes tomorrow?"

Hailey's jaw had dropped, and her face had turned red. As soon as the sound engineer had removed her microphone, she'd stormed over to Hanna. "Do *you* think I'm doing a good job? Because your opinion is the only one that matters."

It had been Hanna's chance to say something, but she'd felt so cornered. She'd given Hailey a closed-mouth smile and nodded feverishly, not trusting her voice.

Hanna repeated her lines again and again, tinkering with her movements and blocking. On the third try, she even felt her eyes well with tears. *I am kind of good at this*, she thought, feeling satisfied. Then she gathered up her things and slipped out the side door.

Even though it was only five o'clock, the sky was surprisingly pitch-black. Wind swirled, kicking up dry leaves, and the rain pelted down in sideways sheets. Hanna peered down the long alley that led to the parking lot. It seemed full of shadows, and all at once, she thought she heard a faint sniff. She whipped around, looking this way and that, but the alley was empty.

Taking a deep breath, she started down the metal ramp to her car. Halfway down the alley, she felt herself hurtle forward, and suddenly she was on the ground. Her palms stung from the impact, and it felt like the wind had been knocked out of her. She scrambled to her knees and looked up, but all she saw was the almost-black sky above. She looked at the ground again and gasped. There, written on the pavement, was a message in chalk. *BreAk a leg, Hanna*, it said. The *a* in *break* was capitalized, bigger than the other letters.

"What do you want?"

Hanna screamed. Someone else *was* in the alley, their body in shadow. When the figure moved into the light, Hanna realized it was Daniel, Hank's strange assistant—the one who'd practically snuck into Hailey's dressing room to retrieve them a few days before.

"W-what are *you* doing here?" Hanna bleated. He'd come out of *nowhere*. "Did you shove me?"

Daniel's eyes narrowed, and they looked even more beady and hollow than ever. "No, but I saw you fall. You shouldn't be here right now, Hanna. Hank sent everyone home."

Then why are you *here?* Hanna wanted to ask, but she didn't. "I—I was just going over my lines," she said weakly, jumping to her feet. She glanced down at the chalk *A* again, her heart pounding hard. "And I'm leaving now."

"Good." Daniel was looking at her with an expression

Hanna couldn't quite identify. "A girl like you shouldn't be alone anywhere. After everything that's happened to you, I would have thought you'd be more careful."

Hanna nodded, then scuttled to her car. It was only once she'd locked the doors that she realized that his expression had kind of been *ominous*. She thought again about the flash of blond hair in the crowd scene the other day. Could Daniel have helped her, somehow? Could an Ali Cat be on the *Burn It Down* crew?

Hanna's phone beeped, and she screamed again. She glanced at it in her lap.

Ali just attacked me at school, said a message from Emily. *Come now!*

Hanna threw the car into drive, her mind suddenly switching gears. She certainly couldn't worry about Daniel right now. All she could think about was getting to Emily as fast as she could.

The sky was an ugly gray and the air was peppered with low rumbles of thunder when Hanna pulled into the Rosewood Day parking lot next to Emily's Volvo. In the distance, she could see Emily sitting on one of the swings on the Lower School's playground. Her head was down, her hair shiny and wet, and it looked like she was in a bathing suit. A nervous bolt surged through Hanna once more.

Spencer and Aria were pulling into the parking lot at the same time, and all the girls rushed toward the swings. Emily didn't look up at them, her gaze fixed firmly on the ground. Her feet were bare and muddy. Her skin looked slightly blue. There was a hooded sweatshirt balled up in her hands, but for whatever reason, she hadn't put it on.

"What happened?" Hanna bellowed, dropping to her knees next to her friend and touching her hand. Emily's skin was cold and covered in goose bumps. She smelled overwhelmingly like chlorine.

"Are you okay?" Spencer sank into a swing next to her.

"Was it really *her*?" Aria wrapped her arms around Emily's shoulders.

Emily indicated a purplish bruise on her neck. "It was definitely her," she said, her voice tinged with sobs. "She tried to kill me."

She told the girls what had happened. With every sentence, Hanna's heart began to bang faster. By the time Emily got to the part about Ali pushing her under the water, she could barely breathe. "I shouldn't have swum alone," Emily moaned when she finished. "It was the perfect place for Ali to find me."

"And then she just stopped holding you under?" Spencer repeated.

"That's right." Emily shrugged. "All of a sudden, she pulled up and ran off."

"And she disappeared?" Aria asked.

Emily nodded miserably. "I don't know how it's possible, but she was suddenly gone."

"How did she . . . look?" Hanna asked, her voice catching.

Emily's head rose for the first time. Her eyes were red-rimmed, and her mouth was drawn. "Corpselike." She grimaced, then looked down at the hoodie she was holding. "I managed to pull this thing off her before she got away."

Hanna shut her eyes. Maybe the girl she'd seen on the film set wasn't a figment of her imagination—and maybe Ali herself had written that note in chalk outside the soundstage. Where *else* had Ali been in the past two weeks? Maybe she'd never left Rosewood. Maybe she'd been watching them this whole time.

More rain began to fall. Aria paced around the swings, her booties splashing in the mud. "Okay. *Okay.* First things first. Emily, do you need to go to the ER?"

Emily shook her head vehemently. "No."

"Are you sure?" Spencer looked surprised. "Ali practically drowned you. The bruises on your neck are as big as plums. And you're *really* shivering. You might be in shock."

"I'm *fine*," Emily insisted, crossing her arms over her chest.

But then her teeth started chattering. "Let's get her in my car," Hanna instructed.

Hanna lifted her by her arms. The others rushed to help, and they hurried through the rain and tumbled into Hanna's Prius, settling Emily into the front passenger seat. Hanna turned on the engine and twisted the heat to high. Aria found a blanket in the backseat and piled it around Emily's legs. Spencer peeled off her jacket and wrapped it around Emily's shoulders.

After a few moments, Emily's lips looked a little less blue. "I told you I was fine," she insisted.

"Still. This is a big deal. I'm not a fan of handling this at all, but we can't handle this alone." There was a steely look on Spencer's face as she reached into her bag and pulled out her phone. Her brow furrowed, and she scrolled through her contacts for a number. A tinny ringing sound pinged through the speaker.

"Who are you calling?" Hanna demanded.

Spencer held up a finger. An attentive look crossed her face when whoever it was answered. "Agent Fuji?" she said into the phone. "This is Spencer Hastings."

"*Spencer!*" Emily whispered, trying to grab the phone away.

Spencer ducked to the side, making a face. *We have to do this*, she mouthed.

But Hanna wasn't sure about the decision, either. Jasmine Fuji was the FBI agent in charge of Tabitha Clark's murder case. She'd seemed to take their side when they told her about A tormenting them, but then she'd had them arrested for Tabitha's murder when that fake video came out. Sure, Fuji had made amends after Nick revealed himself, but Hanna didn't trust her.

Spencer nodded into the phone. "Listen, something happened I need to discuss with you. It's about Alison. Actually, Emily can tell it better."

Then she shoved the phone at Emily, putting it on

speaker. Emily shook her head vigorously, but Spencer made an imploring face. *Talk*, she mouthed.

Emily lowered her shoulders and retold the story. Hanna hid her eyes. It was just as hard to hear the second time around.

"Did you happen to see where this person ran off to?" Fuji's voice blared through the speaker when Emily finished.

Emily cleared her throat. "No. By the time I got through the door to the hall, she was gone."

"But it was definitely Alison," Aria piped up. "Emily wouldn't make something like that up. Actually, we've all felt Alison's presence, but none of us have been entirely sure. Emily made eye contact, though. Alison *spoke* to her."

"That's right," Emily said. "She said, 'Did you really think I'd leave for good?'"

There was a long pause. Static crackled through the phone, and Hanna thought they'd lost the connection. Then Fuji sighed. "Okay. We're obviously going to take someone attacking Emily very seriously. I'm going to call a team out to Rosewood Day to check it out right now, and we're going to figure out what happened—"

"What *happened*?" Spencer interrupted. "We just told you!"

"Girls," Fuji said, her voice suddenly firm, "you've been through a lot of trauma. And I completely understand why you think you saw Alison the night with

Nicholas in that basement when you were drugged. But I can only tell you so many times: Alison is *dead*. She died in the Poconos. Whoever you saw in the pool was someone else. Maybe someone who was impersonating her. Maybe someone in one of those Alison fan clubs. But not Alison herself."

"How do you know?" Hanna wailed, her heart pounding fast. The blasting heat was beginning to make her feel faint. "Emily saw her. Do you completely disregard all your victims' testimonies, or just ours?"

Spencer pinched Hanna's arm, but Hanna felt totally justified in saying what she'd said. She was so freaking *sick* of Fuji and every other adult who thought they were just scared, paranoid kids seeing ghosts. Ali was out there. She was a real, viable, terrifying threat. If someone didn't act, she was going to do something awful . . . probably to one of them.

"I have her hoodie," Emily said in a small voice. Her gaze dropped to the sweatshirt she'd had in her hands on the swings. "She wriggled out of it to escape. Can't you test it for DNA?"

Fuji sighed. "Fine. Bring it into the station." She sounded annoyed. "Can you come in now?"

Everyone said yes, despite the fact that Fuji's office was all the way in the city. Then the agent hung up without saying good-bye.

No one spoke. A lawn mower grumbled far in the distance. Spencer scowled at her phone. "She's such a bitch."

Aria cleared her throat. "Why do you think Fuji keeps insisting Ali's dead? Do you think she has evidence she's not telling us about?"

"I doubt it," Hanna said sharply. "She just doesn't want to be wrong." She leaned over and picked up the hoodie. When the heat hit it, Hanna got a whiff of something sour, sweaty, and vanilla-ish from the fabric. It was sickening to think that was *Ali's* smell.

Then she noticed a single, long blond hair attached to the sleeve. "Guys. *Look.*"

Aria noticed it, too. "Be careful! It might be our only link to Ali!"

Hanna carefully placed the hoodie back on the floor, but then her fingers clamped down on something that made a crackling sound. It felt like paper. She plunged her hand into the pocket and extracted a small receipt.

TURKEY HILL, it read at the top in purple ink. That was the name of a local mini-mart—Hanna loved its homemade iced tea. Below that was printed an address in Ashland, a town about forty-five minutes away, along with a date and time from several days ago. A few items had been purchased, though they came up as generic beverages and hot food items. The bill had been paid in cash.

"My mom loves the outlets in Ashland," Emily said softly. "What do you think Ali was doing there?"

"Probably not outlet shopping," Hanna deadpanned. Her eyes lit up. "Maybe it's where she's hiding out?"

"That could make sense," Spencer said slowly. "No

one would be looking for her all the way up there. But it's not *so* far away that she couldn't pop down here."

"There's a SEPTA bus that runs there, too, in case she doesn't have a car," Aria said.

"But where is she sleeping?" Emily asked. "In a barn?" She made a face.

Aria shrugged. "Don't forget, she and Nick were staying in that bombed-out shack next to Hanna's dad's office. A barn probably seems like the Four Seasons."

Everyone looked at one another. Hanna could tell they were all having the same thought.

"DNA testing might take a while," Aria said cautiously.

"But if Ali visited that Turkey Hill once, she might go there again," Emily added.

Hanna nodded excitedly. Spencer sighed. "Looks like we're going on a road trip," she said in defeat.

Everyone squeezed hands, knowing what was coming next.

10

MAXI STALKING AT THE MINI-MART

The girls took one car to Philly to drop off the hoodie, but Spencer insisted on taking her own car up to Ashland—partly because Hanna's driving made her carsick, and partly because she only felt 100 percent comfortable when she was behind the wheel. It was almost dark by the time she pulled into the mini-mart's parking lot, and her mood was just as ominous and muddled as the low-hanging clouds.

Their trip to the Philadelphia FBI office to drop off the hoodie hadn't exactly been encouraging. Agent Fuji hadn't even *been* there, leaving instructions with her assistant to deposit the sweatshirt with a thuggish guy named Fred who worked in Evidence. Fred had barely looked at the girls when he'd taken the hoodie from them, manhandling the thing into a ziplock bag and tossing it in a bin. "Please be careful!" Hanna had cried. Fred had stared at her, a wisp of a smirk on his face.

Now Spencer turned into a parking spot. The windows

of the Turkey Hill Mini-Mart were slathered with posters for the signature ice cream and iced tea, Marlboro cigarettes, and two-liter bottles of Mountain Dew. There was also a poster that said ROSEWOOD RALLIES in red letters at the top. A FUND-RAISER TO BENEFIT DISADVANTAGED AND TROUBLED YOUTHS. It gave directions to the Rosewood Country Club and said that tickets were $100 apiece. Spencer doubted that people up this way would spend their money on *that*.

Her phone beeped. Two messages had come in from the bullying site. One was from DominickPhilly. *You just can't stand it when you don't have all the attention, can you? That's why you're doing this site. Not because you care.*

Spencer felt a sting. Obviously Dominick hadn't read the tab of the blog called "My Story." Spencer had written about Ali as plainly and soberly as she could, hitting on the emotional aspects of how it felt to be picked on day and night by a bully so rabid and determined she'd actually burned down multiple properties in an attempt to kill Spencer off. Or maybe Dominick had, and he still thought she was a phony?

The next note was from Greg Messner, the same boy who'd contacted her the other day. *How did you get to be so brave?* he'd written. *I would kill for a tenth of your strength.*

She smiled. It was almost like Greg had read the horrible Dominick email and found the perfect thing to make her feel better. *Thank you,* she wrote back. *Sometimes I doubt myself. It's nice to know someone cares.*

She put her phone away, then spotted Hanna's Prius

across the lot. Her friends were sitting in it, staring at the mini-mart.

Spencer crossed the line of gas pumps and tapped on Hanna's window. Hanna unlocked the doors, and Spencer climbed into the backseat. "What's going on?" she asked. "Did you go in yet?"

Hanna shook her head. "We decided to stake out the place for a while. Maybe Ali will just . . . show up."

Spencer bit her thumbnail. "With the Prius right here? Ali's smarter than that, guys. She can probably see us coming from a mile away."

Hanna frowned. "What do you mean?"

Spencer knew she couldn't forget about Ali anymore, not after she'd hurt Emily. But she wasn't sure about this plan. It seemed like a good idea to retrace Ali's steps in theory, but what if Ali had planted that receipt in the hoodie pocket? Perhaps she'd wriggled out of that hoodie willingly to lead them here. She glanced nervously at the gas pumps behind them. What if Ali materialized with a lit cigarette and sent the whole place up in flames?

"Ali's a mastermind," Spencer said aloud. "She knows by now that we found that receipt. She'll probably never come by here again."

Aria's eyebrows furrowed. "Well, we're already here. We might as well do *something*."

Spencer peered again at the mini-mart. A bunch of preteen boys on BMXs hung out by the doors, passing around a cigarette. Inside, the cashier leaned behind the counter, her chin in her hands. It looked like she might fall asleep at any moment.

"I guess we could ask questions," Spencer suggested, climbing out of the car and striding across the parking lot. "Maybe someone knows something."

She passed the BMX boys and pushed open the door, and was greeted by a very loud Faith Hill song on the stereo. The air smelled of burnt coffee and microwaved burritos, and there was a yellow A-frame sign on the floor warning that the place had recently been mopped. An older man was standing at a wall of beef jerky. Of course there was no Ali.

But she *had* been here—days ago. Spencer tried to imagine it. Had Ali taken her time, walking up and down the aisles, trying to figure out what she wanted to buy? Or had she darted in and out fast, afraid someone might recognize her? *Had* anyone? Maybe not recognized her, per se, but brushed against her, or gave her change, or held the door for her on the way out?

Emily walked to the counter, and Spencer followed. The sleepy woman she'd seen from the car was now reorganizing a display of Trident gum.

"Um, excuse me," Emily asked politely. The woman looked up for a brief second, then returned to the gum. "I'm wondering if you've seen a blond girl in here. About my height. Kind of . . . rough-looking. Missing some teeth. She might have acted cagey."

The woman, whose nametag said MARCIE and who had

oily hair and a smooth, lineless face, folded her hands. "When was this?"

"Three days ago," Emily volunteered. "Around three in the afternoon."

Marcie shook her head fast. "Nope."

Spencer's heart sank. "Is there someone else who was working here at the time who might remember?" She tried to control the edge in her voice. "Someone you can call?"

Marcie's eyes narrowed. "Why do you want to know, anyway?"

"This girl is a really good friend of ours," Emily piped up quickly. "But she, um, ran away. And we really want to find her."

Marcie stared at them long and hard, her mouth twitching. Spencer wondered if she recognized them and was trying to place why. Even though all charges against them had been dropped, they were still kind of notorious . . . and their pictures had been everywhere. Maybe this was a bad idea. Marcie might call the police. Fuji would scold them for making trouble.

The cashier shrugged. "We get lots of people coming in and out of here. One blond girl buying water is the same as the next."

"What about surveillance tapes?" Aria asked desperately. "Can you show us those?"

Marcie looked at them like they were crazy. "Honey, why do you think *I* would have access to those tapes? I think the management uses them to watch the staff." She turned back to her register. "Go to the police if you're really worried. Girls your age shouldn't have to find a runaway on your own."

Then she peered behind them, smiling. Mr. Beef Jerky was now in line, holding several long sticks of Slim Jims. There was nothing else to do but move aside and let him pay.

"Shit," Hanna muttered as they trudged out of the store. "Now what do we do?"

"I don't know," Spencer said, feeling aimless.

Emily kicked a pebble on the sidewalk. "That hair on that hoodie had better be a DNA match. Then we could get Fuji up here. *She* could access those surveillance tapes."

Hanna put her hands on her hips and faced the road. "Maybe we could drive around and look for random barns. We could get lucky."

"In the dark?" Spencer scoffed. "I doubt it."

"Party pooper," Hanna mumbled, slumping back into the car.

The other girls climbed in, too, leaving Spencer alone in the parking lot. Hanna looked out the window at her. "Maybe we should all sleep at my place tonight. I don't like the idea of us being apart. We could be easy targets for Ali."

"Yes," Emily said quickly. "There's no way I can sleep alone."

"I'm in," Aria agreed.

"Me too," Spencer said. It was a wonderful idea—in case Ali showed up again, four against one were much better odds.

They promised to meet at Hanna's in an hour. Then Spencer retreated to her car, sinking heavily into the leather seat. The whole day felt wasted. The only thing they'd learned was that Ali was alive . . . and furious. And they already *knew* that.

Her phone buzzed loudly, jarring her from her thoughts. Spencer stared at the unfamiliar 212 number on caller ID. Swallowing hard, she answered.

"Spencer Hastings?" said a woman's voice. Spencer said that she was. "My name is Samantha Eggers. I'm the head of the National Anti-Bullying Council in New York City. It's a new initiative created by Congress last year."

"Of course," Spencer said, sitting up straighter. "I know about you." She'd researched all the bullying out-reach programs available to teens while putting together her website. "You're doing great stuff."

"No, *you're* doing great stuff," Samantha said, her voice mirthful. "I'm a huge fan of your website. You're giving kids a voice." She rushed on. "Listen, I'm calling because we're making an anti-bullying film that will be used as a tool at schools nationwide next year. I'm look-ing for voices on bullying, and your name kept coming up among my staff."

"Really?" Spencer pressed a hand to her chest. "I mean, I only started my website last week. I'm really flattered."

"So that means you'd like to be part of our video?" Samantha asked, her voice rising. "We'll film in New York on Tuesday evening. You're not too far, right? Just an Amtrak ride away? We'll cover the costs."

Spencer pushed her hair off her forehead. "That sounds awesome." She pictured her face in classrooms all over the country, including Rosewood Day. And this was just another way to impress everyone at Princeton.

"Perfect!" Samantha cried.

She gave Spencer the details and directions. After they hung up, Spencer pressed the phone between her hands, her mood buoyed again. *Your name kept coming up.* She pictured everyone talking about her. Lauding her. She couldn't wait to tell someone about this—but who? Her friends would appreciate it, of course, and Greg flashed through her mind, too, but that was crazy. She didn't even *know* him.

The door to the mini-mart swung open, and Spencer looked up. A man in work pants and a plaid shirt sauntered to his car parked at pump number three. Then her gaze fixed on the registers inside. Something the cashier had said suddenly turned over in her mind. *We get lots of people coming in and out of here. One blond girl buying water is the same as the next.*

They'd said they were looking for a girl. They'd said Ali was blond. But they hadn't said what she'd been buying—they weren't even sure themselves. Why had Marcie mentioned water specifically? *Did* she know something?

She shut off the ignition and climbed out of the car again. When she was halfway to the mini-mart, something behind her made a loud, sizzling snap. She turned and stared. The lights at the pumps flickered off. A shadow passed behind one of them. Faint footsteps sounded from the back of the building. And then she noticed a parked car she hadn't seen before. It was a black Acura. It seemed so out of place up here in the land of pickup trucks and practical Subarus.

She thought of the Acura keychain she'd found in her stepfather's trashed model home. They'd found that car, hadn't they? Or did Nick have more than one?

Then something flashed in the front seat. It was a head of *blond hair.*

Spencer's heart pounded. She crept toward the car, knowing she had to see who was inside. With every step, her chest felt tighter and tighter, and her nerves crackled and snapped. Finally, she approached the car from the side. She steeled herself, then took one more step forward to peer into the front window.

The alarm went off, sending her jumping backward. It was a deafening sound, all whoops and buzzes. Spencer staggered a safe distance away, then stared into the window for real. Only now, the blonde was gone. *No one* was in the car. She ran her hands down her face. It made no sense. She'd definitely seen a blond head . . . *hadn't* she?

It felt like a sign. Spencer fumbled for the door

handle and climbed back into her car. She'd turned out of the Turkey Hill lot even before the alarm was silenced.

And before whoever was watching her could do anything worse.

11

ARIA'S FIRST FEATURE

The next morning, Aria stood in the cramped back room of the gallery, watching as Ella carefully swathed the sold Ali painting in Bubble Wrap. They were shipping it to the buyer in New York by a courier truck waiting outside, and they wanted to ensure it got there in one piece. Aria couldn't wait to get rid of it.

Ella paused. "This is how you imagined she would have looked if she'd lived, right?"

Aria fiddled with a piece of packing tape. Ella had been in the hospital room the first time they'd protested to Fuji that Ali had been part of Nick's attack, and she'd also heard Fuji shoot down the theory. It was easier for her family to believe that Aria had imagined seeing Ali instead of considering that the crazy girl was at large.

Aria's gaze moved to Ali's haunting eyes in the painting. She wasn't sure how she'd managed to capture so precisely Ali's furious, insane, and unraveled expression—it was as if something demonic had taken hold of her brush.

Why had a highbrow art collector in New York City been so captivated by it? Aria had Googled John Carruthers last night; there were numerous pictures of him attending charity events at the Met, the Whitney, and the MoMA. A *New York Times* profile said that he and his family lived in a penthouse on Fifth Avenue and Seventy-Seventh Street with views of Central Park. His two young daughters, Beverly and Becca, had the FAO Schwarz life-size piano from *Big* and an authentic Keith Haring mural in their playroom. Hopefully he would hang Ali's face somewhere the girls would never see it.

And what *about* Ali? Surely she'd found out that a painting of *her face* had sold; the deal had even gotten a mention on the *Art Now* blog. That worried Aria a little. Was Ali totally pissed off that Aria was profiting—hugely—off her image? Should Aria pull out of the transaction?

Stop worrying, she told herself as she helped Ella wrap the rest of the painting. She couldn't let Ali run her life.

Ella whistled for the courier, who was waiting in the main gallery space, to haul it to the truck. "So," she said, turning to Aria after he left, "what are you going to do with all that money?"

Aria took a deep breath. When she'd come to work this morning, her mom had announced that the money had been wired into the gallery's account; in a few days, it would be in *her* bank account, minus a small gallery fee. "Give you money for a new car so we don't have to drive that Subaru anymore, for one thing," she said with a chuckle.

Ella scowled. "I can take care of myself, honey. I say you use it for college."

It *was* probably the right thing to do. But the only schools Aria was interested in were art schools—and did Aria *need* art school if she was already selling paintings? "*Or* I could put it toward an apartment in New York," she suggested, giving her mom that sweet, pleading smile that always seemed to work.

Ella seemed skeptical. She raised a finger, ready to probably make a point about how college was invaluable and if she let too much time lapse after high school, she might never go. But then a tall, young guy in a slightly rumpled plaid shirt and olive-green skinny pants appeared in the doorway. He carried a leather bag on his shoulder and had a pair of Ray-Bans propped on his head, and he was breathing heavily, as if he'd been running.

"Um, hello?" the guy said in a sonorous, not-too-high but not-too-deep voice. "Are you Aria Montgomery?"

"Yes . . . ," Aria said cautiously, standing up straighter.

The guy stuck out his hand. "I'm, um, Harrison Miller from *Fire and Funnel*. It's an art blog that—"

"I know it!" Aria interrupted, her eyes wide. She was a frequent visitor of *Fire and Funnel*, a Philadelphia-based indie art site, and was impressed by the blogger's keen eye and intuition—he seemed to know what was going to be hot months before it hit the mainstream. She hadn't known the blogger was so young.

Harrison smiled. "Well, cool. Anyway, I'd like to do a piece on you and your artwork. Do you have a sec to chat?"

Aria tried not to gasp. Ella thrust out her hand. "I'm her mother, Ella Montgomery—*and* I'm the assistant director at this gallery." She used the brand-new title her boss, Jim, had given her yesterday. "I was the one who facilitated the sale of Aria's painting."

"Good to meet you." Harrison looked uncomfortable. "So . . . is it okay if I talk to Aria alone? I'll try to put the gallery in the story if I can, though."

"My little girl is growing up!" Ella crooned, pretending to wipe away a tear. Then she waltzed out of the room. "Of course you can talk to Aria. Take all the time you need."

Then she shut the door so swiftly the Monet calendar hanging on the back rose in the air before settling softly back down. Aria turned back to Harrison. He smiled at her, then perched on a small, cluttered table in the corner and rummaged through his leather bag. "I heard about the purchase of your painting on *Art Now* yesterday. It's a huge deal."

"No, *this* is a huge deal." Aria couldn't control the starstruck tone in her voice. "I'm really flattered you thought of me."

"Are you kidding?" Harrison's face brightened. "Selling a piece to John Carruthers at eighteen years old? That's unheard of." He tapped his notepad. "I'm an art history major at Penn, and I do a little painting myself. A big buyer like Carruthers taking an interest in you is huge."

Aria ducked her head. "I hope he didn't buy it just because I was, like, on the news and whatever."

Harrison waved the notion away. "Carruthers buys based on talent, not celebrity." He paused, studying her intensely. "*Sometimes* he buys a painting if the artist is pretty, though. Did he come here himself?"

Aria blushed, her mind sticking on the word *pretty*. "No, it was his buyer—and he was on the phone. I wasn't even here."

"Interesting." Harrison's blue eyes gleamed. He held Aria's gaze for a moment, and her stomach flipped over. To be honest, he was cute. *Really* cute.

Then he looked back down at his pad. "Okay. I want to know everything about you. Not the Alison stuff, but *you*. What you're into, who your influences are, where you've traveled, what your plans are, if you've got a boyfriend . . ." His cheeks flushed.

Aria giggled. She was pretty sure he was flirting. For a split second, Noel's face flashed through her mind, but then she thought of his awkward expression outside the gallery. *I need my space.*

"No boyfriend," she said softly. "Not anymore."

"Aha," Harrison said, scribbling on his notepad. "Very good."

Then Aria told him about her creative process, her parents' artistic background, and her travels to Iceland—though she left out the last trip, where she'd gotten mixed up with Olaf/Nick. It was easy to talk to Harrison. She loved the way he stared at her as she spoke, like she was the most important person he'd ever talked to. He laughed at all her jokes, and he asked all the right questions, too. She also liked how sexy and artsy he looked as he snapped pictures of her work with his long-lensed SLR camera, checking the screen after every shot to make sure he got what he'd wanted.

"And what are your future plans?" Harrison asked, setting the camera back down.

Aria breathed in. "Well . . ." Suddenly, what she said next seemed so permanent and definitive. *Should* she move to New York and try to make it as an artist? What if she did and it was a horrible failure?

Her phone rang. Aria's stomach lurched, wondering if it might be Fuji—they hadn't heard anything yet about the hoodie's DNA results. But it was a 212 number. NEW YORK CITY, said the caller ID.

"Do you mind if I grab this?" she asked Harrison. He nodded, and she answered tentatively.

"Aria Montgomery?" said a gruff woman's voice. "This is Inez Frankel. I own the Frankel-Franzer Gallery in Chelsea. I just heard on *Art Now* about your painting selling. You're hot, girl—but you probably already know that. Do you have any other pieces to show?"

"Uh . . ." Aria's mind spun. "Well, I have other pieces *completed*."

"And I'm sure they're awesome. Listen, send me some JPEGs of them, could you? If we like them—and I'm sure we will—I want to offer you a three-day show starting next Tuesday—we can move some stuff around and squeeze you in. We'll make it worth your while, honey. Lots of promo. Tons of press. A big party during the opening. Everything will sell—at my gallery, it always does."

"Ex*cuse* me?" Aria squeaked, astonished. A *gallery* show? In New York City?

Her other line beeped. Aria glanced at the caller ID again; this time, a call was coming in from a 718 area code: Brooklyn. "My name is Victor Grieg, from the Space/Think Gallery in Williamsburg—I saw your story on *Art Now*," a fast-talking man with a heavy foreign accent said. He asked the same questions about Aria having other works for sale. Then he said, "We want to give you a show, like, *now*. Who's your agent?"

"I—I don't have an agent," Aria stammered. "Can I call you back?"

She hung up on both galleries. Harrison looked at her curiously, and Aria grinned. "Two galleries in New York want to give me shows!" she announced gleefully. The statement hardly seemed real.

Harrison gave her a knowing look. "This is your start!" He leaned forward like he wanted to hug her, then seemed to change his mind and hung back. "So when do they want to show you?"

"N-next week. Starting on Tuesday." The reality struck

her. Aria glanced at her other paintings stacked in the corner. Did she have enough? She couldn't sell the ones of Noel—that would just be too weird. Then her gaze settled on the all-black canvas, Ali's sixth-grade smirk covered over. She couldn't use *that* one, either. She definitely needed to paint more over the next few days.

Harrison beamed. "Well, I'll let you finish up with the galleries—I think I've got all I need for my post. But hey, I never like to miss a gallery show of the artists I feature—maybe I could snag an invite?"

"Of course!" Aria cried, wondering if she should ask him if he'd be her date. She'd only just met him, though.

Harrison looked pleased. He stood, rummaged in his pocket, and handed her a slim white card. The swirly *Fire and Funnel* logo was at the top, and below was his name in gray ink. Her fingers brushed his as she took his card. Aria moved toward him, wanting to get in that hug after all, but now Harrison was fiddling with his bag. When he looked at her again, she felt shy.

So she stuck out her hand. "Great to meet you."

"Absolutely." Harrison shook her hand, his fingers pressed against hers for an extra beat. Aria was pleased to note that her stomach did a little flip. "See you soon," he added.

When he was gone, Aria turned back to her phone, eager to call the galleries back. Which should she go with? Who would give her a better show? She felt like a princess who had too many suitors to choose from. It was crazy to think that just moments before, in her interview, she'd been unsure about how to answer the question about her future. Now it was like it had been served to her on a silver platter, every detail falling into place. *This is your start*, Harrison had said to her excitedly.

And suddenly it felt like the truth.

12

NOTHING SAYS SEXY LIKE A
GUARD-SUPERVISED DATE

The Ulster Correctional Facility rose above a forest of dark green trees, gray and bland against the cloudy sky. On Tuesday afternoon, Emily pulled her car through a set of electronic gates toward a sign that said GUEST PARKING. The lot was desolate, save for a rusty Toyota pickup truck in the last spot. A gust of wind pushed a Coke can across the pavement. Even though it was summer, the trees on the prison lot were bare.

Emily cut the engine and sat for a moment. Her head pounded from all the coffee she'd had to get her through the long drive to the prison outside New York City. Her heart was beating fast, too, though she doubted it was from caffeine. In moments, she was going to walk into a prison. And see Jordan.

Deep breath.

She climbed out and glanced over her shoulder into the scrubby woods. The whole drive, she'd felt like someone was following her, but whenever she'd checked her rearview mirror, she'd always seen a different car—or no car at all. Ali could be anywhere right now, though. Why had she run off without killing Emily? Why hadn't Fuji gotten back to them with the DNA results? How long did testing take, anyway?

She thought, too, about a blog post she'd read this morning on one of the most popular Ali Cat sites. The poster, whose name was an androgynous WeWillAlwaysRemember, had written: *Any enemy of Alison is an enemy of mine. She was a VICTIM. If you hate her, I hate you. I think you know who I'm talking about.*

The post worried Emily. What if Ali Cats were more than twisted freaks who worshipped a psychopath? What if they actually had it out for people who didn't like Ali— namely, Emily and the others? She'd forwarded it to the others . . . and, after some thought, to Fuji. Of course Fuji hadn't responded.

She crossed the lot and pulled open a heavy metal door marked ENTRANCE. The latch caught loudly behind her, and she was greeted by a sad-sounding country song on a tinny radio. A woman in a navy uniform looked up from behind a gated window. "ID," she said to Emily in a bored voice.

Emily slipped her driver's license through a small opening. The woman inspected it, her eyes droopy and tired.

"You're here to see Jordan Richards?" the woman asked. Emily nodded, too afraid to speak.

She was given a guest pass with her name on it. There was a loud buzzing sound, and the woman directed Emily into another hall, where a guard who looked like a weathered, hardened version of Tina Fey patted her down. Emily had done a little reading on the prison last night; unlike the prison *she'd* been stuck in for a day when she'd been falsely arrested for Tabitha's murder, the Ulster Correctional Facility was only for women and only employed women. The only other information she could get out of the place was that it provided educational services to inmates, which meant it couldn't be all *that* bad, right?

Then again, the air smelled like a mix of mustiness and ammonia. Fluorescent lights buzzed loudly over Emily's head, and everything from the slamming doors to Emily's footsteps to the sound of one guard's furious gum-chewing had a hollow, lonely echo. Haggard Tina Fey gestured for Emily to follow, and they passed through a series of unadorned halls with puke-green cinder-block walls. As they passed one door, Emily caught a whiff of what she could only describe as rotten mashed potatoes. Jordan had once told her that her family was so well-off and she was left alone for so much of the time as a girl that she usually ordered takeout from the five-star French restaurant down the block. How on earth was Jordan surviving?

The guard punched a set of numbers into a keypad, and after another loud *buzz*, the latch gave way. They walked into a large, windowless room peppered with tables and chairs. A water fountain sat in one corner. A door to a bathroom was on the far wall.

A burly, red-haired girl in an orange prison jumpsuit was sitting at a table with a girl in a denim jacket and a hood pulled tight around her head. Both stood up as soon as Emily arrived and rushed in opposite directions. The hoodie girl used the door through which Emily had just come; a frizzy-haired guard took the redhead's arm and led her toward an interior door, presumably back to her cell. But before she made the turn into the hall, the redheaded prisoner pivoted and stared at Emily, her eyes moving up and down her body. She was eyeing her up, maybe . . . or checking her out. Emily wasn't sure she liked either prospect.

"Sit." Emily's guard pointed to one of the tables. Emily did, and the guard crossed the room to a second interior door. Then, a familiar figure stepped through. Emily drew in a breath. Yes, Jordan was in an orange prison uniform, and yes, her hair looked a little greasy and her face was a little drawn, but she was still the beautiful girl Emily remembered.

All sorts of memories rushed back at once. The two of them floating on that stolen boat in the San Juan harbor. Snuggling in the bed in their stateroom as the cruise ship drifted toward another port. How good it felt to kiss her. How wrenched she'd felt when Jordan jumped overboard.

Jordan met Emily's eyes and smiled. Emily shot to her feet, unable to control her excitement. She never thought she'd see Jordan again. She never thought Jordan would *want* to see her. And here she was. It was just so . . . *incredible.*

"Fifteen minutes," Haggard Tina Fey said gruffly. "Time starts now."

Jordan rushed over to Emily. "H-hey," she eked out, her mouth wobbling. Up close, she smelled like soap. The same tiny freckles were sprinkled across her cheeks. Emily wanted to touch each one. "You're . . . here."

Emily let out a choked laugh, so overjoyed to hear Jordan's voice. "I'm here," she answered, caressing Jordan's shoulder. "I'm so glad to see you."

Jordan's eyes widened, and she glanced nervously at Emily's hand. "We're not supposed to touch," she whispered, pulling away slightly.

A lump formed in Emily's throat, but she tucked both hands in her lap as she sat down. Jordan sat across from her, her hands on the table. It took everything in Emily's power not to grab them and never let go.

"So," Emily said once she found her voice. "I–I missed you."

Jordan swallowed hard. A tear ran down her cheek. "I missed you, too."

"I'm so glad you wrote to me." Emily smiled at Jordan so hard her cheeks hurt. "I mean, all I do is think about you."

"Same." Jordan stared bashfully at the tabletop.

Emily's heart did flips. *I'm so glad you don't hate me,* she wanted to say a thousand times. "Are you . . . okay?"

she asked instead, then wanted to slap herself. Of course Jordan wasn't okay. She was in prison.

Jordan shrugged, twisting her mouth in that adorable way Emily remembered. "I've been better. But it's not *that* bad." She leaned forward a little. "What about *you*? I had no idea what you were going through, Em. It sounds awful. You're okay now, right? Everything's good?"

Now it was Emily's turn to look down. A lot of people had inked their initials into the wood, including someone who called himself or herself FlameGirl. "Not exactly."

Jordan's eyes widened. "What do you mean?"

Emily winced. She hadn't planned on getting into this in the limited time she and Jordan had together, but now Jordan was staring at her plaintively. Emily had no choice but to explain how Ali had attacked her at the pool. She left out a lot of the details—like how Ali had said *Say you still love me!*—but by Jordan's stunned expression, it was clear she got the gist.

Jordan's jaw dropped when Emily finished. She gestured to the bruises on Emily's neck. "Is that what *those* are from?"

Emily nodded miserably. Her parents had asked a lot of questions about the bruises, too; she hadn't known what to tell them.

"Did you go to the police?" Jordan asked.

"We did, but they don't believe us. They still think she's dead." She sighed and stared at the ceiling. The lights in the room were so bright they hurt her eyes.

"So what are you going to do?"

There was a tinny taste in Emily's mouth. Just rehashing the attack brought all her feelings of frustration, fear, and rage to the surface. This needed to *end*. "Find her," she whispered savagely. "And kill her."

Jordan paled. She glanced across the room at the guards. Both women didn't seem to be paying attention, but suddenly, Emily felt wrong-footed. What was she doing talking about murder in a prison?

"I'm not serious," she backpedaled. "I just get so mad."

Jordan nodded, but she still looked concerned. "I wish *you* didn't have to find her on your own."

"So do I, but we don't know what else to do."

"Just promise me you'll stay safe." Jordan reached forward to grab Emily's hand, but then she remembered the no-touching rule and pulled away. "Because I have some news. I have a new lawyer named Charlie Klose. There are some loopholes in my case that he wants to pursue."

Emily cocked her head. "Like what?"

"I wasn't read my Miranda rights either time I was arrested, for one thing." Jordan drummed her ragged nails on the table. "And they searched my car without a warrant, and they mistreated me when I was still a minor. Serious stuff, actually. Combined with the fact that I'm repentant and willing to repay for all the damage I've done, he thinks I have a really good chance of getting off on parole."

Emily's mouth dropped open. "Really?"

Jordan grinned excitedly. "There might still have to be a trial, but he's really positive." She slid her hand forward and touched the very tip of Emily's fingers. "In a few months, I might be a free woman."

Emily leaned forward eagerly. "And . . . *then* what? For you and me, I mean?" She hoped it wasn't a premature question to ask. Jordan had so newly forgiven her, after all. Maybe they needed to take things slow.

Jordan offered a tiny smile. "I want there to be a you and me, Emily. For real. But it can't be on an island, like we talked about before—not if I'm on parole. I'll have to stay around here and check in with my parole officer. I want to stay on the straight and narrow this time—really build a life and start over." She looked at Emily shyly. "With *you* . . . if you're up for that."

"Of *course* I am," Emily bleated emphatically. She let it sink in. A life. With *Jordan*. It was something she hadn't dared to hope for even days ago. She shut her eyes and pictured her and Jordan waking up every day together. Jordan was right: They didn't need to be in a tropical paradise to be happy. Just being with her was paradise enough.

"So I need you to stay safe," Jordan added, clasping her hands together. "Will you? For me?"

Emily nodded fast. "Of course. Cross my heart."

"Good," Jordan said.

"Time!" The loud voice stopped Emily's heart. The guard lumbered toward the table and extended her arm toward Jordan.

Jordan glanced at Emily, her expression both hungry and tortured. Before she could stop herself, Emily shot forward, pulled Jordan toward her, and kissed her hard on the lips. Her mouth was soft and tasted as minty and delicious as always. Emily closed her eyes, savoring the milliseconds of contact. Every cell in her body seemed to reawaken.

But then the guard pulled Jordan away. "No *touching*," she grumbled, holding Jordan tightly by the arm and pulling her out of the room.

Jordan waved good-bye, shuffling out the door. Emily watched her go, feeling both wrenched and happy at the same time. The kiss still tingled on her lips. The heat of Jordan's body seemed to radiate within her. She would have to hold on to those feelings, she knew, until next time. But there was going to *be* a next time—she could feel it. Jordan was going to get out.

And they were going to be together.

13

(IT) GIRLS GONE WILD

On Tuesday night, Hanna stood in the aisle of the Amtrak Acela train as it creaked and wobbled into Penn Station in New York City. The doors opened, and she followed the line of weary travelers toward the escalators, careful not to trip in her five-inch stiletto heels. She was also careful to pull the hem so that her sequined miniskirt covered her butt. A bunch of passengers in business suits had given her outfit strange looks, probably because she'd paired it with the dramatic shoes, a sparkly clutch, and some enormous sunglasses that she was still wearing even though the sun had set. She didn't mind the looks, though, because she was going out on the town with Hailey Blake, movie starlet extraordinaire. Hanna had tried to work it into every conversation on the train—with the ticket collector, with the older woman sitting next to her, and even with the man who served her a Diet Coke in the café car.

She reached the top of the escalator, elbowed through the teeming crowd of people waiting for outbound trains,

and spilled onto Seventh Avenue, momentarily overwhelmed by the rush of people, cabs and buses, and neon
lights. Someone supporting the pro-life movement stood
at the curb, holding a placard talking about when a baby's
heartbeat began in the womb. Someone else passed by
pushing a pretzel cart. Then, through the crowd, Hanna
saw another sign: ALI CATS UNITE! She blinked hard, trying
to find it again through the sea of bodies.

But it was gone.

"Hey, bitch! Over here!"

Hanna's head swiveled to the left. A white stretch limo
was parked behind a pretzel cart. Hailey, her blond hair
streaming, waved wildly out the back window. "Stop acting like a lost tourist and get in here, crazy girl!"

Hanna jogged over, her heart doing a flip. It was still
hard to believe that *the* Hailey Blake had sent her a text
last night that said, *Hey, I'm in NYC tomorrow doing press
interviews—wanna come up after your scenes and meet me? We
can hit the kill or be killed premiere party!* Hanna was never
going to delete that text as long as she lived. *Kill or Be
Killed* was only *the* most hyped movie out that summer—
she couldn't believe she was lucky enough to be there.

But then again, maybe Hanna shouldn't think of it
as luck. She was fabulous and cool, too. After all, ever
since the news had broken that Hanna was part of the
Burn It Down cast, her phone had been ringing off the
hook. The local news wanted to do a profile on her life.
Main Line Living magazine wanted to feature her closet

in an article about fashionistas in the Philadelphia area. She had a ton of new friends on Twitter, and the owner of Otter, Hanna's favorite boutique, had contacted her asking if she wanted to be in the runway show for the fall line. *Hanna*, a model. Maybe she totally deserved to be hobnobbing with Hailey.

And clubbing tonight was the perfect way to forget about Ali. After hitting a dead end at the Turkey Hill, Hanna and the others had decided to revisit the case this weekend, as they all had exciting plans tonight they couldn't postpone. Not that Hanna was sure there was anything *to* revisit. It wasn't like Fuji had gotten back to them with DNA results. And though Spencer had shared the Freudian slip by the woman behind the convenience store counter, Hanna wasn't sure it was actually a clue that she knew anything. Maybe she assumed all blond teenage girls bought water at gas stations.

And the chalked A message at the studio? It had probably been all her imagination. That Ali Cat sign she'd just seen? What*ever*.

She slid into the back of the limo next to Hailey, who was wearing a similarly short dress and high heels. Her eyes were heavily made-up with a winged, cat-eye effect, and her lips glimmered with shiny pink gloss.

"Hanna, this is my driver, Georgio," she said, gesturing to the limo driver behind the wheel. "He's an up-and-coming male model. This is just his side job."

"She flatters me," said the man behind the wheel in

a sexy Italian accent. He wasn't much older than Hanna, with wavy dark hair and seductive eyes. Hanna bet he had great abs, too.

The limo pulled away from the street, and Hailey gave Hanna a mock-slap. "So thanks for meeting me!" she gushed. "When I sent you that text about coming up, I didn't know if you'd be into it."

"Are you kidding?" Hanna said as the limo halted at a stoplight. "I never miss a chance to come to the city. And a premiere party sounds great."

"I figured we'd have more fun here than boring old Philly," Hailey said, rolling her eyes. "I mean, what is there to do there except look at the Liberty Bell?" She snorted and undid the latch of a compartment in the center console, unveiling two mini bottles of champagne and two small crystal flutes. "C'mon! We gotta pregame!"

Hanna grabbed a glass and took a sip. Hailey offered another glass to Georgio, but he refused, reminding her he was driving. "Party pooper!" she bellowed, and she and Hanna laughed.

Streets whizzed past as the car descended downtown. Hanna stared out the window, taking in the lighted stores and crowded streets. As the fizzy champagne bubbles played on her tongue, her phone buzzed inside her clutch. Hanna checked the screen; the first text was from her mom. *Did you get into New York okay?*

Hanna leaned back into the leather seat. Last night, after she'd received Hailey's invite, she'd regaled her mom with stories about the actress, painting Hailey as a sweet girl who had good, clean fun. Ms. Marin had allowed Hanna to come to New York for a few hours.

In limo right now, drinking Perrier, Hanna wrote back. It wasn't like her mom would ever know the truth.

The next text was from Aria. *At gallery, freaking out. I wish you could be here.*

Hanna's new friend regarded her curiously. "Who are you texting?"

"My friend Aria." Hanna beamed. "She has an art opening tonight. We're all really proud of her." She wished she could make a brief stop at the gallery, but Aria had told her the guest list was überstrict—she'd had to pull strings even to get her *parents* on it.

Hanna began to type a reply text, but Hailey made a face. "Don't you, like, talk to Aria all the time?" Her voice was high and thin. "This is *our* night together, isn't it?"

Hanna dropped her phone to her lap, surprised. She'd figured she'd be part of a huge Hailey entourage. How special was it that Hailey wanted her all to herself, though?

"You're totally right," she said, tapping a quick *Good luck! You'll be great!* text to Aria and then slipping her phone back into her Lauren Merkin clutch.

Hailey opened a compact and applied red lipstick to her lips. "I am *so* excited to blow off some steam," she said. "I don't know about you, but the movie we're working on is a total *grind*."

Hanna stared down at her nails. She found the experience amazing, even the boring parts where they had to sit around while the camera people got the lighting right. "Is anything bothering you in particular?" she asked.

"Hank and his minions, obviously," Hailey groaned. "That dude has had it out for me since day one. He's, like, *always* insulting my performance. Haven't you noticed?"

Hanna pretended to be fascinated with the giant Whole Foods out the window. If only she could covertly hint that, perhaps, Hank had a point. But she had no idea how to say that without sounding mean.

Hailey sighed dramatically after Hanna didn't reply. "I just wish they'd fire him and find someone new. Between you and me, I wasn't sure if he and I would mesh from the start. I took the film, though, because I thought it would be a good opportunity. Working with some of the actors, doing a more serious role—it seemed like the right thing to do. That's my whole philosophy in life, really—*never pass up an opportunity.* You never know where it's going to take you." She leaned back in the leather seat. "It's how I got my big break, you know. A talent scout spotted me in the mall and asked if I wanted to do a commercial for Barbies. I was like, *Uh, I'm ten!* Barbies were for babies. But I did it anyway, and look where it got me."

"Totally," Hanna agreed, then squeezed Hailey's hand. Maybe Hailey's performances would improve as the movie went on. They *had* to.

Then she thought about the weird situation at the

set the other day, after everyone had gone home. Okay, maybe *BreAk a leg* hadn't been intended for her, but Daniel had definitely been spooky. She was about to ask Hailey what she knew about Daniel when her friend rose up in her seat and squealed, "We're here!"

The limo pulled along the curb on an unassuming block on the Lower East Side. Low-slung buildings hunched around them, the Williamsburg Bridge twinkled in the distance, and the street was strangely light on traffic, but bass thundered from somewhere nearby, and the scent of Asian spices wafted through the air. A spotlight shone on a line in front of a velvet rope; hipsters, drag queens, divas, and statuesque model-types waited on the sidewalk. Hanna looked around for a sign that said this was, indeed, the *Kill or Be Killed* after-party, but then she figured no event as exclusive would have to *announce* itself like that.

Hailey blew a kiss to the limo driver and swung out of the car, careful to keep her long, thin legs pinned together. She pulled Hanna out with her, and the two tumbled up to the bouncer, an intimidating-looking guy with squinty eyes, pale blond hair, and a black patterned tattoo near his left eye.

"Sven, my boy!" Hailey bleated, throwing her arms around his burly neck.

The bouncer grinned and lifted the rope. "For you *and* your gorgeous friend."

Hailey flounced in, and Hanna followed her, feeling

everyone in the line glaring. "Who is that with Hailey?" came the whispers. "Where do I know her from?" "She's got to be famous."

Hanna grinned.

They walked into a room whose walls were covered in mosaics and whose glossy tables held explosions of fresh flowers in large, bulbous vases. Plushy booths packed with fabulously dressed people lined the walls, and bartenders scurried behind a bar that looked as if it was made entirely of gold. Everyone Hanna passed was more beautiful than the last. They all turned to Hailey with huge, welcoming smiles.

"You're back, girl!" said a guy who Hanna was almost positive was the model for Armani. He leaned toward Hailey and gave her air kisses.

"Come to our table!" cried a girl with big, beautiful doe eyes and the most gorgeous, long black hair Hanna had ever seen. After a moment, Hanna realized she was a Victoria's Secret model named BiBi. Mike totally had a crush on her.

BiBi yanked Hailey toward a banquette, but Hailey planted her feet. "Maybe in a bit, Beebs. I want to spend some quality time with my bestie here," she said, squeezing Hanna's arm. "This is Hanna, my costar—*and* the most awesome girl in the world."

"Great to meet you, sweetie," BiBi said in her French accent, kissing Hanna lightly on the cheek. Hanna wanted to respond—maybe something about how Mike was her biggest fan, or what it was like to wear those Victoria's Secret angel's wings—but Hailey yanked her toward a small, cordoned-off area marked VIP, at the back of the club. Inside, people who were somehow even *more* beautiful mingled around a horseshoe-shaped, platinum-colored bar.

Hanna tried to remain cool, but her stomach was swooping. She'd never been in a VIP section before. There had better be a celebrity blogger in there, or maybe someone from *Us Weekly*. She needed people to know about this.

Hailey winked at the bouncer, and he lifted the VIP rope for both of them. She sauntered toward an empty banquette, and Hanna followed. On the way, Hailey snatched a bottle of champagne from a waiter's tray. She pulled at the cork with her fingers, and it eventually gave way with a festive *pop*. Foam spilled from the lip and onto the floor. Hailey tipped up the bottle into her mouth, then passed it to Hanna. Hanna looked around, feeling a little foolish, but took a swig, too.

Then they fell into the velvet seats. At each place setting was a small, quilted gift bag. Hanna eagerly looked inside. There was a (big!) bottle of Bond No. 9 High Line perfume, a small box of Godiva chocolates, an advance DVD copy of *Kill or Be Killed*, and a gift card to Bliss Spa. Hanna squealed with delight.

Hailey examined her gift bag, too, then regarded Hanna eagerly. "So? Is this okay?"

Hanna almost coughed up a swallow of champagne.

"Are you *kidding* me?" She gestured around. "I feel like I've died and gone to heaven."

"Good." Hailey looked relieved. "I hope this is the start of a whole bunch of fun girls' nights."

Once again, Hanna was touched. It was so sweet that Hailey wanted to do all this for *her.*

A waiter appeared, and Hailey ordered everything on the menu in tasting portions. More champagne was poured, and every few minutes, someone Hanna recognized—a famous magazine editor from *Project Runway,* a breakout fashion designer, a guest host from *American Idol,* that guy who'd won a bunch of gold medals in swimming in the last Olympics, and, of course, a bunch of the *Kill or Be Killed* actors—stopped by to give Hailey props. Hailey introduced Hanna to each of them, and the more champagne Hanna drank, the more outgoing she felt. Soon enough, she was chatting with this season's It Model about the beauty of T-straps. When a hot, up-and-coming singer-songwriter asked Hanna to dance, she got up and whirled around for three blissful minutes, her cheeks hot and her head light.

There was more dancing, more friends, and more champagne, and at one point, Hailey climbed onto the bar and did a few seconds of twerking before she dizzily climbed back down. Hanna helped Hailey to her feet, and they tumbled into their seats to find that their food had arrived.

"*Perfect,*" Hailey whooped. "If I had any more champagne on an empty stomach, they'd have to peel me off the floor." Then she pushed a bunch of plates toward Hanna. "Try these. They're all amazing."

Hanna dug into a plate of what looked like spring rolls. Hailey selected a dumpling and cut it delicately with her fork. Then Hailey's eyes widened. "Over here!" she squealed, motioning for someone across the room.

Hanna followed her gaze. Jared Diaz, the boy who was playing Mike in *Burn It Down*, and Callum Yates, who was playing Noel Kahn, appeared from the crowd. Both were dressed in smart button-downs, perfectly fitting jeans, and cool leather sneakers. They wove through the club as if they'd been here before.

"I texted them to stop by," Hailey yelled to Hanna across the table. "I hope that's okay?"

Hanna felt a teensy dart of annoyance—worried it might look like a double date. But the guys were nice. And this was what she'd wanted, after all—to hobnob with her costars. To be part of the It Crowd.

"I'm so glad you guys made it!" Hailey chirped as the boys reached the table. She patted the seat of the banquette, and Callum slid in next to her. "Jared, you sit next to Hanna!"

Jared did as he was told, giving Hanna an excited smile. Hanna, feeling loose and friendly from the alcohol, gave Jared a huge hug and offered him a bite of spring roll, which he graciously accepted, using her fork.

"Were you in New York for press interviews, too?" she asked Jared as he chewed.

Jared rolled his eyes and wiped his mouth. "It took *all day.*"

"Oh, cry me a river." Hanna waved her hand. "I'm totally jealous."

Jared glanced at another spring roll, then raised an eyebrow for Hanna's permission to take it off her plate. She nodded. "Actually, everyone was asking about you," he said.

"Me?" Hanna touched her chest.

Jared popped another spring roll in his mouth, his eyes searching her face. He was as cute as Mike, though in a trendier, Justin Bieber sort of way—not really her type. "A lot of the reporters wondered why you weren't part of the press junket, too. People kept asking me who would make a better Hanna Marin—Hailey or the *real* Hanna." He grinned slyly. "I told them the best person to ask was Hanna Marin herself."

Hanna stared down at the table. It was a good thing it was dark in the club, because her cheeks were blazing red. She could feel Jared watching her carefully, but it didn't seem like he was baiting her. Had *he* noticed Hailey's pitiful Hanna performance, too?

Suddenly, she felt a rush of uninhibited courage. She scooted closer to Jared and leaned into his ear. "Between you and me? *I'd* make the better Hanna."

Jared cocked his head flirtatiously. "Oh really?"

Hanna's gaze slid toward Hailey and Callum, who were deep in conversation about which New York City gym was swankier—La Palestra or Peak Performance. She

glanced back at Jared and put a finger to her lips. *Don't tell.*
To which Jared pretended to lock his lips and throw the
key over his shoulder.

Hanna giggled, and he held her gaze for a moment.
Then, all of a sudden, he leaned forward and kissed
Hanna full on the mouth. He tasted like bourbon, and
his lips felt totally different than Mike's. A full three seconds passed before Hanna realized what was happening
and pulled away, but she'd already sensed a camera flash.

"Yeah!" Hailey called from across the table, her phone
raised. "Super sexy! Do it again!"

But Hanna had already drawn back. She wiped her
mouth. "What was *that* for?" she asked Jared, fully aware
of her squeaky voice.

Jared crossed his arms over his chest, looking pleased
with himself. "Well, now I've kissed *both* Hannas." He
eyed Hailey across the table. "And I have to say, you're
both pretty awesome."

Hailey threw her head back and laughed. "Jared, you
are a *trip*!"

But Hanna's cheeks burned. She had a *boyfriend*. What
if this got out? Should she tell Mike this instant?

But when she looked around, no one was paying attention to her. And less than five minutes after it had happened, Jared was talking to Callum about some club in
LA like he'd forgotten the whole thing. She felt her heart
slow down. Maybe what had just happened didn't matter
in the least. It wasn't like Jared had dragged her to a back

room and torn off all her clothes. In fact, perhaps Hanna should feel flattered that a huge star wanted to give her a harmless little peck.

She sat back in the chair and popped a spring roll in her mouth. There was absolutely no point in telling Mike what had just happened. He'd freak out, after all, and her night would be ruined. All Hanna wanted, she realized, was to have an unforgettable evening in an unforgettable VIP room with unforgettable people. No complications. No scandals. No A. Just . . . fun.

She smiled at the others around the table. The volume on the sound system turned up another notch, and everyone was spilling onto the dance floor. "What are we waiting for, party people?" Hanna said, dropping her fork, taking a final swig from her drink, and pulling Hailey to stand. "Let's dance!"

And off they went.

14

OPENING NIGHT

On the west side of New York City, in the trendy Chelsea neighborhood, Aria exited a bathroom stall and examined herself in the long, narrow mirror. Her dark hair was pulled off her face, revealing her clean, flawless skin. Her eyes shone, and her naturally-pouty lips looked especially shiny with gloss. She'd bought a sleek, sophisticated black dress for the occasion, pairing it with strappy gladiator heels and a bunch of studded bracelets. She was going for the "cool girl on the town, out for a night of gallery-hopping" look.

Until she pushed through the bathroom door, looked around the gallery space, and remembered. Every painting on the wall was *hers*. Lots of them had soft gray stickers on them to mark they'd already been sold.

Portraits of random people around Rosewood she'd quickly painted in the last few days were along the far wall. Colorful abstracts lined the space near the bar. The "dark series," as Aria called the paintings she'd done after Nick's attack, took up another wall. Each painting was numbered, and a discreet price list was available by request. Aria had been almost too afraid to look at the prices they'd set, but Ella had forced her. Her largest painting, one of her mother laughing, was for sale for *two hundred thousand dollars.*

It was unreal. As were the invites to underground art parties in Brooklyn, phone calls from indie bands who wanted Aria to paint their next album covers, and the fact that her name, all alone, had become a hashtag on Twitter. As in: *Scored an invite to #AriaMontgomery opening tonite. Huge deal!*

The gallery director, Sasha, dressed in black skinny pants and an asymmetrical, fashion-forward crop top that showed off her immaculate abs, glided toward Aria and took her hands. "Everything looking good, my dear?"

"Of *course*," Aria gushed, gaping at the crowd that had begun to gather. It had felt like a dream to actually sign all the paperwork that permitted this gallery to give her a show. Aria had feared Sasha would sour when she saw Aria's other works, but she whooped with pleasure as she unwrapped canvas after canvas. "Gorgeous," she'd trilled, again and again.

Then Aria smiled at her father and Meredith, who'd also come. The two of them stood proudly near the bar, glasses of red wine in hand. "Thanks for getting my family on the guest list, too," she said bashfully.

"Yeah, well, *I* would have rather let in a few more

reporters, but I understand you need your people by you on tonight of all nights," Sasha said, giving her a playful swat. "Speaking of which, there are, like, a zillion people who want to talk to you. Art agents, buyers . . ."

"Is John Carruthers here?" Aria asked. She'd heard he came to a lot of openings, and she was eager to meet him. And maybe even ask why he'd bought the portrait of Ali.

Sasha scanned the crowd. "Er . . . no. I think he's still traveling." She patted Aria's arm. "But don't worry. There are plenty of other people who want your work. You're the next big thing, my dear!" Then Sasha's eyes lit up. "Oh! I forgot to mention. A blogger has been asking about you nonstop. Let me just . . ."

"Harrison?" Aria asked, her heart lifting. He'd said he'd try his hardest to make the trip from Philly.

"No, a woman from *ArtSmash*."

Aria's eyes widened. *ArtSmash* was probably the biggest art blog around. It was so popular and influential, in fact, that the site hosted art events around New York, Los Angeles, and Philadelphia, and was often a sponsor of exhibits at edgy galleries in Brooklyn and Philly's Fishtown neighborhood.

Sasha signaled to someone in a black suit at the bar. The woman raised an eyebrow and sauntered over. She stuck out her hand. "Esmerelda Rhea," she said in a loud, bossy voice. "I'm with *ArtSmash*. I'd like to do a profile on you. An exclusive."

Aria's stomach dropped. "Um, it can't be an exclusive.

I've already given an interview with Harrison Miller."

Esmerelda's expression went blank. "Who's Harrison Miller?"

"From *Fire and Funnel*?" Aria said tentatively. "It's kind of indie. But really cool."

Esmerelda looked unimpressed. "Well, we can just tell this Harrison person not to post it, okay? An exclusive with us will actually *mean* something."

Aria blinked. "But it's a good interview." She'd read a draft last night: Harrison had called her art "fascinating," "mature," "soulful," and "provocative." He'd also said Aria was "enchanting in person, as artful, graceful, and deep as her paintings." How could she turn *that* sort of press down?

Esmerelda chuckled. "You're so green. It's so sweet!" She gave Aria a condescending smile. "I'll handle Harry, if you'd like."

"Harrison," Aria corrected.

As if on cue, Aria spied Harrison's tall, familiar figure ducking through the front door. He had the same battered leather bag on his shoulder, and he had an earnest, eager look on his face. He gazed across the room and noticed her. His face lit up, and Aria grinned back.

"There he is now," Aria said in a strong voice, motioning him over.

A few paces away, Harrison noticed Esmerelda and paled. "H-hello, Esmerelda," he stammered when he was close. He looked kind of wary. "It's nice to see you again.

When was it last? That MoMA party?"

"Mm-hmm," Esmerelda said tightly, her beady eyes narrowing. *Interesting*, Aria thought. Moments before, Esmerelda had pretended she had no idea who Harrison was. Then she let out a huffy little breath. "So. Aria's been telling me that you spoke to her already. *We* want the exclusive, though. That can be arranged, can't it?" She stared at him steadily, her eyes unblinking.

Aria's mouth dropped open. She turned to Harrison. He looked cowed and miserable—maybe as if Esmerelda had done this to him before. She was nothing but . . . a *bully*, Aria realized. And Aria certainly knew how *that* felt.

She stood up straighter. "Harrison's posting my story," she said in a strong voice. "My exclusive is with him."

Esmerelda looked like she'd been slapped. "Are you *serious*?"

"Yes," Aria said, hoping she wasn't making a huge mistake. Perhaps having an exclusive with *ArtSmash* might advance her career faster, but she couldn't let this lady push people around.

Esmerelda sniffed. "Well, it's your career to sabotage." She glanced around at the paintings on the wall. "And honestly, this stuff looks like a senior-year art show anyway." She elbowed around a bunch of people coming in, almost tripping over someone's discarded umbrella.

Once she was gone, Aria turned back to Harrison. He

looked astonished. "You didn't have to do that. *ArtSmash* is, like, *huge*."

Aria shrugged. "Well, maybe I like *Fire and Funnel* better." She offered him a small smile.

Harrison licked his lips nervously. "Well, *Fire and Funnel* likes you, too."

Aria felt herself blush. "I'm glad you came tonight."

Harrison didn't break his gaze. "I wouldn't have missed it for the world."

They stared at each other. Then, slowly, Harrison moved his hand toward Aria's. She felt his fingers entwine with hers and squeeze. She squeezed back. She was too numb and overwhelmed to know how she really felt about it or Harrison, but she told herself to stop overthinking and just relax.

Then her phone, which was wedged into her envelope clutch, began to buzz. She glanced at it, registering the familiar Philadelphia number. It was Fuji. *The hoodie.*

"I–I need to take this," Aria said, holding up one finger. "I'll be right back."

She ducked through the crowd and into the hall to the bathroom. Her heart pounded as she hit ANSWER and said hello.

"Aria," Fuji barked through the receiver. "I'm sorry to call you so late. I have Emily and Spencer on the line, too."

"Hey," Emily and Spencer said in unison.

"H-hi," Aria answered shakily, her heart hammering hard.

"I've tried to reach Hanna, but she isn't picking up," Fuji went on. "I have some news you might want to hear."

"About Ali?" Aria said eagerly, unable to control her anticipation. Of *course* it was about Ali. There was no other reason Fuji would be calling. "Did you finally get the DNA results?" *They came back a match. That hair is Ali's. Finally, finally, they understand that she's still alive.*

"I'm sorry it took so long, but yes, we got them," Fuji said in a clipped voice. "The hair on the sweatshirt is Spencer's."

Aria's mind went blank.

"What?" Spencer sputtered.

"It might have stuck to the shirt when you girls were examining it," Fuji explained. "I'm sorry, girls."

"I can't believe this," Spencer said faintly.

"B-but you tested the rest of the sweatshirt, right?" Aria pleaded. "There was something else on there, maybe? Ali's skin cells? *Another* hair? An eyelash?"

Fuji sighed. "My team looked over the sweatshirt very thoroughly, but we didn't find anything else that could be tested. You girls should also know that Rosewood Day had disabled their surveillance cameras in the pool area for the summer, so we have no record of the intruder. To be honest, no one should have been in there at all— including you, Emily. You're lucky they're not thinking of pressing charges on you for trespassing."

"But . . . ," Emily said emptily, trailing off. "It's my *school*. I was there for a class. I wasn't exactly trespassing."

Aria sank against the wall. "So you have no video evidence?"

"No." Fuji sounded frustrated. "We'll keep looking around and asking questions, though. But as far as it being Alison, that's simply impossible. Please let Hanna know."

Aria listened to the dull *click* as Fuji disconnected the line. Then she stood back, her magical day suddenly ruined.

That was it. They were back to square one.

15

STAND CLEAR OF
THE CLOSING DOORS

"Okay, fifteen minutes to air," said Samantha Eggers, a pointy-chinned woman with dark-framed glasses, as she poked her head through the doorway. "Everyone good?"

Spencer and the other kids on the anti-bullying panel nodded, and then Samantha—the same woman who'd called Spencer and invited her to be on the panel—disappeared through the door. She'd stuck everyone in the green room, as she called it, where they could wait and relax as the crew got everything ready. It was basically a conference room in the Time-Life Building on Sixth Avenue near Fiftieth, which also housed *Time*, *Entertainment Weekly*, *People*, and aired a CNN morning show on the street level. The green room was full of chairs, couches, and magazines, and a long table held bowls of pretzels, a plate of cubed cheese, and a cooler full of sodas. The sweeping windows looked out onto Sixth Avenue and Radio City Music Hall's old-fashioned neon sign.

There were supposed to be six kids on the panel, but not everyone was here yet. There were two girls besides Spencer, one of them equally fussily dressed and poised-looking as Spencer was. The other girl was Asian and reminded her of Emily: She wore no makeup, her dark hair was simply pulled back, and her plain black dress revealed strong-looking calves. Two boys sat on opposite sides of the room, cagily looking at their phones. By their slight frames and nervous demeanors, Spencer wondered if they'd been bullied. Maybe she'd even talked to them on her site.

She wanted to ask, but her mind was still on the call from Fuji. Why did Fuji shoot them down again and again? *Now* what were they going to do?

Everyone gathered at the door. Samantha led them into another conference room on the floor. It was filled with lights and cameras and a small stage area in front of a black curtain. There were a bunch of kids Spencer's age sitting on folding chairs in the back. Samantha had told her there would be an audience, and she'd reached out to her blog readers and mentioned how psyched she was to be on the panel and wondered what sorts of questions they'd ask as audience members. A lot of people had replied; she hoped she'd receive questions half as insightful tonight.

Suddenly, someone tapped her on the shoulder. "Spencer Hastings?"

A tall, athletic, tousled-haired boy had stood up from his chair in the front row. He wore a pale blue shirt, a tie, dress pants, and shiny loafers, and on the back of one hand was a tattoo of what looked like a soaring falcon peeking out of his sleeve. He was one of the handsomest strangers Spencer had ever seen.

"It's Greg Messner," he said after a beat. "I've emailed you a few times?"

Spencer blinked. "*You're* Greg?"

He touched his chest. "You remember me?"

How could she not? This was the guy who'd bolstered her up, telling her that her blog's message was powerful and uplifting. But Spencer had had no idea he was so *gorgeous*. "W-what are you doing here?" she stammered, nervously running her hand through her hair. Did it look frizzy? Should she have worn a different dress?

"I saw your post about the panel, and I called to see if I could be in the audience." Greg ducked his head. "I wanted to support you."

Spencer's insides flipped. "Thank you," she blurted, stunned that he cared so much.

Greg smiled and leaned forward, ready to talk more, but they were interrupted by Samantha as she clapped her hands. "Okay, folks! We're ready!"

Greg stepped back and gestured for Spencer to go to the stage. "Good luck!" he said excitedly. "You're going to be great."

Samantha directed the panel to the chairs in front of the curtain. Makeup artists flitted around, brushing each of them with high-definition-camera face powder. Spencer tried to play it cool, but every so often she peeked into the audience at Greg. He was staring at her every single time. Her heart pounded wildly. Up close, Greg had even *smelled* good, like the men's side of the Aveda salon she often frequented.

Not that she had a crush on him or anything. She barely *knew* him.

"Now, we're going to be fairly informal," Samantha explained, standing in front of the panelists. "One of the producers will ask a question, and then anyone can jump in. The audience can respond, too." She gestured to them, though they all were nameless, uninteresting faces besides Greg's. "Just be yourselves, and be proud of what you've accomplished. Remember, you all are the voices on anti-bullying measures, and we're very supportive of your efforts. *All* of you."

Spencer locked eyes with Greg again, and he gave her another encouraging smile. Then the cameras started to roll. One producer, a thin, graying man named Jamie, asked everyone to share their stories. The panelists went around the room, explaining how they or someone they loved had gone through a particularly horrible experience. The two shy boys had been tormented—one because of his sexuality, the other because he was on the autism spectrum. The athletic girl, whose name was Caitlin, was on the panel for starting an outreach program after her brother, Taylor, killed himself after being picked on violently. And Spencer briefly told her story about Ali, but

she mostly made it about her website and how she wanted
to help other people share their stories.

From there, Jamie asked more questions about the
emotional toll bullying took on people, where bullying
stemmed from, and how to stop it. The panel took turns
giving answers, and every time Spencer spoke, she felt the
weight of her words. *Every classroom* would see this for
years. She was leaving a legacy.

When Jamie asked a question about whether bullying seemed to be on the rise in the age of digital media,
the panelists looked at one another. Spencer cleared her
throat. "Social media can expose your pain to a height-
ened degree. On Facebook, *everyone* sees what you're
going through, not just people who happen to be in the
hall when whoever it is tortures you. Everyone can 'like'
a mean comment about you. It might make you feel like
it's you against the world."

She passed the microphone, catching Greg's eyes in
the audience. *Nice*, he mouthed. Her spine tingled pleasantly.

But then someone in the audience coughed. "That is
such bullshit."

Samantha's eyebrows shot up. Cameras swung around
to face the audience member. "Excuse me?" Jamie said,
squinting into the darkness. "Can you stand up so we can
see you, sir?"

A figure in a bulky red hunter's plaid jacket rose. He
was a dark-haired, square-faced guy with quirked eyebrows

and a turned-down mouth that made him look angry. When he glanced at Spencer, his eyes hardened even more. "You people sound like those parents who blame violence on video games. Social media isn't to blame. Oversensitive people are."

Everyone on the stage murmured worriedly. Spencer blinked at the figure in the audience, a puzzle piece slotting into place. She recognized his face from a profile picture. It was DominickPhilly, the jerk who was always trolling her site.

Why the hell was *he* here?

Jamie placed his hands on his hips. "Maybe you'd like to elaborate on that?"

Dominick shrugged, his gaze still on Spencer. "The more power we give this whole anti-bullying thing, the more power we give bullies. You don't think bullies haven't been around since, like, the dawn of time? And maybe, I don't know, some people *deserve* to get picked on."

Everyone on the stage gasped. Samantha, who was sitting on the sidelines, leapt to her feet. "This is inappropriate. I think you should leave."

"What about freedom of speech?" Dominick protested.

Samantha's eyes blazed. "We're trying to help people get through terrible ordeals. What we *don't* need is someone invalidating their feelings."

"Wah, wah, wah." Dominick simpered, rolling his eyes.

"That's it." Samantha signaled to a man Spencer hadn't

noticed in the corner, and he swept forward, pushing into the aisle and taking Dominick's arm. Everyone watched as the guard pulled Dominick up the aisle and out the exit.

Just before the door closed, Dominick turned around and glared at Spencer—and only Spencer. "I hope you're happy, little liar," he said ominously.

Spencer flinched. "Hey," Greg said gruffly, leaping up. He looked like he was about to jump off the stage, but Jamie waved at him to sit back down.

"Sorry about that, folks," Samantha said after the door slammed shut. "I guess it shows that bullies are every-where, huh?" She chuckled uncomfortably. "Let's get back on track, shall we? We'll edit all that out."

Spencer was able to finish the video, even staying focused, but she had to hide her shaking hands under her thighs. She could feel Greg sneaking peeks at her, and she kept a smile pasted on her face.

After another half hour, Jamie signaled for the cameras to stop. He beamed at the panel. "You guys were amazing. I think we have everything we need and more."

"Celebratory party at Heartland Brewery!" Samantha crowed happily, bursting into applause. "You all deserve it!" She glanced at the audience. "You all are welcome, too."

Spencer stood and followed the others off the stage. Greg caught her arm on the way to the green room. "You going to the party?" he asked.

Heartland Brewery, Spencer had heard, was where

all the *Saturday Night Live* cast members had their after-parties. But when she thought about attending a party, her heart started to pound. Dominick had unsteadied her. She didn't want to be in a crowd.

Greg cocked his head, studying her. "Or we could go somewhere quieter?" he suggested. "I know a great coffee place in the Village. It's only a subway ride away."

"That sounds perfect," Spencer breathed. This Greg was the same as the guy from the emails: intuitive, sympathetic, and understanding of just what she wanted without her having to explain a thing.

Which was exactly what she needed.

They descended the concrete stairs below the huge office building to the subway station. As they walked through a tunnel toward the F train, Spencer kept trying to think of something to say to Greg, but all she could think about was Dominick. Greg had called up and gotten into the audience easily; clearly, Dominick had, too. But why? Expressly to yell at Spencer? To humiliate her?

"So was that guy an ex or something?" Greg asked as he bought them both MetroCards.

Spencer's head swung up. It was stupid to play dumb; the stress from Dominick was probably obvious on her face. "His name is Dominick. I only know him from my blog—he has it out for me for some reason. I don't know why. Some people are just haters."

Greg walked toward the stairs leading to the downtown

platform. "Well, try to forget about him. You did a great job tonight. You're so comfortable on camera."

"Well, I've been interviewed enough times that I'm used to it," Spencer said, laughing bashfully.

They stepped onto the downtown platform. A sign said that the local train, which they were waiting for, would pull in on one track, and the express train would arrive on another. At the moment, there was no train on either track. The uptown trains were across the platform, separated by a bunch of steel beams and dangerous-looking rails. For the most part, the platforms were desolate, with only a few people wandering up and down, wearing earbuds or scrolling through their phones. Spencer began to pace the length of the station, gazing at the posters on the walls. There was one for a new HBO drama series coming out; someone had blacked out the main actress's teeth and given her devil horns.

Then she looked at Greg, realizing something. "How do you know about this place in the Village, anyway? I thought you lived in Delaware."

Greg nodded. "My parents divorced when I was seven, and my dad moved here. I visited sometimes."

"That must have been fun."

He shifted his jaw. "I was really sporty growing up, so usually I was pissed that I was missing football practice. For a long time, I didn't appreciate what the city had to offer. *And* I hated my dad's new wife. Cindy."

Spencer rolled her eyes. "My parents split up, too. But

my stepdad is okay. Maybe it's easier because I'm older."

"Maybe." Greg stared blankly at the subway tracks. Spencer hated looking there for fear she'd see a rat. "Cindy used to bully me, actually."

"Your *stepmom*?" Spencer blurted. "How?"

Greg raised one shoulder. "She was insulting and manipulative. But she was sly about it—she acted like she loved me whenever my dad was around, and she denied it whenever I told him she'd been mean. *No one* believed me."

"That's awful," Spencer whispered, feeling a tug in her heart. "What did you do?"

Greg shoved his hands in his pockets. "I just . . . took it, for a while. And then, when I had a say, I told the court that I didn't want to visit my dad anymore. I was an idiot, though—I didn't tell the court what Cindy was doing. I thought it would shatter my dad—they would have investigated her *and* him. But he found out eventually—Cindy drunkenly confessed everything shortly before she left him. He apologized up and down, but it was too little, too late." He shuffled his feet. "I always say I stood by and watched other kids get bullied, but it's not the truth. I'm too embarrassed to tell *my* story. She was, like, half my size. And *old*."

"That doesn't matter," Spencer urged. "Emotional abuse is emotional abuse, no matter where it comes from."

Greg nodded slowly. Then he raised his eyes to Spencer's, his face a little blotchy like he was about to cry. "It's why I got this." He showed her the tattoo of the bird on his hand. "I felt like it gave me . . . power or something. I don't know." He swallowed hard. "I've actually never told anyone about Cindy," he admitted.

"Well, I'm glad you told me," Spencer said softly, feeling touched.

Greg nodded. "I'm glad, too." He rubbed the bird tattoo with his fingers. "If I can ever return the favor for you, I'm here."

Spencer's insides bounced and flipped. It would be nice to talk to someone other than her friends. He would believe her, she knew. About *anything*. She leaned forward and touched her lips to his cheeks. "Thank you."

Greg grabbed her hands. He stared into her eyes meaningfully, and Spencer knew they were going to kiss for real. Her lips parted. She moved closer. It felt like it was only the two of them, wounded and broken but resilient, against the world.

A gust of wind kicked up. A local uptown train raged through the tunnel, and Spencer pulled away from Greg. She chided herself, feeling ridiculous. What was she doing, kissing a complete stranger? Hadn't she *just* sworn off boys?

The train cars rumbled loudly over the tracks far across the station. The cars came to a stop, and the doors whooshed open. Passengers got on and off in a jumble, the platform suddenly very crowded. Spencer stared idly at the commotion so she wouldn't have to make eye contact with Greg. A flash of blond shifted next to a pole inside a car. Spencer did a double take.

It was *Ali*.

She was skinny, ashen, and greasy, like Emily had described. Ali stared at Spencer challengingly, a smirk on her face. So bold. So brazen. Sort of like, *Fuck you, Spencer. I can do whatever I want.*

"Hey!" Spencer screamed out, rushing to the edge of her platform. But she couldn't actually *get* to Ali—she was blocked by a whole set of tracks and rails.

"*Look!*" Spencer pointed furiously at the girl in the car opposite them. A few people on the platform glanced at Spencer as she pointed. "It's *Alison!*" she shrieked, but her words were suddenly swallowed up by a subway train rushing into the station. It was the train Spencer and Greg were waiting for, the local going downtown.

"Spencer?" Greg said, touching her arm. Or at least Spencer *thought* that was what he'd said—it was impossible to hear him for sure.

She turned and pointed to the open doors across the platform. *Alison!* she mouthed, hoping he'd understand. *She's on that train!*

Greg's brow furrowed. He shook his head, then pointed to his ear. Spencer gestured furiously, and Greg *looked* in Ali's direction, but more people had crowded into her car. Her face vanished from view. "Alison!" Spencer said over and over. A few other people glanced over, too, but most of them looked at Spencer like she was crazy. Then Ali reappeared again, still in the subway car. She stared out from the window, her eyes bright and cunning. An alarm blared. "Stand clear of the closing doors, please," said a recorded announcement.

Slowly, horribly, the subway doors shut, sealing Ali in. She grinned at Spencer through the glass. And as the subway pulled away, she raised a few fingers to wave. *See ya,* she mouthed.

And then she was gone.

16

PARADISE LOST

For the first time in what felt like years, Emily woke up in her bed in Rosewood with a huge smile on her face.

Jordan was her first and only thought.

The possibility that she might be free and that Emily might get to spend time with her—*real* time, without sneaking around—overshadowed Ali. It trumped the disappointing phone call from Fuji last night that it was Spencer's hair on the hoodie. It even trumped Spencer's text that said she was sure she'd seen Ali on a New York City subway train. All Emily could think about was lush, beautiful, irresistible Jordan. All night long.

Humming to herself, she drifted across the bedroom and stared at her dreamy expression in the mirror. *Jordan, Jordan, Jordan.* She definitely had to arrange for another prison visit soon. And write her letters for sure. And maybe buy her a present. But what? Emily wondered what one could give a prison inmate. A book, perhaps? A non-dangerous piece of jewelry?

She glided down the stairs to the breakfast table, where her parents were watching TV. "There are eggs," Mr. Fields said, gesturing to the stove.

"And coffee," Mrs. Fields added.

"Thanks," Emily almost sang. "But I'm not hungry." She was too hyped-up for food. And she certainly didn't need anything artificial like coffee to make her feel more awake or alive.

She sank into the chair, smiling vaguely at the chicken-shaped napkin holder in the center of the table. Had she ever told Jordan about her mom's chicken fetish? She'd probably think it was so funny. There was so *much* Emily needed to tell Jordan, minor things that only Jordan would want to know. Maybe, soon enough, Emily would have all the time in the world to do that. She let out a wistful sigh, savoring how wonderful that was going to be.

Mrs. Fields sipped her coffee. "So, do we need to get you a new dress for the Rosewood Rallies fund-raiser?" she asked Emily across the table.

Emily looked up and blinked. For a moment, she had no idea what her mom was talking about. "Oh, I'm fine," she said after she remembered. "I'm sure I've got something in my closet."

"It should be a lot of fun," Mrs. Fields said, a small smile on her face. "Are you planning on bringing anyone?"

Emily smiled dreamily. If only she could bring Jordan. They'd have *so* much fun there, dancing, stockpiling delicious desserts, sneaking off to make out . . .

"Emily?" Mrs. Fields gazed at her curiously. "You all right?"

Emily smiled. She was tempted to tell her mom about Jordan, especially because she might be free in a few short months. But maybe it would be better to wait a little while longer, until her mom recovered a bit more from her heart attack.

"I'm just glad it's Wednesday!" she chirped, staring wistfully at the ceiling.

Her parents exchanged a nervous glance. Mrs. Fields cleared her throat. "We're worried about those bruises. *Where* did you get them again? The pool?"

Emily touched her neck. She'd almost forgotten about them. "It doesn't matter," she said faintly. "I'm fine."

Then, Mr. Fields shifted forward in his seat. "Oh dear," he said with a grunt, his brow furrowing at something on the TV screen.

Emily followed his gaze. The mug shot of Nick appeared. It was an update on the murder case.

"Nicholas Maxwell's lawyers have informed us that Maxwell will try to plead insanity for all the murders," a male reporter in an ugly sweater-vest announced. "He has been a patient at mental hospitals in the past, and his counsel is confident he wasn't a mentally stable member of society when he committed these crimes."

"What?" Emily squeaked, frustrated. It didn't seem fair that Nick could plead insanity—he'd just be thrown back into The Preserve or something. She wanted him to rot in jail.

Mrs. Fields glanced anxiously at Emily. "Maybe we should turn this off."

"It's okay," Emily said quickly. She wanted to see the rest.

Then came a still shot of the Maxwells' house, a large estate in New Jersey. Emily had actually visited the house with Iris only a few weeks ago. Iris had had an unrequited crush on Nick—she'd known him as Tripp—while they were at The Preserve, and she'd wanted to go through his things to see if he'd felt the same way. While they searched the house, they found an old phone of his; Ali's picture had been on it. It had been the only clue that Ali and Nick were secretly linked.

"This is the home where Maxwell grew up," the reporter's voice said, the big house still on the screen. "Since the story broke, vandals have broken windows and tried to damage the property in other ways. Protesters have done the same thing to the Maxwells' other homes in the area. The family has had a long history of making real estate investments and flipping homes, having several properties on the market at any given time."

The news moved to a story about an overturned

tractor-trailer on I-76, but Emily couldn't pay attention. Something about the story stuck in her brain. Suddenly, she realized what it was: She hadn't realized the Maxwells owned a lot of properties in the area. There was a town-home, though: the one that featured the surveillance photo of Ali outside it. Spencer's friend Chase, who'd run a website about the Ali case, had found that photo, and he and Spencer had tracked the town house down—not that they'd found any evidence of Ali inside. But it *had* belonged to Joseph and Harriet Maxwell—Nick's parents, not that they knew that at the time.

But where else were their homes? Could Ali be hiding in one?

Gritting her teeth, Emily slowly rose from the table and looked aimlessly around the kitchen, as though some-thing in the room would give her an answer.

But nothing was coming to her. She darted out of the kitchen. "Emily?" her mom called after her. "You should eat something!"

"I'll be back," Emily yelled over her shoulder.

A spoon clattered in a bowl. "She's acting so *strangely*," Emily heard her mother whisper.

Emily continued to climb the stairs and walked down the hall to her bedroom. She shut and locked the door, flung herself on the bed, and looked at her laptop. A while ago, Spencer had shown her the link to the county register's office, which listed the names of every real estate transaction throughout the Philadelphia area, all on public record. She pulled it up and typed in *Maxwell*. A series of hits popped up, and she quickly narrowed her search. Sure enough, the town house in Rosewood was on the list—it was now for sale. There was another house in Bryn Mawr, as well as a bunch of properties that had already changed hands. And then, at the bottom of the page, her gaze fixed on a final listing. *Ashland*. Its status was: *For Sale*.

Her mind went still. The Maxwells had a house in Ashland. As in the Ashland they were in five days ago. She thought again of the slip the convenience store clerk, Marcie, had made about a blond girl buying water. Maybe the cashier *did* know something. Maybe Ali was a regular customer.

She clicked on the link, hoping it would list an address, but there were no further details. How could she find out where the house was?

One by one, she dialed Spencer, Aria, and Hanna, but not a single one answered. She dropped her phone in her lap, feeling anxious. She needed to talk to someone about this. Something had to be done—*now*. This felt like a vital clue. But she felt too scattered to think clearly or make a decision.

Jordan. Perhaps she'd have some advice. Maybe she could help Emily think of ways to work through how they could find Ali without anyone getting hurt.

The number for the Ulster Correctional Facility was still on the call list in her phone. But were prisoners even allowed phone calls? It wasn't like summer camp, where parents or friends could call on the office phone and campers could call them back; prisoners could probably only talk to their lawyers.

Would Jordan's lawyer help? Emily remembered his name—Charlie Klose—and she'd looked up information on him after she left the prison. He was as renowned and respected as Jordan had purported. Maybe she could call Charlie and ask that he place a call to the prison. And then he could patch her through.

Propping herself up against several pillows, she pulled up Charlie's law firm's website and found the office number. Emily tapped her fingers nervously against the back of the phone as the line rang.

Finally, a man's voice answered. "Charlie Klose."

"Mr. Klose?" Emily's voice squeaked. "Um, my name is Emily Fields. I'm a friend of Jordan Richards's."

"Emily Fields." Charlie Klose's voice hitched over her name. "Yes. Jordan told me a lot about you. You're the girl who went through all that nonsense in Rosewood."

"That's right." Emily's heart was thudding hard. It seemed like an opening, though—at least he knew who she was. "Well, anyway, I have a favor to ask, if you don't mind. Is there any way you can call up Ulster and patch me through? I know it's not really allowed, but I really need to talk to her. It's not about her case. And it will only take a few minutes—I promise."

There was a long pause. A lump grew in Emily's throat. He was going to tell her no. She could sense it. How could she be so stupid? In his eyes, she was a silly teenager.

"I don't know how to tell you this, Emily," Charlie said, his voice cracking. "But something has happened at the prison. Jordan's . . . gone."

"*Gone?*" Emily shot to her feet. "What do you mean? She *escaped*?" It had happened before: Jordan had broken out of her prison in New Jersey and stowed away on the same cruise ship Emily was on. That was how they'd met. But why would Jordan bust out now? She'd seemed so optimistic about the case. And had she left Emily for good?

"No, she didn't escape." Klose sounded choked up. "I—I don't know the details, so I can't tell you everything, but she was . . . *killed*. Last night."

Emily blinked hard. Her fingers loosened around her phone, and it slipped from her palm. "Pardon?" she asked faintly, lifting it back to her ear.

His words were hurried. "There was an altercation with an inmate named Robin Cook. . . . I don't know who she is or what their relationship was. But Jordan is gone. Her parents have already identified her body."

Bile rose in Emily's throat. "Why would someone want to kill her?"

"I don't know. But Robin Cook was found missing from her jail cell this morning. *She's* the one who escaped."

"*What?*" Emily shrieked.

"I'm really sorry to be the one to tell you this, Emily," he said quietly. Then he hung up.

Spots formed in front of Emily's eyes. *It's a lie*, she thought. It had to be. Jordan couldn't be dead. Emily had just *seen* her.

She stood in the silent, empty bedroom, staring at her bureau, then her desk, then her bed. She'd had this same stuff since she was a child, but it suddenly seemed so unfamiliar. *Everything* seemed so unfamiliar, even her shaking hands, even the old Rosewood Day T-shirt she was wearing.

Jordan is dead. Jordan is dead.

Like a zombie, she walked toward the closet and opened it. She kicked aside the shoes strewn at the bottom and ducked through her hanging pants and dresses. She sat down on the floor, curling her knees in. And then she pulled the door shut behind her. The closet was dark. It smelled like rubber. It felt like a grave. Her thoughts tried to veer to Jordan, but she couldn't go there. Her mind actually stopped moving forward, as if a physical wall were up. Her body wasn't remotely ready to cry, either. It wasn't really even ready to breathe.

Then Spencer's text from last night swirled back to her. *Ali is in New York.* Emily had received that text at about nine o'clock. Ulster Prison was only an hour or so away from the city . . . and according to the lawyer, Jordan had died last night. Emily's heart began to pound.

None of that seemed like a coincidence.

17

THE LAIR

Hanna drove as fast as she could to Ashland, the back roads mercifully light on traffic. Many of the turns were sharp, and the CD she was listening to skipped when she sailed over the rickety covered bridge. She couldn't think of a single thing on the drive, though there were several good reasons for that. One, she had a staggering hangover—she'd taken the latest Amtrak back to Rosewood last night and had gotten only four hours of sleep. In the only fitful dream she recalled, she'd been on a date with Mike and had leaned over to kiss him, but when she drew back, it had been Jared smiling at her instead. Why had she let Jared kiss her at *all*? What if Mike found out?

But more than that, she was distracted because of Emily's tearful, blubbering, almost-unintelligible voice mail this morning: *Jordan's dead. I think Ali did it.*

After what seemed like a zillion miles of highway, Turkey Hill loomed in the distance. Hanna flicked on her turn signal to pull into the gas station. The mini-mart was empty. Hanna searched the register area, hoping to see the same woman from the other day behind the counter, but there was a large guy with a long goatee instead. She wasn't sure why Emily wanted to meet all of them here to discuss Jordan's death, but she certainly wasn't going to argue with a girl who'd lost her true love.

As she drove past the gas pumps, her phone beeped. It was Hailey. *Last nite was so fun! Check it out!*

She'd sent several pictures of them at the premiere party. The very last one was of Hanna and Jared in liplock. Hanna squeezed her phone in horror. *Please delete that!* she texted back immediately.

Got it. Your secret's safe with me. Hailey added a winking emoticon. And then: *Hey, can you talk right now?*

Hanna was about to call Hailey, but then she noticed Emily's car in the lot. It was in the last space near the Dumpsters. Hanna could make out Emily's silhouette in the driver's seat through the window. She was staring straight ahead, totally expressionless.

Sorry, Hanna replied to Hailey, and dropped her phone on the seat, climbed out of the car, and jogged to Emily, the strings of her Ugg slippers flapping on the pavement— she'd been so scattered this morning that she'd forgotten to put on proper shoes. The Volvo's engine was still running, and the air blew into Emily's face. Even so, Emily was shivering. Tears ran down her cheeks. Hanna's heart broke into a thousand pieces.

Tires screeched behind her. Spencer and Aria, in

Spencer's car, skidded into the lot, got out, and ran to Emily, too. Like Hanna, both of them looked exhausted. Aria was still wearing a lot of makeup, presumably from her art opening the night before. Spencer wore jean shorts and an oversize black sweater; there were dark circles under her eyes. Hanna wanted to ask them how their evenings were—they'd both had big, exciting nights. But it seemed inappropriate, considering what had happened to Emily.

Hanna flung Emily's door open. Her friend didn't even look up at her. "Em," Hanna said, taking Emily's hand. It was freezing cold. "I'm so sorry. What happened?"

More tears spilled down Emily's cheeks. "It's all lies," she said emptily. "Jordan's lawyer is saying it was senseless prison violence. An accident. But I know the truth. This was Ali. She was in New York—Spencer saw her on the subway. She must have gone to the prison afterward. She got in, and she murdered Jordan."

Hanna blinked hard. That didn't make any sense. "So you're saying she, like, broke into prison and killed Jordan?" she asked gently.

"Yes," Emily said, setting her jaw. She sounded so certain.

"But aren't prisons *really* secure?" Aria asked, climbing into the backseat. "You're saying that Ali not only got inside the place, but also made it back to the prison cells themselves?"

"I guess so," Emily said stubbornly. "Or maybe an Ali Cat did it."

Spencer sniffed. "You think one of them is in prison?"

"I don't know!" Emily sounded exasperated. She paused to wipe the tears from her face with a Kleenex from a small, snowman-printed package. "Didn't you read that post on the Ali Cat site I sent you? It was about how some of them hate whoever hates Ali, and how they're willing to hurt any of Ali's enemies. Maybe they're crazy enough to murder for her. Ali *has* to be behind this, you guys. She saw that I was happy, and she needed to ruin that." She paused and swallowed hard. "When she cornered me in the pool, she was like, *Say you still love me.* I couldn't do it. All I could think of was Jordan. And the look on her face when I said no—well, she was furious. That's why she pushed me under, but it's also why she let me go. Killing me wouldn't have been satisfying. She had to kill the person that I was now in love with. She wanted me to live and suffer."

"Oh my God." Hanna clapped her hand over her mouth. The others looked just as stricken. Emily hadn't told them about the "Say you still love me" stuff before.

Emily looked around ominously at the others. Her chin was shaking wildly. "She's going to ruin your happiness, too. Mark my words."

Hanna shivered, her thoughts instantly zinging to the kiss with Jared last night. Ali couldn't know about *that*, could she?

Emily pulled another Kleenex from the pack. "We have to get her, you guys. Before she does anything else."

"How?" Spencer asked. "The hoodie was a dead end, remember? We have no idea where she's living or how she's tracking us. We're stuck until we see her again."

"Maybe we could find out from the prison if any visitors came in or out last night?" Aria suggested.

Spencer scoffed. "Somehow I don't think Ali signed herself in with her real ID."

"Or maybe we could look at this." Emily reached into the footwell and pulled out a real estate magazine Hanna often saw displayed at the organic grocery store in Rosewood. She flipped to a page marked with a Post-it and pointed to a picture of a majestic-looking stone house that looked a lot like Frank Lloyd Wright's Fallingwater. ASHLAND, read the address. *Secluded hideaway, on ten acres,* read the Realtor's description.

"The news mentioned that the Maxwells have a lot of properties in Pennsylvania," Emily explained tonelessly. "I did some digging, and one of them was a wooded estate in Ashland, and it's for sale. I scoured the internet, and this is the only thing that matched. It's got to be the one."

Spencer reached for the magazine from the backseat. She studied the picture for a long time, then said, "And since the Turkey Hill receipt was from here, you're thinking Ali's maybe staying there?"

Emily nodded. "Ali probably knew about all of Nick's family's houses. And if it's been unoccupied for a while, maybe she figured it would be a good place to hide."

Aria squinted. "But wouldn't the cops have searched

the properties? Nick's, like, a mass murderer. They might have wanted to make sure there weren't more bodies or evidence."

"They might have," Emily said, "but the report didn't say anything about that. And it's not like they have the places on twenty-four-hour surveillance. Ali could have slipped in after the search."

Hanna gestured to the magazine. "This seems so obvious, though. I mean, first we find a receipt leading us to Ashland, and we *already* know Ali was staying at the Maxwells' town house. It feels too easy."

"Or maybe Ali's getting sloppy," Emily suggested. "She doesn't have Nick anymore to watch her back. Maybe she doesn't realize we've made the connection. I think we should check it out."

Aria twisted her mouth. "I don't know, Em."

Hanna agreed, though she didn't say so. It seemed like Emily was trying to force mismatched puzzle pieces together.

But on the other hand, she *got* it. Hanna recalled Emily's light, chirpy, beyond-excited voice when she'd told Hanna about Jordan potentially being released from prison. It wasn't an exaggeration to say she'd never, *ever* heard Emily so happy. A carpet had been ripped out from under her—a whole *life*. No wonder she was acting this way.

Spencer wound a piece of hair around her finger. "We would be trespassing. And it could be a trap."

Emily's eyes flashed. "I knew you guys would be like this. She ruined my life. I'm willing to go to the ends of the earth to find her. And if I have to do it alone, then that's what I'll do." She gripped the steering wheel purposefully.

Hanna glanced at Spencer and Aria worriedly. Both of them had the same shocked expressions on their faces. "Hey," Hanna said quickly, touching Emily's shoulder. "You're not doing this alone. We'll all go, okay?"

"We're not going to let you get hurt," Spencer added.

"But promise us that if anything seems creepy, we're out of there," Aria chimed in. "Deal?"

"Uh-huh," Emily said robotically, but the tough look in her eyes made Hanna think that Emily was ready for all *kinds* of creepy. What if Spencer was right? What if Ali knew they were coming? What if she was waiting for them?

What were they in for?

Despite punching the address from the real estate listing into the GPS on Spencer's phone, Emily still took several wrong turns before finding the Maxwells' estate. The only marker to the house was a small red mailbox poking through the trees, but Emily finally made the correct left turn. A long gravel driveway led almost straight up, the tires crunching noisily on the rocks. The car was hemmed in on either side by tall, camouflaging oaks and pines. At night, the place was probably pitch-black, the trees obscuring the stars and the moon.

They pulled up to the house, which looked exactly like it did in the magazine's picture: lots of levels, planes of stone, sheets of long, huge windows. The front porch was clean and swept. Flowers poked through mulched beds in the front yard. Tube-shaped wind chimes hung from the eaves. Hanna picked up a slight marshy, algae-like scent; maybe there was a creek back in the woods. There was a Realtor's sign in the front yard and a lockbox on the door.

Emily immediately leapt out and started to look around. Hanna followed, not wanting Emily to go too far alone. "No one's here," Hanna called out quickly. "I guess we were wrong."

"Yeah, let's go," Aria said, her voice quavering. "I've seen all I need to see."

But Emily didn't seem to hear them. She touched the peeling white bark on a birch tree in the front yard, then went up to one of the windows and peered inside the house.

"Em, there's a lockbox on the door," Spencer, who'd also climbed out of the car, called out. "Ali wouldn't be stupid enough to still be hiding here if potential buyers are viewing this place, you know?"

"And I bet this house has a pimp security system," Aria added, her eyes darting back and forth around the property. "An alarm would go off if Ali tried to get inside."

"See? There you go," Hanna said, heading back to the car. "Let's get out of here."

But then Emily pointed to a path in the side yard. "What's that?"

She jogged toward the back of the house. Hanna and the others exchanged another worried glance, then followed reluctantly. A long wraparound porch extended all the way to the backyard. Jutting beyond that was a huge slate patio, complete with low-slung furniture and a granite fire pit. There was also an in-ground, oval, infinity-edge pool, its winter cover still on.

"This place is nicer than the Kahns'," Aria mumbled, eyeing a massive stone waterfall and three large Grecian statues of buxom naked women.

Something cracked behind Hanna, and she turned and peered at the sky. Tree branches swayed. Something shifted in the woods. The hair rose on the back of her arms. Once again, she thought of that chalk message on the sidewalk outside the studio. *BreAk a leg, Hanna.*

"You guys . . . ," she started nervously.

Emily was marching beyond the pool, seemingly impervious to danger. Hanna scurried after her, watching as Emily walked purposefully down a small path, pushing branches aside and stepping over thick roots. In moments, they were facing a square, two-story building hidden in the woods. Half-rotted barn-style doors sealed off the front. Cobwebs dominated the porch. Most of the windows were covered. Dead leaves and broken branches blanketed the roof, and one of the shutters flapped noisily.

"What is this place?" Aria said breathily, staring up at the eroded roof.

"A pool house, maybe," Spencer said. "Or maybe some sort of work shed."

"You can barely *find* it," Emily remarked. Her eyes were suddenly bright. "Ali might not be ballsy enough to stay in the main house. But what about *here*?"

The prickly feeling on Hanna's skin had intensified. This *did* feel like somewhere Ali might hide. She turned toward the sound coming from the woods again. Someone could be in there, watching them as they discovered this.

Before anyone could stop her, Emily leapt up the stairs and peered into a small part of the window that wasn't covered in cardboard. "I can't see anything," she said. She moved to the door and tried the knob.

"Em, don't!" Aria screeched, covering her eyes. Hanna leapt forward to grab her hand.

But Emily shrugged Hanna off and jiggled the knob roughly. It turned, and the door swung open into the room. Hanna winced and jolted back, afraid an explosion would go off. Or, even worse, *Ali* would appear.

But there was only silence.

Everyone waited a beat. Spencer coughed. Aria peeked between her fingers. Hanna gazed into the dark space, unable to make out anything.

Emily squared her shoulders. "I'm going in."

Spencer groaned and scampered behind her. Aria was next. Hanna scrambled up the porch steps, definitely not hanging outside alone. As she crossed the threshold, the wind shifted, wafting a familiar smell into her nostrils. Her heart stopped. Aria turned around and stared at her. Her eyes were wide, too.

"Vanilla," Aria whispered.

"*See?*" Emily hissed.

Emily pulled a flashlight out of her backpack and flicked it on. Hanna cringed again, terrified at what they might see, but the room was mostly empty. Huge silken spiderwebs spanned the corners, many of them peppered with trapped, dead insects. At the far end of the room stood a small counter, a sink, and a rusted refrigerator whose smell Hanna could only imagine. A small table sat by the counter, its matching chair missing a leg. Underneath the table was a pile of dead leaves. Another room shot off to the left, and there was a narrow door at the right. Stairs led to a second level.

No one moved except for Emily, who rushed over to the counter and opened the single cabinet and drawer. Both of them stuck a little, probably warped shut. Then she opened the fridge—empty—and felt around the windowsills and tried the water tap—it didn't work. Hanna peeked in the second room, using her phone as a light. Inside was nothing but an old bureau. She knew she should look in the drawers, but she was too scared. *We should leave*, a voice kept hammering inside her. *This isn't right.*

Emily opened the narrow door and gagged; a filthy toilet and a rusted sink stood behind it. After opening the single cabinet, she shut the door again and darted up the stairs. Hanna heard her footsteps; before anyone could follow her, she was back down. She held something between her fingers. *"Look."*

She shone the flashlight on a plastic wrapper. It was a bag of Rold Gold pretzels. "Remember how Ali ate these the day of the DiLaurentises' press conference?" Emily asked excitedly, almost hysterically. "You know, when they announced that Ali had a twin?"

Hanna would never forget that bizarre day. Courtney—really *Ali*—had appeared on a stage outside the DiLaurentises' new house, and the family had explained that they'd brought Courtney home from the hospital to help her heal. *Lies, all lies.* If only they hadn't set her free. None of this would have happened.

After the press asked questions, Ali summoned the others inside—it had been the beginning of her plot to win them over, make them think she was their old friend. They'd sat around the kitchen table, and Ali had eaten pretzel after pretzel, her crunches the only sound in the room. *I promise I won't bite*, she'd said with a spooky, knowing smile on her face.

Now Aria cocked her head. "A lot of people like pretzels, though. And Rold Gold is a common brand."

"Yeah, I'm not sure what that proves," Spencer said softly. "It probably doesn't have any fingerprints on it."

Emily glowered at all of them. "Don't tell me she wasn't here. I *know* you all smell the vanilla."

"We do," Hanna said, surprised by Emily's aggressive tone. "But we can't go to the cops with this. It's not enough."

"So what are we supposed to do?" Emily shrieked, her eyes wild. "Wait for her to come back? Because I will. I'll sleep on this floor to make sure I catch her."

"Em." Spencer placed her hand on Emily's shoulder. Emily was suddenly shaking. "You can't do that. You have to calm down."

Aria propped her hands on her hips and looked around. "Maybe we can watch this place somehow—without us getting hurt."

Hanna didn't like the sound of that. "What do you mean?"

Emily's face lit up. "What about video surveillance?"

"That could work," Spencer said cautiously. "My stepfather has cameras on all of his model homes. You can access them remotely, even on an iPad."

Emily nodded hurriedly. "We could plant some here. Today."

Spencer glanced at the others. Hanna wanted to say no—that would mean getting all the gear and then coming *back* here—but she feared what Emily would do if they didn't agree. Sleep in the woods, maybe. Sit on the porch all night, waiting for Ali.

"I guess so," Spencer said. She pulled out her phone. "I think Best Buy sells whole kits of stuff that's easy to install."

"And then . . . what? We watch from afar?" Aria asked.

"That's right," Spencer said. "We could take shifts, each of us watching the house at different times. If we see anything, we go to the police."

Hanna ran her tongue over her teeth. It certainly seemed safer than facing Ali directly. And a video of Ali would be enough to prove to the police she was still alive.

"Let's do it," Emily said. "Let's go *now*."

She shone the flashlight on the door leading to the yard, and as it creaked open, Hanna braced herself again. She blinked in the silent, empty yard. The tree branches waved softly. The sun glittered high in the sky. The shadows Hanna thought she'd seen in the woods weren't there anymore.

Maybe they'd never been there. Maybe Ali really *didn't* know they were here.

And maybe, this time, they were really going to catch her.

18

THE STING OPERATION

Everyone spent the next few minutes pacing around the old pool house and deciding where to place the surveillance cameras once they bought them. The idea was that they'd come back here later with all the equipment and a ladder and mount everything, carefully concealing it with tree branches. Hopefully, by that night, they'd have a whole surveillance operation up and running.

But halfway through the strategizing, Aria padded back to the car and climbed inside. Moments later, Hanna joined her. The two of them silently passed a bottle of water back and forth, the only sounds the water sloshing in its container and the two of them noisily swallowing.

"Are we really doing this?" Hanna whispered.

Aria gulped. Hanna seemed as freaked as she was. "I guess so."

"Do you actually think Ali's staying there?"

Aria shut her eyes. "I don't know. I *want* to believe it, for Em's sake. And there was that smell of vanilla, I guess. . . ."

"I'm worried about her," Hanna blurted.

Aria opened her eyes. Hanna looked like she was about to cry. "I can't imagine what it must feel like to have the person you love most in the world die," Hanna said haltingly.

"I know," Aria said, tearing up just thinking about it.

"But, I mean, I'm afraid Emily's going to do something . . . *destructive*. And I'm scared we won't be able to help her this time."

Aria swallowed hard. She had a feeling Hanna was talking about Emily's suicide attempt. Aria would never be able to forget that day, seeing Emily on the edge of that bridge. The expression on her face had been haunting: It was like she'd just . . . given up, standing there, ready to plunge into the water. Thankfully, they'd been able to talk her down, and Emily promised she'd never do something like that again.

But that was three weeks ago, and now Emily seemed unhinged again. Except instead of throwing in the towel, she was acting kind of . . . *crazy*.

"We'll keep an eye on her," she said, touching Hanna's hand. "And hopefully this will be over soon."

She was about to say more, but then Spencer and Emily appeared around the side yard and climbed back into the car. Spencer looked frazzled, but Emily's expression was still focused, charged, and alert. "Okay," Emily said as she swung into the driver's seat. "Off to Best Buy."

Emily started down the long, hilly driveway toward the street. Aria glanced over her shoulder, back at the house, feeling a strange pull in her stomach. What if Ali really did use this property as her secret hideout? *Had* Ali killed Jordan? Was Ali coming after them next?

She slid her cell phone from the pocket and checked the screen. Her new agent, a woman named Patricia, had sent a text about the success of last night's show. *Four buyers interested in pieces*, she'd written. She'd received a note from Harrison, too. *I've gotten a ton of site traffic because of my exclusive with you!*

Her stomach did an excited flip at all this news—especially that Harrison had signed off with a dozen *X*s and *O*s. But she didn't feel as excited as she should. They really, *really* needed to get Ali before she ruined everything in their lives.

Suddenly, Emily slammed on the brakes, sending Aria flying against her seat belt. The bottle of water she and Hanna had been sharing rolled to the floor, the cap popping off and liquid pouring everywhere.

"What the hell?" Spencer called out.

"Look." Emily pointed at a woman strolling down the path that paralleled the road. She had dark hair and wore denim shorts and a faded blue T-shirt. A golden retriever with a bandanna around its neck walked beside her, its tail wagging. "I bet she lives here," Emily added.

"So?" Hanna hissed. "That's no reason to give us whiplash!"

Emily pulled to the side of the road, killed the engine, and got out of the car. Spencer gave Aria a nervous look. *What's she doing?* she mouthed. Aria pulled her bottom lip into her mouth and climbed out of the car.

Emily jogged up to the woman. "Excuse me, miss?"

The woman turned and squinted at them. She was older than Aria had first thought, her face lined and weathered, with ropy tendons sticking out on her neck. She pulled on the leash for the dog to stop. "Can I help you?"

Emily jutted a finger at the Maxwells' red mailbox. "Have you seen anyone coming in and out of there? A girl, maybe?"

The woman stared at the mailbox for a long time. A gust of wind blew up the ends of her hair. The fingers of her left hand kneaded into the dog's fur on his back. "I don't think so."

"*Think,*" Emily insisted. "It's really important."

Aria touched her friend's arm warningly. Emily sounded kind of pushy . . . and they didn't know this woman at all.

A light went on in the woman's eyes. "Yes. I saw a girl, actually. A blonde, I think."

"When?" Emily cried in a loud, somewhat aggressive voice.

The woman flinched. "I—I don't know. Isn't she their daughter?"

"When did you last see her?" Emily pressed.

The woman suddenly looked trapped. Aria grabbed Emily's arm and pulled her away. "We should go." She smiled politely at the woman. "Sorry."

The woman drew her dog closer to her. Two deep parentheses formed at the corners of her mouth, and then she started down the road. "You should be," Aria thought she heard her mumble.

When they got back to the car, Aria saw that Spencer's face was bright red. "Em, what's gotten into you?" Spencer cried. "You can't assault people!"

"She knew something!" Emily cried. "What if *she's* hiding Ali? What if she's bringing her food? She could be an Ali Cat!"

Emily tried to break free and run after the woman again, but Spencer grabbed her tighter. "Em, come on. You have to calm down."

Emily's tense form slackened. She laid her head on Spencer's shoulder and started to sob. "I can't take this," she blubbered, barely able to get the words out. "I just want to *find* her and end this."

Aria stepped forward and caressed Emily's back, trying to understand how awful it must be to lose someone that important. Of course Emily was beside herself. Of course she wanted answers. "We know," Aria said gently. "And we're here for you."

"And we're *going* to find Ali," Spencer insisted. "We're going to put up those cameras, and we're going to catch her. Okay?"

"Okay," Emily blubbered.

Gently, Spencer took the keys from Emily's hand and settled her into the passenger seat. Then she moved into the driver's seat herself. Aria thought it was a good move—Emily was way too distraught to drive. Spencer slowly pulled away from the curb, passing the woman and her dog down the road. Aria turned her head away, too embarrassed to make eye contact.

In thirty minutes, they'd reached the Best Buy outside Rosewood. They walked into the store, which smelled like rubber and had Miley Cyrus blasting loudly over the speakers. "So we'll buy four cameras," Spencer was saying as they walked through the aisles. "They'll be in four quadrants on the screen. And we'll have a server so that we can watch even when we're in the car, or in class—whatever. We don't even have to find a wireless signal."

"That sounds good," Aria said, nearly colliding with a turning rack of headphones in order to keep up. "And I think . . ." She trailed off and stopped short. A familiar figure stood a few feet from her, staring at the selection of computer mice. A thin girl with long blond hair and expensive-looking wedge sandals stood next to him, her arm slung around his waist. Aria's heart froze in her chest.

It was Noel.

A small sound escaped from the back of Aria's throat. Noel turned and saw her, his features tensing, his Adam's apple bobbing.

"H-hi," Aria blurted. Her cheeks reddened. She stared at the girl's thin, tanned arm around Noel's waist. She couldn't help it.

Noel glanced at the blond girl, too. "Oh. Scarlett, this is Aria."

The girl smiled tightly, a territorial look flashing across her face. After a beat, she extended her hand. "Scarlett Lorie. Nice to meet you."

Aria nodded, her mind scattering in a zillion directions. She didn't know that name or recognize this Scarlett person at all. Was she Noel's *girlfriend*? For how long? Why were they shopping for computer mice together? Why did Noel look so *happy*?

Spencer swept up to Aria with a cart full of boxes. "We're all good," she said in a perfunctory voice, then noticed Noel and Scarlett, still standing there, their arms entwined. "Oh. Hi, Noel." She grabbed Aria's hand and pulled her away. "Come on. Let's go."

Aria turned and gave Noel a parting glance, but he didn't wave. He just . . . *stared* at her, and Scarlett wrapped her arm around him tighter, leaning forward to whisper something into his ear. Aria bit down hard on the inside of her cheek as the cashier rang Spencer up and she handed over a stack of twenty-dollar bills—it was better to pay in cash, they'd decided, so no one could track them down later.

When the transaction was finished, she peeked at Noel once more. Now the two of them were laughing flirtatiously. Maybe at *her*.

Aria jerked away, facing the front of the store. Whatever. It didn't matter. Noel could date anyone he wanted.

Even a ditzy blond idiot who looked, disturbingly, like Ali.

19

SPENCER'S GOT A FAN. . . .

"More coffee, miss?"

Spencer jumped and hid her iPad with a napkin. A petite Asian girl wearing a pink apron that said SUE'S held a carafe of coffee.

Spencer shook her head. "I'm okay for now, thanks."

She waited until the waitress drifted away before looking at the iPad again. She'd been so lost in concentration on the video surveillance they'd set up yesterday, she'd forgotten that she was watching from this little café in Philly and not in her bedroom.

Not that the surveillance cameras had yielded any activity yet. It had been hard to conceal the cameras in the trees, first of all, so only one view really showed the inside of the house. The other three angles showed the porch, the side yard, and an angle facing the big house—they might be able to catch someone on their approach. There hadn't been the slightest movement on any of the cameras, though. Only a few deer drifting past, some leaves blowing. Her friends hadn't seen anything during their shifts, either.

We've only been at this one day, she told herself, nervously rearranging the sugar and Sweet'N Low packets in the small ceramic holder in the middle of the table so they all faced the same direction, something she often did to calm herself down. Maybe Ali was still in New York.

"What's all this?"

Spencer jumped again. Greg stood above her, smiling bashfully.

"Oh!" Spencer hid the iPad screen with her hand. "Just some dumb thing on Vine. So how are you?" she said, trying to act casual.

"Fine." Greg pulled out a chair. "You been here long?"

"Uh, traffic was light." Spencer peeked at the iPad screen. Nothing. She quickly logged out of the server and shoved the device in her tote bag. "I love this place, by the way."

Greg smiled. "I'm glad. It's the only place I know in Philly, actually. I don't get to the city much."

He'd texted last night wanting to see her, and when Spencer had said yes, he'd mentioned Sue's and said he had time at 10:00 AM. Sue's had quaint, mismatched tables, miniature tea sets on high shelves along the walls, and stacks and stacks of books and board games that overtook a lot of the floor space. There was something so pleasantly haphazard about the café, like you were drinking coffee in a professor's living room.

"Well, thanks for coming all the way to Philly," Spencer said after the same waitress poured Greg a cup of coffee.

Greg smiled. "Delaware is about as far from Philly as Rosewood. And anyway, thank *you*. I wasn't really sure you'd want to after, you know, New York."

A too-hot sip of coffee slid down Spencer's throat. She'd thought Greg wouldn't want to see *her*. After Ali's train had whooshed into that dark, obscuring tunnel, Greg had asked what Spencer had been trying to tell him. But by that point, Spencer knew she'd sound insane if she said anything, so she'd kept quiet. But Ali's face hadn't left her thoughts. She'd been distant the rest of the night, heading back to Rosewood early.

Now Greg stared at her intently, perhaps waiting. Spencer looked down. "I guess I owe you an explanation, huh?"

"Only if you want to."

She gazed at the books on the shelves. Did she? She wasn't sure.

When she tried to get more words out, they wouldn't come. Greg's shoulders heaved up and down. He took a long sip of coffee. "You probably have a lot of people nosing around your life right now, wanting to know more about you. But what I saw the other night in the subway station was . . . *panic*. I want to help. I just want to make sure you're okay."

"I know. And that's sweet." She tried to smile. There

were worse things in life than having a gorgeous guy care about her well-being.

"You seem really scared to me. I've *lived* that, Spencer. I know how it feels and what it looks like. So can you tell me what happened?"

Spencer stuck a spoon in her coffee and slowly stirred. She thought again how Greg had been so willing to listen. He seemed completely guileless. She realized that even though she barely knew him, she trusted him.

She shifted forward a little. "Okay. I don't think Alison's dead."

Greg's eyes widened. "Alison DiLaurentis." It came out like a statement, not a question. "You're *sure?*"

Spencer swallowed hard, glancing around to make sure no one was listening. That was the beauty about this place, though—no one was *here.* "Yes," she whispered. "We're pretty sure."

She told Greg that Ali had haunted her, Hanna, and even Aria, in a way, and then how she almost drowned Emily. "I had an eerie sense I'd see her in New York some-where," she explained. "And then I did—on the subway. I never thought it would be somewhere so public. I started yelling like that because I wanted someone else to see her, too—so we could prove it to the cops. But it was so loud . . . and everyone in New York thinks everyone else is crazy, and no one was paying attention to me. And then the train rolled away. She was gone."

Greg laced his fingers together. "So she was just . . . *riding* the subway? And you randomly saw her?"

Spencer shook her head. She'd been pondering that a lot. "I think she got on at Rockefeller Center, like us. She *wanted* me to see her—getting on at another station and trying to time it doesn't really make sense. Maybe she was lurking around the Time-Life Building, waiting for us to be done. And then, when we went to the subway, she hid on the uptown platform until she was positive I was looking."

"But why didn't she attack you in the subway station? Why merely scare you from across the platform? From what I've heard, Alison seems more ruthless than that."

"Because she doesn't want to draw attention to herself. The cops think she's dead—she doesn't want anyone else to know it's her. I guess she didn't plan on me freaking and trying to point her out." Spencer pushed her hair out of her eyes. "Ali's been doing this to all of us—appearing randomly, letting us know she's still around. Well, except to Emily—Ali actually *hurt* her. And she killed Emily's girlfriend."

Greg's jaw dropped. "She *did*?"

"I mean, we don't know for sure," Spencer backtracked. "Jordan was in prison. But it's way too much of a coincidence." She lowered her eyes, realizing that last part sounded insane. Maybe she shouldn't have mentioned it.

Greg fiddled with a little stirring spoon. "Why don't you tell the cops?" he asked.

She shrugged. "The cops think she's dead. And I'm the

only one who saw her in New York."

"Well, maybe there are cameras in the subway. Or the station."

Spencer thought about this. "There could be. But you'd need police permission to get those. And like I said, the police don't believe Ali's alive." It was the same reason they couldn't go to Jordan's prison themselves and ask for surveillance records. Besides, Ali was too smart to let anything get on camera. Only, did that mean she was too smart to let herself be seen on the cameras they'd set up around the pool house, too?

"The cops are assholes." Greg looked angry.

"Yeah." Spencer pretended to pick lint off her T-shirt.

"Well, *I* believe you."

Spencer looked up as Greg took her hand. A lump formed in her throat. It felt so good to hear someone say those words. "Thanks," she said softly. "It's nice to hear that."

Greg shook his head. "It's a horrible thing to feel like you have no one to turn to and no one who will listen. But I will *always* listen. You can always talk to me. What's your plan?"

"We have no plans," Spencer said automatically. There was no way she was telling him about the pool house or the surveillance cameras. But his voice was so tender that tears came to her eyes. "Thank you, though. For . . . being here."

"You're welcome."

They stared at each other meaningfully. Then Greg moved into the seat next to Spencer and touched his lips lightly to hers. The coffee smells and faint French music fell away, and all Spencer felt was his soft mouth. Her head throbbed with pleasure. She pulled Greg closer, his firm, strong chest pressed against hers. She could feel his biceps through his shirt, his strong back muscles, too. Even his body felt safe. He really *would* protect her. And maybe, unlike the other boys she'd known, he wouldn't leave when things got scary.

They pulled away, grinning at each other. Spencer sought for something cute and witty to say, but then she blurted, "Will you go to a benefit in Rosewood with me?"

Greg looked amused. "I'd be honored. When is it?"

"Tomorrow." Spencer grimaced guiltily. "I'm sorry I'm inviting you so late. But I would love it if you could make it. It's for troubled and disadvantaged youth around Rosewood. Apparently, I'm their honored guest—maybe because I'm so troubled." She winced.

"Ooh," Greg said. "Well, in my book, you're *always* the honored guest."

Spencer was about to playfully punch him, but her buzzing phone threw her off. She glanced down into her open bag. NEW EMAIL FROM DOMINICKPHILLY.

She groaned. What could *he* want? She knew she should ignore it, but she was still thinking very much about Dominick's presence in New York. Especially how he'd sauntered out of the room saying, *I hope you're happy, little liar.*

"Excuse me," she said to Greg, reaching for it. Slowly, she pressed the button to bring up the message. Her face fell.

"What is it?" Greg asked.

Spencer swallowed hard. "A new note from Dominick."

"That guy who heckled you?"

She nodded, then turned her phone to show him. Greg's brow furrowed as he inspected the screen. "*You can run to Philly,*" he read aloud, "*but you can't hide from the fact that you're a fraud.*" He set his jaw. "How does he know you're in Philly?"

She ran her hands down the length of her face. "I don't know," she said shakily. She stared out the window, half expecting to see him on a park bench across the street, glaring. But the park's only visitors were some pigeons. "Maybe he's following me," she said softly.

"But . . . why?"

Suddenly, Spencer had a horrible thought. She turned to Greg. "Have you heard of the Ali Cats?"

Greg frowned. "That Alison fan club?"

"Yeah. I haven't wanted to think they're dangerous, but who knows? Maybe Dominick is one of them." Spencer had discounted Emily's theory until she'd reread the Ali Cat post. The person who'd said they hated all enemies of Ali *did* seem pretty vehement. There were a lot of crazy people out there in the world—and Dominick seemed right up there.

"So he's out to get you?" Greg looked skeptical.

"I don't know." Spencer felt like she might cry. She blinked again and again, trying to wipe away the image of Dominick's scowling face.

Greg curled her hand in his. "I do know, Spencer. I get it, I promise." He slung his arm around her shoulders and pulled her close. "I won't let anyone hurt you, Spencer," he said in a warm, soft voice.

Spencer sank her face into his chest, holding on to him tightly, wishing she would never have to let go.

20

ROCK BOTTOM

Emily's sleep was interrupted by knocking from somewhere muffled and far away. She opened one eye, then the other, and then looked around. Clothes on hangers loomed over her head. A dirty sneaker lay on its side next to her nose. She'd fallen asleep in her closet. *Again.*

She uncurled from a tight ball and kicked open the door. Sun streamed through the window onto her neatly made bed. Then she heard the knocking again. Someone was at her door. "Emily?" came her mom's voice. "Something came for you."

She glanced around her room, noticing the heap of blankets in the closet, Jordan's picture on her bed, and the surveillance video screens already up on her laptop—it wasn't her turn to monitor yet, but somehow she felt safer with them on all the time, and so she'd left the feed up all night. She tucked Jordan under the mattress and closed her laptop lid, then padded across the room and opened it a crack.

Mrs. Fields held a box in her hands, a concerned

look on her face. "You got something from the Ulster Correctional Facility?"

A chill went through Emily's body. "Thanks," she said quickly, grabbing it and shutting the door.

Her mom stuck her foot in the gap before Emily could close the door completely. "Didn't you get a letter from there, too?" she went on, her voice cracking. "Do you . . . *know* someone from there?"

Emily hugged the box tightly to her chest. EMILY FIELDS, it said on the top. "No," she mumbled. It was the truth, after all.

"Then why is someone from a *prison* sending you things?"

See? *That* was why Emily hadn't told her mom anything. Sure, she was dying to explain that the love of her life was gone . . . and that Ali had done it . . . and that she felt like she was falling into a dark, deep chasm that she'd never be able to climb out of. But her mom wouldn't hear any of that. She wouldn't hear anything past the fact that Emily had loved someone in *prison*. She wouldn't absorb any of Jordan's good qualities, or that she would have been freed soon. So why even bother getting into it?

Emily turned around jerkily and walked back to her bed. "I'm really tired."

She hoped her mom would take that as a hint to leave, but Mrs. Fields remained in the doorway. A moment later, Emily heard a sniff and turned. Mrs. Fields's face was red, her eyes full of tears. "What's wrong with you, honey?"

she begged Emily. "Please tell me."

"Nothing," Emily groaned. *Now go away so I can open this box*, she wanted to scream.

Mrs. Fields still didn't move. Her gaze drifted to the bruises on her neck. "You're going to explain those right now," she demanded, now sounding angry. She often took on an angry tone, Emily knew, when she got *really* scared. "Otherwise, I'm going to think someone hurt you."

Emily balled up a fist. "I did it myself," she blurted before she could think.

Her mom's eyes widened. "You deliberately *hurt* yourself? Why?"

"It doesn't matter!" Emily roared. She stomped back to the door and closed it tight. "I'm fine, Mom! Just give me some space!"

She twisted the lock on the knob and waited. She could hear her mother standing outside, sniffing a little, her clothes rustling. And then, without saying another word, Mrs. Fields turned and padded down the hall. Emily listened as she walked down the stairs. She heard a jingle of keys, then the rumble of the garage door rising. Where was her mother going? Emily wasn't sure she'd been out since her heart attack. But maybe it was a good thing. She'd asked for space; now she was getting it.

She looked at the box, then felt under the mattress and pulled out the picture of Jordan she'd hidden. Jordan smiled happily up at her, blissfully unaware of what her future would hold. Emily stared at the picture until her eyes blurred, trying to imagine that Jordan was still alive. But all she saw when she closed her eyes was Jordan's body on a cold, hard slab in the morgue. Gone.

Slowly, she opened the box. On top of a layer of Bubble Wrap was a small typewritten note. Emily picked it up and examined it closely. *Jordan Richards's possessions*, it read. And then, *Delivered to: Emily Fields*.

A knot formed in Emily's chest, and she shut the box tight. This must be the stuff Jordan had on her when she was arrested. For whatever reason, Jordan had wanted *her* to have it, not her parents. What was inside? A watch, maybe. Some earrings. *Personal* items, things Emily couldn't bear to see right now. Or maybe ever.

She needed noise, news, *something.* Carrying her phone and the laptop with the surveillance feed, she padded downstairs. The house was quiet, the TV in the den off and the breakfast dishes stacked neatly in the drying rack. Emily switched on the TV in the kitchen and stared at a commercial for a local car dealership. A plate full of Danish from the local bakery sat on the kitchen table, probably a hint that Emily should eat something. But she couldn't imagine putting food in her mouth, and swallowing, and feeling full. She wasn't sure she'd be able to eat anything ever again.

The commercials on TV were over, and the news was back on. "We have new developments from the disturbing murder of the young woman in prison known as the Preppy Thief," the anchor, a generic-looking blond woman with an ascot around her neck, was saying.

Emily's head snapped up. It was as if the news were showing this just to torment her. On the screen was a picture of Jordan on a boat dock, her long hair blowing in the wind, a huge, brilliant smile on her face. It was gut-wrenching to look at. Jordan seemed so *alive*. So vibrant. Emily moved zombielike toward the TV and touched Jordan's cheek, the TV zapping her with static.

"The assailant is Robin Cook, who'd been incarcerated for assault and battery. Miss Cook went missing from her prison cell a few days ago. Citizens in the Ulster County area are on alert to be on the lookout for her—she could be violent and dangerous."

A picture of the killer appeared, the very first one Emily had seen—she'd scoured Google for any information on Robin Cook but had found nothing. Emily studied it hard, then stood back. She knew this girl. It was the burly red-headed girl she'd seen in the visitation room the day she'd talked to Jordan. The one who'd looked Emily up and down, like she was checking her out.

That was Jordan's killer? She and Jordan had barely *looked* at each other. No animosity had passed between them.

Then Emily thought about Robin Cook's visitor that day. It had been a girl in a hoodie, right? Emily couldn't really remember her; the girl had hurried so quickly out of the room when Emily arrived. It had seemed like Emily spooked them.

What if that was because the visitor was *Ali*?

Emily's thoughts started to whirl. Was it possible? Maybe, somehow, Ali knew this girl. And maybe she'd met with her that morning to plan how Robin was going to kill Jordan. Maybe Hanna and the others were right: Ali *hadn't* broken into prison and killed Jordan. She'd had someone else do it—and then, presumably, she'd broken that someone out of jail.

Robin was an Ali Cat.

She placed her palms on the table and let out a scream. The sound echoed satisfyingly through the room . . . but it wasn't nearly satisfying enough. Suddenly, she felt antsy, as if her clothes were made of hair. A harsh and dangerous feeling awoke inside her, something she barely recognized but immediately embraced. That was *it*. The final straw. She stood up and grabbed her keys. It was time to actually *do* something.

She was going to that house. She was going to find Ali, no matter what it took.

An hour later, Emily sat in her car, her fingers squeezing and squeezing the leather steering wheel like a stress ball. Trees, hills, open space, and occasional barns swept past, but she didn't pause to look at the scenery. And her phone, which sat on the passenger seat, kept buzzing.

It was her friends, checking in on her. Maybe they'd seen the Jordan/Robin news on TV, too. But Emily couldn't answer their calls—there was no way she could tell them she was driving to Ashland alone. They were already worried about her. Something about seeing Robin's face—and knowing she'd been right *next* to Emily the day Jordan died, and that Emily could have *stopped* her, maybe—changed something in her. Now all she could imagine was seizing Ali and squeezing her hard around the neck. Harder, then harder still, until she couldn't breathe. She pictured Ali's eyes bulging wide, her mouth gasping for air she couldn't breathe. Ali finally turning to Emily and begging her to stop.

And would Emily stop? *No, she wouldn't.* At least, not in her fantasies. She wasn't ashamed of feeling that way, either. She felt like she'd passed some point of no return, and couldn't go back.

She turned at the red mailbox marked *Maxwell* and climbed the steep hill up the driveway. The main house stood tall and proud, a FOR SALE sign now in the front yard. Emily parked the car under one of the big birch trees, got out, and grabbed the metal baseball bat from the backseat, the only weapon-like item she could find in her house. Then she looked around. Leaves swished playfully on the branches. Somewhere, a dog barked. It was so quiet up here. So peaceful.

And so horrible.

Emily hurried around to the pool house. Adrenaline coursed vigorously in her blood as she marched up to the windows. She cupped her hands and peered inside. The room was dark. But Ali *had* to be here. Emily would accept nothing less.

Emily's brain snapped and fizzed. When she kicked the door open, it felt like it wasn't her body doing it, but someone else's—someone strong and brave. The door swung open into the empty room, and she stepped inside, nostrils flaring, bat poised. The room still smelled sickeningly of vanilla soap. Emily never wanted to smell vanilla again.

"Ali?" Emily bellowed, prowling around the room like a cat. She pictured the sound registering on the surveillance cameras. But it didn't matter: It was her shift now. No one else was watching. "Ali? Where are you?" she growled.

She stopped and listened. Nothing. But all she could picture was Ali hiding in a closet, holding her hand over her mouth to stifle a giggle. Maybe Robin was with her—maybe they were laughing together. Emily poked her head into the second room on the first floor. That same empty bureau, that maddeningly dusty floor. She pulled open a closet door, then slammed it hard. *Nothing, nothing, nothing.*

She stormed up the stairs and glared into the two small rooms. Dark. Filled with spiderwebs. She could practically hear Ali's cackles.

"Ali!" Emily screamed, spinning around, a pulse throbbing hard and fast in her brain. "I know you're near! And I know what you did to Jordan! *I know it was you!*"

But she received no answer. The same as *always*—Ali was always ripping something away from them, and there was never, *ever* a way to truly get it back. How much had Emily lost since this ordeal began? How much had Ali ruined? How could one person continue to get away with this? How could such a sick, black, despicable soul continue to persevere?

It felt like there was a huge buildup of pressure inside her. She let out a keening wail and stumbled down the stairs, her vision blurred. First she darted toward the drawer in the makeshift kitchen, pulling it out. It felt satisfying to throw it to the floor and hit it with the baseball bat. She pulled at the cabinet next, grunting as she ripped it off its flimsy hinges.

She used the bat to smash a vase in the kitchen. Then she hacked away at the wooden railing. She yanked the only set of curtains off the walls, tossed them on the ground, and stomped on them.

There wasn't much to trash, but she destroyed all she could. When she was finished, she stood in the center of the room, breathing hard. Sweat ran down her face. There was dirt under her fingernails and blood from the broken glass on her arms and legs. She could feel splinters in her hands. She looked around, still sensing Ali was close. "*How* did you do it?" she whispered to the ceiling. "Why did you do this to me?"

It was a stupid question to ask, because Emily already knew the answer. Sobs rippled through her body. "I will never love you!" she shrieked to the empty room. "Never, ever! And I will kill you! You will pay for this!"

The words rang out through the room, too true but also too raw. The bat slipped from her sweaty fingers. All at once, Emily felt horrified by what she'd said. It *was* what she wanted . . . and she knew she was capable. But she couldn't believe she'd turned into this person.

Then she looked around the decimated room with fresh eyes. *What had she done?* Her friends would see the remains of this during their surveillance shifts. They'd think it was a lead . . . and Emily would have to tell them the truth. What if the Maxwells or a Realtor checked in on the place? What if they found this?

She jumped to her feet, wiped her bloody hands on her jeans, and quickly gathered up all the cabinets and drawers and put them back on their hinges as best she could. Then she used her hands to sweep the glass into a pile. *You're a terrible person, you're a terrible person*, she thought, the words like punches. How could she say she was going to kill someone? How had Ali driven her to *this*? All at once, she wondered if Ali had succeeded in her master plan. She had twisted Emily into a lunatic. She had changed her from the sweet, sensitive, cautious girl she once was into someone *exactly like her.*

By mid-afternoon, she'd cleaned up entirely, and she emerged from the house sweaty, bloody, and exhausted. She scuttled to her car and threw herself into the seat, barely noticing all the blood she was getting on the steering wheel. She stared blankly through the windshield, for a moment not having any idea where she was going to go.

She felt drained, used up, finished. She felt ready to wave the white flag.

"I surrender, Ali," she said in monotone as she drove down the steep hill to the main road. "You win."

And *that* was a terrible thing to say aloud, too.

21

I'LL BE YOUR BEST FRIEND. . . .

"And *that's* why we're not friends anymore, Hanna Marin," Hanna said harshly, eyeing Hailey under the hot set lights. Her Naomi Zeigler wig tickled her scalp, but she resisted scratching it. "Because you're *crazy*. And you're a liar. And there's only so much a girl can take."

Instead of Hailey looking shocked, as the script dictated, she stared glassily at the wall, almost asleep. A beat too late, she snapped to attention. "But, Naomi," she whined. "You don't, like, know the whole story."

"Cut!" Hank bellowed. "The lighting is all wrong."

The bell rang. Everyone snapped out of character, and Hailey fell gratefully into a raffia couch. "Oh my God," she murmured, slinging a hand over her eyes. "I feel like death."

"Late night?" Hanna asked cautiously. Hailey did look exhausted. Despite hours in hair and makeup, her hair was limp and her face was sallow and puffy. And even when she smiled, she seemed pissed off, like she was ready to lose it.

"Yeah, but super fun." Hailey pulled her hand away from her eyes and peered at Hanna. "I was going to invite you, too, but you never texted me back."

She sounded hurt. Hanna suddenly remembered Hailey's "can you talk" text that had come in just as she'd pulled into Turkey Hill yesterday. She had completely forgotten to call Hailey, though maybe that was a good thing. Right now the last thing she needed was to get in more trouble. Every time she talked to Mike on the phone during his breaks at soccer camp, that horrible image of her and Jared kissing swirled in her head.

Hank made his adjustments, then ducked behind the wall again. "I need you to reply more quickly this time, Hailey," he shouted out. "You missed your cue."

Hailey rolled her eyes. "What does *he* know?" she murmured to Hanna under her breath. "*I'm* the one who's been in twelve major motion pictures and two hit TV shows."

Hanna stuck her tongue into her cheek. How much longer could she watch Hailey butcher her character? She said nothing as she walked back to her first marker.

Hank called action, and they started the scene again. This time, Hailey not only missed her cue, she completely bungled most of her lines or else breezed through them tonelessly. Hank yelled cut again. Hailey fell onto the couch once more. "How long is this going to *take*?"

Hank ran out from behind the wall and walked right

up to Hailey, towering over her. "What are you doing?" he demanded.

Hailey's eyes narrowed. "Huh?"

"You missed your cue." Hank placed his hands on his hips. "*Again.* And I couldn't even make out most of your lines. You had no inflection. And your eyes were completely dead."

Daniel, Hank's assistant, rushed up behind him with the scene's script fastened to a clipboard. Hanna took a small step away from him—he still creeped her out—but he was paying no attention to her. His long finger searched down the page, finding the line. "Halfway through, you were supposed to say, 'Naomi, there's something you need to know,' not just 'Hey, Naomi.'"

Hailey made a face. "So?"

Hank looked at the cameraman. "Okay, we're going to have to retake that. *Again.*" He rolled his eyes and started back to his chair, muttering something under his breath. It sounded like, "And this time, Hailey, try not to show the world you're hungover."

Hailey straightened up. "Excuse me?"

Hank trundled on, still muttering.

"Hey!" Hailey called after him. "I asked you a question!"

Hank still didn't answer. "Uh, may I remind you that *I'm* the star here?" Hailey bellowed. "And you're just the overweight, washed-up director!"

Her words rang out through the room. Hanna gasped.

She was pretty sure everyone else on set did, too.

Hank wheeled around, eyes blazing. "You're out of line, Hailey."

Hailey raised her chin. "That's what you get for talking behind my back."

Hank gritted his teeth. "Maybe you deserved it. Your head isn't in this. Your behavior is unacceptable. You're always late, you're always hungover, and your bad performance after bad performance is bringing down the quality of this whole production."

His voice rang out through the high-ceilinged room, and after he finished talking, there was dead silence. Hailey blinked hard, as if Hank had just punched her in the stomach. She opened her mouth to speak, but then shut it fast, tears welling in her big blue eyes.

Hanna's stomach swirled around and around. She'd prayed for Hank to finally get through to Hailey, but hated that it was going down like this. This was so public. So embarrassing.

Hank sighed heavily, closed his eyes, and seemed to center himself. "Either you straighten up and actually listen to me, or you're gone," he said in a calmer voice. "You understand?"

Hailey turned away slightly. "You can't fire me."

"Hailey . . . ," Hank warned.

Hailey raised her hand to cut him off. "Because I *quit*."

Then she wheeled around, shoved Daniel out of the way, and stormed to her dressing room, slamming the door so hard some of the high overhead lights shook. In seconds, Hanna could hear her on the phone with some-one—her agent, maybe. Hailey sounded furious.

Hanna dared to look around the set. Every single actor stood stock-still, awkward looks on their faces. The cam-eraman gripped the sides of the camera, his jaw slack. The hairstylist's mouth was a perfect O. The production assis-tants nudged each other, and one of the guys in catering was already typing away on his phone.

It suddenly felt so hot inside the room. Hanna turned and fled for the side door, needing some air. She exited into the same alley that had spooked her the other day, though it was now bright, airy, and completely unthreat-ening. She peered down at the pavement. The *BreAk a leg, Hanna* message was gone.

"*Ouch*," said a voice. Hanna turned around. Jared had stepped out onto the ramp next to her.

Hanna nodded, gesturing to the building. "Should I go to Hailey's dressing room and see if she's okay?"

Jared shook his head. "Let her cool down. Call her tomorrow." He ran his hands over his thick hair. "It sucks, though. They'll have to replace her on such short notice."

Hanna rolled her jaw. She hadn't thought about that. "Who do you think they'll get?"

"I don't know, but hopefully someone way better."

Hanna's thoughts began to churn. Maybe that was a good thing. Hanna's character would be redeemed. No one would make fun of her once the film came out. And Hailey would find something else, wouldn't she? She was a huge star. Her agent probably had something lined up already.

"Like Lucy Hale," she suggested, suddenly excited. "Or maybe that cute girl on that Netflix series?"

"Actually, I think *you* should go for it."

Hanna blinked hard. Jared was staring at her with a completely serious expression. "Excuse me?" she blurted.

Jared sidled closer. "I'm serious," he murmured. "You're good—really good. Hank can't stop talking about you. And we both already know you make a better Hanna Marin than Hailey. . . . "

He smiled leadingly, one eyebrow raised. Hanna lowered her eyes, feeling guilty about what she'd said to Jared about Hailey's performance—and about the kiss.

But it *was* true. Hanna thought about how Hank had done nothing but praise her after every scene. Sure, the Hanna role was more demanding and time-consuming than the Naomi part, but Hanna could handle it. Anyway, why hire another actress when the real Hanna was right here, ready and waiting?

Was Hanna ready and waiting? Could she ask for the role? She thought of something Hailey had said in New York: *Never pass up an opportunity. You never know where it's going to take you.*

Jared shifted his weight. When Hanna looked up, he was studying her closely, a whisper of a smile on his face as if he knew what Hanna was thinking. "Talk to Hank," he urged. "All he can say is no." And then, patting her arm, he turned on his heel and went back to the sound-stage.

22

A TOUR AND AN *A*

Thursday evening, Aria stood on the steps of the Philadelphia Art Museum as the sun set. Though the museum was almost closed, visitors were still lingering, eating pretzels from the cart at the foot of the steps, racing up and down the stairs like Sylvester Stallone in *Rocky*, or listening to a saxophone player belt out a rendition of "Let It Be."

Then a neon-green car with PHILADELPHIA QUICK CAB printed on the side pulled up to the curb, and Harrison, dressed in crisp jeans and a gingham button-down, climbed out. When he spied Aria, his whole face lit up. Aria waved happily.

"Hey!" he cried after bounding up the stairs to meet her. He leaned forward and gave Aria a hug. Aria sighed happily, inhaling the sandalwood smell of his coat.

"Ready for this?" Harrison asked when he pulled away.

Aria ducked her head, suddenly feeling shy. "A private tour in the museum? Of course I'm ready."

"It's the least I could do," Harrison said earnestly.

Harrison had sent her a text this morning telling her how many comments the article had already received, though she'd been too afraid to look at them herself. He'd also added that he'd scored several new advertisers and had been asked to be an "expert" on an art-scene retrospective the *New York Times* was writing for its Sunday edition. At this rate, he'd said, he could actually start making money from the blog and quit his part-time bartending job.

As he reached for her hand, he looked intimately into her eyes, and Aria held his gaze. She wanted to go slowly with Harrison, but whenever he looked at her like that, it felt like there were horse hooves pounding in her chest. Which was a welcome feeling, especially after seeing Noel and Scarlett in Best Buy.

Not that she was really dwelling on that or anything.

They started up the stairs toward the museum. Everyone was streaming out instead of going in. "How'd you manage to score an after-hours tour, anyway?" Aria asked.

Harrison smiled. "The perks of being just the teensiest bit connected. A lot of art critics get to go after-hours to all the museums—that way they can really see the works without fighting the tourists. All it took was one phone call—*and* a mention of your name."

Aria gasped. Her name had clout?

Harrison held the door open for her. "But actually, I was hoping *you'd* give me the tour. The Philly Art

Museum, Aria Montgomery–style."

Aria cocked her head. "I'd be honored, Mr. Überblogger."

They walked into the lobby, which Aria knew like the back of her hand. It was strange to see the place so empty, no hustle and bustle of kids racing for the armor and weaponry rooms or the gift shop. An echo spiraled from high above, and then came a loud *clank*. Aria looked around nervously. She didn't like the idea of being *totally* alone.

But then a guard appeared from around the corner. A girl stepped out of the coat-check room, shrugging into a jacket. Aria breathed out.

She and Harrison walked past a table of flyers about upcoming events and a large desk about membership opportunities. Then Aria felt the slightest pang. She and Noel had come to the museum a few months ago, and they'd stood right in front of the membership desk, arguing about what to see. Of course Noel wanted to visit the ancient hatchets and swords, but Aria had insisted on seeing a new exhibit of eighteenth-century children's apparel first. In the end, she'd gotten her way.

She winced. Was she always that pushy? Was that why Noel didn't want to see her anymore? Maybe he'd taken stock of all their differences and realized how little they really had in common. That had to be it, because last night, when she'd stalked Scarlett on Facebook–the girl had been *asking* for it by giving her last name–she'd discovered that she went to a preppy private school in Devon, was totally into horses, was the captain of her cheerleading team, and almost certainly had no idea what differentiated a Kandinsky from a Rothko. In other words, the complete opposite of Aria.

She caught herself. *You don't care.* She was here with a boy, after all. *She'd* moved on just like Noel had.

A docent rushed up to them, a big smile on her face. "Mr. Miller! Ms. Montgomery! It's lovely to see you. I'm Amy, and I'm so thrilled you made it." She pinned little buttons that had pictures of the museum's winged-horse logo on their shirts. "Do you want a guided tour?"

"No, we'll be all right on our own," Aria insisted.

Amy scuttled off, saying she'd check on them later.

"Come on," Aria said to Harrison, skipping up the marble steps, suddenly filled with confidence. "Our tour starts now."

She led him to her favorite part of the museum, the contemporary-art wing. The rooms were empty, and only one guard stood at the main entrance, tapping on his phone. At first, Aria and Harrison walked around the perimeters, silently studying the art. Then Aria began to pick out her favorite pieces. She pointed at *Three-Part Windows*, by Robert Delaunay, a Cubist masterpiece of shapes signifying the Eiffel Tower views out a window. "I *wish* I could paint something like that," she sighed. "It's so evocative."

Then she moved on to another Cubist work, *Nude*

Descending a Staircase, by Marcel Duchamp, then pointed at some of the graphic compositions by Jean Hélion. "For whatever reason, I was always drawn to these," she said.

"Mmm," Harrison said, his chin in his hand.

Aria swallowed hard, suddenly unsure. All at once, she remembered how cool and opinionated and cultured Harrison was. Were her choices small-timey? Prosaic? "I mean, there are probably works in here that are better examples of the form, or the time period, or a particular movement," she said quickly. "I'm no art-history major."

Harrison looked at her. "Art is subjective. You know that. You like what you like." He squeezed her hand. "You know, this is why you're so unique. You're so . . . *humble.* I'm around self-obsessed artists all day—it's really refreshing. And you're not like a high school kid, either. You're so mature."

Aria blushed. "Well, thanks, I guess." She wasn't used to receiving so many compliments.

Then she walked toward a room full of sculptures, her heels clacking loudly on the marble floor. "I used to come here when I was younger, like, in fourth and fifth grade, and sit here for hours," she murmured. "And when I was older, my junior high class came as a group. I wanted to see all these paintings again—they felt like my friends. But my *real* friend, the girl I was with, wanted to go back to the steps and flirt with some boys from Penn. I was kind of bummed."

A sour feeling filled her. She'd told that whole story

without being totally cognizant that the friend had been
Ali. Not *crazy* Ali, but Courtney had been crazy—and
pushy—in her own way.

Harrison clucked his tongue. "I used to think the
paintings were my friends, too. I never knew anyone else
thought like that."

Aria blinked hard. "We seem to have a lot of funny
things in common."

"A lot of *cool* things." Harrison stepped toward her.

Aria's heart pounded as he stared meaningfully at her.
See, *this* was why she was attracted to him. Because they
understood each other.

He moved closer and closer until their chests were
almost touching. Aria held her breath, knowing what was
coming next. When he leaned in to kiss her, she shut her
eyes.

"Is this okay?" she heard him whisper softly, his sweet-
smelling breath on her cheeks. She nodded and felt him
kiss her. His lips were firm and tasted a little fruity. His
jaw felt angular, and there was a smattering of stubble on
his chin. It was a foreign feeling: Noel had always been
clean-shaven. She explored his skin carefully, not sure if
she liked it or not.

Then the guard in the corner coughed loudly. Aria giggled and pulled away, and Harrison's eyes widened guiltily. But then he slipped his hand into hers. Aria squeezed
back, a shaky feeling growing inside her. Maybe it was
excitement. Maybe it was uncertainty. Was it weird that

she'd thought about Noel during their kiss? Why couldn't she just *get over him*?

She pulled back and regarded Harrison. "Will you go with me to a party in Rosewood tomorrow?" she blurted. "It's called Rosewood Rallies, and it supports a good cause. I can't promise it'll be fun or even remotely cool, but you and I could make the best of it."

She needed to ask, she realized. The more dates she went on with Harrison, the more she'd probably like him—and the less she'd think of Noel.

Harrison smiled. "*Anything* you're at is more than remotely cool, Aria. Of course I'll go."

Aria was about to fling her arms around him, but then she heard footsteps. She turned just as a shadow disappeared out of view. She frowned and looked back at Harrison. "Did you hear that?"

He cocked his head. "Hear what?"

Aria walked toward the door. The guard from the doorway was missing; had it been him? The silence pounded in her ears, noisier than any sound. She listened closely for any other noises, and then heard something else. The faintest, lightest, laughter. Goose bumps rose on her arms.

No one was in the hall. Aria crossed into the next room, a long, narrow space filled with huge canvases. Then she heard footsteps again and gasped.

"*That*," Aria instructed. "Those footsteps."

This time they were coming from the main hallway. Aria turned and followed them, her heart beating fast.

"Aria?" Harrison called after her as she turned the corner into the main hall. It was empty. She looked around. As she wheeled to the left, she almost collided with someone bustling out of another wing. She jumped back and screamed. But it was only Amy, carrying a cardboard holder of coffee drinks.

"Sorry!" Amy cried, stepping back. "I was searching for you two. A girl still in the café wanted to treat you to this, Aria. She says she's a friend and a big fan."

She gestured to the coffees. Aria stared down at them. The lids were off, revealing frothy white foam. On the left one, a letter had been etched in the milk—a rapidly disappearing but very obvious *A*.

Her stomach dropped. Before she could quite think it through, Aria took off down the stairs and ran down the hall toward the café, stopping short in the doorway. Workers were clearing trays off of tables. Someone was changing the trash bag in the can by the door. The air still smelled like coffee, but there was no one sitting at any of the tables.

Then Aria saw a flash of blond disappear through one of the back doors. She darted over—only to find a blond cafeteria worker, soaking a large metal tray in a deep, stainless steel sink.

"What are you *doing*?" Harrison asked.

Harrison and Amy stood behind her. They both had strange looks on their faces, especially Harrison. The cups of coffee were gone.

Aria ran her hands down the length of her face. "I'm

sorry," she stammered. "I—I just wanted to find the guest who bought those for us. A-and thank her."

It was a ridiculous excuse, and neither of them looked like they believed her. Harrison stepped forward, slinging his arm around her shoulders. "Let's get you out of here," he said, steering her toward the main entrance. "A friend told me of a great Italian place a few blocks away."

"Sounds perfect," Aria said faintly, grateful that Harrison wasn't making a big deal out of her weirdness. *No more freak-outs for the night*, she scolded herself. The *A* on top of that coffee might have just been an accident, a coincidence. *Ali. Wasn't. Here.*

She would have believed it, too, if it hadn't been for the faint hint of vanilla that suddenly assaulted her as they left the museum, a tiny ribbon of scent that followed Aria, hauntingly, all the way down the long stone steps into the busy city street.

23

SOMEBODY'S OUT THERE

Spencer pulled into the parking lot of the Turkey Hill. She tapped her toe to a Taylor Swift song playing on the stereo by the gas pumps. She started inside, recognizing one of the junior high–age boys hanging out on the curb near the ice machine from her first visit.

"Excuse me," she said to them. All of them held skate-boards, and one had a pack of cigarettes peeking out of his hoodie pocket. They looked at her lazily and mostly unin-terested, though they all did a quick once-over, their gazes resting on her boobs. "Have you seen a blond girl about my age? Pretty, but she's missing some teeth? Probably doesn't say much?"

The boys shook their heads. One of them actually snickered. *Okay, strike one.* Spencer caught the arm of another customer who looked like a local heading inside and asked him the same thing, but he said he hadn't seen Ali, either. *Strike two.*

Inside the mini-mart, she accosted a man by the stacks

of soda—no, he said—and a woman pouring herself a cup of coffee. "Honey, I'm from out of town," the woman told her in a husky voice. "Sorry."

Spencer lowered her shoulders. *Strike three?* Finally, she marched to the counter. "I'm wondering if Marcie is here?" she asked the worker, who had a shaved head and a lazy eye.

He shook his head. "Marcie doesn't work here anymore."

She frowned. "Why?"

He looked uncomfortable. "She passed away, actually. Just the other day. It was rather unexpected."

Spencer blinked hard. "Was she sick?"

He shrugged. "I heard it was a car accident." Then he looked at Spencer expectantly. She grabbed a pack of gum and paid for it, knowing that she had to get away from the counter and stop asking questions. Her heart banged hard. Marcie had slipped about a blond girl buying water . . . and now she was *dead*? From a *car accident*? That didn't seem like a coincidence.

She was starting the engine as the phone rang. ARIA, read the caller ID. "I feel like I'm losing my mind," Aria whispered after Spencer said hello. "I was in the Philly Art Museum, and I swear Ali—or maybe one of her minions?—was following me. Tell me that's not possible."

Spencer glanced at her iPad on the passenger seat. The surveillance feed was up, but as usual, every single camera angle showed nothing. "It's not *im*possible," she said carefully.

Aria made a small, nervous squeak. "I don't understand why Ali's going out in public. I mean, what if someone other than us *does* recognize her and turn her in? She's taking a lot of risks. And using her minions is crazy, too. How can she trust those people not to talk?"

"I know," Spencer said. "Imagine if they *did* talk and they told the cops she was alive. Even though Nick took the blame for almost killing us, the police still have that letter we got from Ali saying she killed her sister. *And* Ian and Jenna. She's still really guilty." She shut her eyes, drinking in the possibility. It would be *so* awesome if that happened. Say Dominick or this Robin Cook person from prison really *were* Ali Cats, but they got tired of Ali's game and talked. It was possible, right? They'd be such heroes.

Aria barked a laugh. "Maybe we should *hope* Ali makes more public appearances. She might mess up." She sighed. "I have to go. My date's probably wondering where I am."

Spencer dropped the phone in her lap and rubbed her eyes, feeling even more hopeless than before. Ali wasn't going to get caught, and her minions wouldn't turn her in. She'd go to the ends of the earth to stay hidden.

Then a flicker on the surveillance screen caught her eye. Spencer's heart lurched, and she snatched the laptop from the seat and brought it closer to her face, gazing hard at the black-and-white images on the screen. The camera pointed at the porch was picking up some movement.

Something big shifted in the corner. It seemed like a person.

Her heart started to pound. She checked the other screens; no one was inside the house, and there was nothing going on in the yard. Then the figure moved again to stand by a window, providing Spencer with a clear view. It *was* a person, dressed in a dark coat with the hood pulled tight. By their height and build, it seemed like a guy.

Dominick. Hadn't he been wearing a dark jacket at the panel interview? This would prove it for sure—he *was* stalking her.

She jammed the key into the ignition and gunned the car into reverse, almost taking out a pickup truck on its way to the gas pumps. If Dominick was an Ali Cat, maybe he could lead her straight to Ali.

She cut the lights of the car and pulled up the driveway five minutes later. There were no cars parked by the house; Dominick must have parked somewhere else. She glanced at the surveillance screens again. He still stood at the window. Was he looking for something? Waiting for someone?

Spencer slipped out of the car as quietly as she could. The wet grass seeped through her canvas shoes as she trudged through the grass, but she paid it no mind. The pool house came into view. Dominick still stood by the window. Spencer halted in her tracks, unsure what to do next. Dominick froze, too, maybe sensing that someone was nearby. Spencer stepped as quietly as she could behind a big juniper bush. She tried not to breathe.

Beep.

It was her phone. She fumbled for it in her pocket to shut it up, then gazed at the screen. It was an email for her bullying site, from a completely unrelated contributor. If only she'd remembered to silence the ringer.

Leaves crunched. Twigs snapped. She looked up. Suddenly, Dominick was slipping into the woods, as if he'd heard the phone.

Spencer took off after him as silently as she could, smacking stray branches out of the way. It was almost too dark to see where she was going. By the time she reached the top of the hill to see where he'd gone, the woods were empty.

She stood still and silent, listening for footsteps, but there were none. The only sound was the wind whistling through the branches. Spencer wheeled around, wondering if she'd gotten turned around in the woods, but all she saw were trees and stumps and bushes. Nothing else. He had just . . . *disappeared.*

Disappointed, she tramped back to the shack, thorns hitting her the whole way. The sky was completely dark, the only lights dim flickers from the road far below. Spencer fumbled in the darkness until she found the window Dominick had been standing at, then reached into her pocket for her phone and shone it on the sill. It was filthy with cobwebs and dirt. Something made of glass had broken on the sill, too; when she picked it up, a bubble of blood appeared on her thumb.

She shone the phone light along the jamb, but she still didn't see anything. She aimed the beam into the room, but it was empty, too. Maybe she would never know what Dominick had been doing there.

But the bigger deal was that he'd been doing something at *all*.

24

SET 'EM FREE, THEN KILL 'EM OFF

The following morning, Emily sat in her Volvo in the Rosewood Day parking lot before chemistry class, on a conference call with Spencer and the others. Mostly, Spencer was doing all the talking.

"There was someone at the pool house," Spencer said hurriedly after describing her heckler. "I ran up to catch him."

"But how could you follow him through the woods?" Hanna shrieked. "You could have gotten really hurt, Spence! You should have called the police!"

Emily murmured in agreement, but she felt guilty—Spencer was getting the lecture *she* also deserved. Her friends didn't know about her freak-out the other day at the pool house, and hopefully, they never would. They could, technically: They could rewind the footage themselves and see everything she'd done. Even thinking about it made Emily feel prickly and embarrassed. All those things she'd trashed. All those awful things she'd said.

"Look, I know it was crazy, but I wasn't thinking straight," Spencer said. "And anyway, I'm fine. But the guy got away." She sighed dramatically. "Which sucks, because I'm almost *positive* it was Dominick. I don't know who else it could have been."

"So who *is* he?" Aria asked.

Spencer briefly described the guy who'd heckled her online and at her panel in New York. "It's part of the reason why I ran up there—I thought it was him, but the camera image wasn't clear, and he ran off too quickly for me to get a better look. I even rewound the surveillance tape, but I still couldn't see his face."

"So how can we find this Dominick guy?" Hanna asked, her voice high and thin. "Do you know where he lives?"

"All I have is the screen name he used to torment me on my blog. He says he's from Philly, but who knows if that's true?"

"What do you think he was looking for?" Aria asked.

"Well, when I watched the surveillance tape again, he seemed to be just standing there," Spencer said. "So I don't know. Maybe he was waiting for Ali. Why else would he be there unless *she'd* been there?"

"So where does this leave us?" Aria asked. "If the Ali Cats are real, and Ali trusts a few of them, does that mean that they're all after us?"

Emily shut her eyes. For the past few days, after her foolish trashing of the pool house, she'd lived in fear that

Ali and Robin Cook would break into her house while she was sleeping and stand over her, laughing, before they smothered her to death. She'd barely slept a wink. "How can we fight something when we don't even know what the something *is*?" she said weakly.

"Let's not panic," Spencer said firmly. "Maybe I can find Dominick and ask him questions. Or maybe we could report him to the police, saying he was trespassing on the Maxwells' property."

"And what if the cops ask us how we knew Dominick was there?" Hanna reminded her. "We'll have to tell them about our cameras. And then *we'll* be in trouble for trespassing, too."

Everyone was silent for a while. Then Aria sighed heavily. "We're all meeting at the Rosewood Rallies charity thing tonight?"

Spencer groaned. "I don't *want* to."

"I don't, either," Emily said.

"Please come, Em," Aria said quickly—so quickly, in fact, that it annoyed Emily a little. She'd noticed how tweaky and twitchy her friends had been around her lately. They were probably worried about her—she knew she'd been acting a little unhinged. But on some level, she wished they'd just leave her alone.

After that, there wasn't really much more to say, and everyone hung up. Emily gripped the steering wheel for a while, a hot feeling welling in her stomach. Several girls crossed the parking lot on the way to class, their ponytails bouncing. For all she knew, *they* could be Ali Cats, too. The whole school could be.

Then she looked at the box that sat next to her on the passenger seat. It was Jordan's possessions from the prison—she *still* hadn't looked at it, but she also didn't like the idea of leaving it at home, where her parents could snoop. One of the flaps stuck up slightly, daring her to peek inside. But she feared the pain she'd feel when she did. Chances were, she'd recognize some of the items in that box: a pair of Jordan's earrings, her driver's license, the shoes she'd been wearing when they caught her. Other people might think that reuniting with these items might make her feel closer to Jordan, but Emily disagreed. They would only make her feel even more disconnected, so much further away.

When her phone rang again, she let out a yelp. An unfamiliar number popped up on the screen. Emily answered with a nervous hello.

"Miss Fields," said a gruff voice. "My name is Mark Rhodes, and I'm a detective from the Ulster County PD. Agent Fuji from the Philly FBI branch gave me your number. I'm investigating Jordan Richards's death."

Emily sat up straighter. "Investigating?" she repeated. "Robin Cook was charged with that, wasn't she?"

The detective cleared his throat. "Well, there have been some rumors around prison that Miss Cook was put up to it somehow, or even framed. And this morning, her body was found in the woods outside a shopping mall in New Jersey."

Emily blinked hard. "She's dead?"

"We suspect there was more at play here than we first thought. You visited Miss Richards the morning she was killed. Did she say anything to you? Mention she wasn't getting along with someone?"

"No . . ." Emily's mind whirled.

"And you don't know of anyone on the outside who might have, say, tracked Miss Cook down, in revenge for killing Jordan?"

Emily shot up. She hated what the detective was getting at. "Absolutely not," she almost shouted. "Jordan—or her *people*—had nothing to do with Robin's death. Alison DiLaurentis killed her."

There was a long pause. "Excuse me?" the detective finally said.

Emily knew she couldn't stop now. "Ali arranged for Robin to kill Jordan—they met the morning of Jordan's death. Then she broke Robin out of jail and killed her to close the loop." Her heart thrummed hard. It totally made sense. This was how Ali was going to keep her Ali Cats from talking. She murdered them.

There was static on the line. "I'm sorry. You're talking about Alison DiLaurentis, the girl who killed her sister and died in that fire?"

"*Yes,* her," Emily practically shrieked. "She's not dead, okay? She's *out* there. I *saw* her."

"Did Jordan *mention* Ms. DiLaurentis when you two

talked?" the detective asked. "Had she seen her? And I don't understand—you're saying that Ms. DiLaurentis was in the Ulster women's prison?" There were sounds of rustling papers.

Emily made a fist. He *so* didn't get it. "Of course Jordan didn't mention her—Jordan never *saw* her. And no, Alison wasn't in the prison. Robin was her contact on the inside, and Ali broke her out somehow. She killed Cook once she was on the outside and they were alone because she couldn't have her telling anyone what happened."

"So Ms. Cook was Ms. DiLaurentis's killing machine."

Now the detective's tone wasn't inquisitive—it was mocking. Emily felt a jolt of frustration. "I know how it sounds," she said. "But look into it, okay? Look at the log of Ms. Cook's visitors—I know for a fact that Ali saw her on Tuesday. Check the surveillance cameras. Dust for fingerprints. Do *something*. Because right now I feel totally unprotected. Just like Jordan was. Do you know I haven't even seen Agent Fuji or anyone else at the school where I was attacked, trying to figure out who *did* do it if it wasn't Alison?"

"Is that so?" The agent sounded worried.

Emily hadn't even thought of it when she said it, but now she stared at the double doors to the natatorium, realizing it was true. She'd been here every day for chemistry class since her attack, and she hadn't seen anyone dusting for prints or asking questions once.

And then it hit her. Maybe Fuji didn't believe her

about *that*, either. Maybe she thought Emily had made up the attack for attention.

A growl rose from the back of Emily's throat. She tossed her phone into the backseat even though the detective hadn't hung up. *They didn't believe her.* No one believed her. Meanwhile, there could be hundreds of Ali Cats looming around them, watching, knowing *everything*. And the police didn't care. Not one bit. *No one* cared about her anymore—not in the way Jordan had.

And she was pretty sure no one ever would again.

25

FAME DOES FUNNY
THINGS TO A GIRL. . . .

On Friday afternoon, Hanna sat in her trailer on the movie set, taking deep breath after deep breath. Her phone buzzed. MIKE, said the caller ID. When she answered, Mike sounded happy and relaxed.

"The Amtrak café worker let me order a beer!" he whispered on the staticky line.

Hanna giggled. "So you're going to be drunk for the party tonight, huh?" He had boarded a train from soccer camp and was due in Rosewood shortly after four, which gave him enough time to get ready for the Rosewood Rallies fund-raiser.

"Nah, only buzzed." Mike sighed wistfully. "I can't *wait* to see you, Han. What are you doing right now? Primping? Getting beautiful?"

Hanna stared at her silver dress, which hung in dry cleaner's plastic on a hook on the closet door. She'd picked it up just before coming to the set, but she wasn't quite ready to put it on yet. "Um, I'm about to start getting ready," she said, feeling too jittery and superstitious to tell Mike about what she was *really* about to do. "I'll call you in a little bit, okay?" She made a kissing sound and hung up.

Then she stared at herself in the mirror, pushing her auburn hair behind her shoulders. "You can talk to Hank," Hanna whispered to her reflection. "You *deserve* to be the next Hanna."

Shortly after Jared put the bug in her ear about taking over Hailey's role, Hanna had crept up the stairs to Hailey's dressing room and knocked lightly on the door. Hailey had let her in, and she'd immediately started railing about what a stupid movie *Burn It Down* was. "The plot is dumb," she said, tossing her possessions into a bunch of cardboard boxes she'd dragged out of the small closet. "The characters are dumb. It won't go anywhere at the box office." She peeked at Hanna. "No offense."

Hanna had shrugged, letting the comment roll off her back. "Well, maybe it's a good thing this happened, then," she'd tried. "You seemed really unhappy."

Hailey nodded vehemently. "Damn right," she said. "I was miserable. This the best career move in a while. I'm so happy this is done."

"And you'll find something else," Hanna added.

"Naturally!" Hailey crowed, raising a fist in the air.

"I'm just sorry I'm leaving you behind, sweetie." Then she told Hanna that she was going to get on the phone with her manager the very next day and have him arrange to fly Hanna out to LA for a visit as soon as possible. "We are going to have so much fun," Hailey whooped, tossing a bunch of dresses into an open suitcase. "The clubs in LA are a zillion times better than the lame-ass ones in New York. And the shopping? To die for!"

Hanna had left Hailey's dressing room with a sense of accomplishment. Hailey was out—and was happy to be out. Chances were, she'd have a new film offer by tomorrow.

And Hanna? Well, maybe, just maybe, she could be in. She just had to ask Hank first.

But before she could move, her phone buzzed again. This time, Emily was calling. Hanna hit the green ANSWER button and cleared her throat. "What's going on?"

Emily took a shaky breath. "Jordan's murderer is dead."

Hanna frowned. "Is that good?"

"Of course it's not good!" Emily screeched. "Hanna, *Ali* killed her! She recruits these crazy minions to work for her, and then she disposes of them like Kleenexes!"

Hanna chewed on her thumbnail. Every time she heard Emily's twitchy, unhinged tone lately, her stomach hurt a little bit worse. "Are you *sure* Ali did it?" she asked tentatively. "Is there any evidence?"

Emily sighed. "That would be too easy. You just don't understand." With a groan, she hung up.

Hanna stared at her phone. Then she dialed Emily's number again, but it rang and rang and rang. Was Emily actually mad at her? Should Hanna have just agreed without asking questions? Thank goodness Emily had already agreed to go to the Rosewood Rallies tonight—at least there they could keep an eye on her.

Then she glanced at herself in the mirror once more, trying her best to push her worry aside. Rolling her shoulders, she stepped out of the trailer, teetered down the steps in her high, strappy sandals, and walked into an adjacent trailer that served as Hank's office—Hanna had chosen to visit him that afternoon because she knew they had a break in shooting and he wouldn't be busy.

She took another deep breath and knocked on the door. There was a cough, and Hank opened it, the smell of cigarette smoke swirling out of the small, cramped space. "Hanna!" he said, raising an eyebrow. "Come in, come in."

Hanna climbed the steps and walked into his trailer, which had a desk, an expensive-looking leather couch, and a bunch of framed awards and accolades on the walls. Hank's computer was humming, and the latest script was on the screen. Papers littered his desk along with what looked like union forms, a collection of Starbucks paper cups, and several black-and-white head shots of pretty girls about Hanna's age. Several of them Hanna recognized from other TV shows and movies. She knew why Hank was looking at them: He was trying to find a new Hanna.

"So." Hank sat down in his chair and placed his hands on his thighs. "What can I do for you?"

Hanna averted her gaze from the head shots, trying not to feel unnerved by how professional they all looked—she didn't even *have* a head shot. "I'd like to take Hailey's place as Hanna. I want to play myself in the movie."

For a moment, Hank's face was blank, and Hanna wondered if she'd made a total mistake. She was an amateur, a silly girl they'd probably only brought in because it was a fun publicity stunt. Those head-shot girls were the *real* actresses. But then Hank leaned back in his chair. "Interesting."

Hanna heard herself say the lines she'd rehearsed all morning. "We haven't shot many Naomi scenes yet, so if you recast someone as her, you wouldn't have lost much time. And I know I'm pretty green at all this, but I'll work really hard, and I won't give you the trouble Hailey did. I know the part because of running lines with Hailey, I've heard all your notes for her, and I think I know what sort of character you're looking for. Plus, I'm way cheaper than those girls." She gestured to the head shots, which she hoped wasn't presumptive. "I just want the chance."

Hank crossed his arms over his chest, looking both uncertain and kind of impressed. He didn't say anything for a few beats, chewing thoughtfully on his thumbnail. Finally, he nodded. "Okay. You've convinced me. Let's give it a shot."

Hanna's jaw dropped. *"Really?"* She hadn't actually expected her pleas to work.

Hank nodded. "But if it doesn't work out, you're back to playing Naomi." He stood and shook her hand. "Congratulations. I'll have our legal team put together the paperwork."

"You won't regret it!" Hanna blubbered, pumping his hand up and down. She backed out of the trailer, blathering again about how this was an amazing opportunity and how she was going to work really, really hard. As Hank shut the door on her, a huge smile spread across her face, and she let out a high-pitched, happy squeal. "Yes!" she cried. "Yes, yes, *yes!*"

"I can't *believe* you."

Hanna whirled around, nearly stumbling down the trailer steps. Hailey stood in front of her, a gray duffel over her shoulder. She was staring at Hanna with a betrayed look on her face, as if she'd just heard the whole conversation between Hanna and Hank.

Before Hanna could say a word, Hailey marched up to her. "How dare you walk over me like this?" she growled.

Hanna blinked hard. "You quit!" she squeaked. "And you said you were miserable!"

Hailey's nostrils flared. "You *convinced* me I was doing the right thing."

Hanna's mouth opened, then closed. "But . . ."

Hailey held her hand up to stop her. "But *nothing*," she hissed. Her eyes were hard and cold. "You're a bitch and a liar, Hanna. I asked you how I was doing time and again, and you lied and lied and lied. '*You're great, Hailey.*' '*Good job, Hailey.*'" She wagged her finger in Hanna's face. "I'm going to *hurt* you. Mark my words."

And then she spun around, heading back to her rental SUV, a huge Escalade she often complained about driving around Rosewood's windy back roads. "Hailey!" Hanna called out weakly. But, to no surprise, the girl ignored her, throwing herself into the front seat, gunning the engine, and pulling out of the lot as fast as she could.

A few hours later, Hanna stood at the Rosewood Amtrak station, glancing again and again at her phone. So far, she'd sent Hailey twelve texts, but Hailey hadn't replied to any of them. *I made a mistake.* And, *I'm sorry.* And, *I'll back out of the role, just say the word.* She'd reached out to Jared, too, hoping he'd tell her Hailey sometimes got like this and would calm down in a few days, but he hadn't replied, either. It wasn't fair: The most wonderful thing had happened. She *should* be completely happy. Instead, she felt antsy and uneasy, with a gnawing pain in her stomach.

At least Mike was due any minute; he'd celebrate with her. *I've got a surprise for you,* Hanna had texted him, though she hadn't told him what it was. She paced up and down the platform, checking her watch again and again. Though it was just a little after four, with hours of daylight left, the spooky, empty station left her feeling uneasy. Something metal clanged on the stairs, just out of view. She whipped around. *Ali?* There was another clang, followed by a long sigh. Her skin prickled. She waited, terrified by who might appear around the corner. But no one came.

A shrill whistle blew. The train puffed into the station, and Hanna waited excitedly as all of the passengers disembarked. Mike brought up the rear, shouldering the Jack Spade bag she'd bought him last Christmas. Hanna let out a squeal and waved for him, but when Mike looked up at her, his eyes were dead. He walked toward her, and then past her, heading up the stairs.

"Uh, hello?" Hanna said, scampering behind him. "How many beers did they give you on the train? Are you so drunk you forgot what your girlfriend looks like?"

Mike reached the top of the stairs, but instead of heading for Hanna's car, he walked toward the auxiliary lot. "Where are you going?" Hanna demanded, suddenly feeling nervous.

"My dad's picking me up," Mike said in monotone.

"Mike." Hanna grabbed his sleeve. "*I* have a car here. What's going on?"

Mike glared at her coldly. His eyes were red-rimmed, as if he'd been crying. Hanna's heart started to beat hard. Finally, he shoved his phone at her. "Is *this* your surprise?"

Hanna stared at the screen. It was the mobile site for

TMZ. BURN IT DOWN COSTARS COZYING UP! read the head-line in garish red lettering. And there, just below, was a picture of Hanna and Jared—kissing at the nightclub in New York.

Hanna could feel the blood draining from her face. "H-he kissed me for *one* second," she blurted. "And then Hailey snapped a picture before I pulled away."

Mike snorted. "Yeah, right." He grabbed the phone back. "Then why does the article say *you* kissed *him*? You would do anything for the attention of a big movie star, even cheat on your boyfriend?"

"Mike, no!"

She reached for him, but he ducked away. "A guy on my floor sent me the link when I was only fifteen minutes away from here. *'Hey, your girlfriend's hooking up with some other guy.'* Some of the comments even said *you* submitted this yourself."

"Of course I didn't!" Hanna roared.

"So who did?"

Hanna blinked hard. All at once, it came to her. *I'm going to hurt you*, Hailey had said. It made perfect sense.

She lowered her eyes. If she hadn't been so ambitious, if she hadn't wanted to be a star so badly, none of this would have ever happened. She couldn't even blame any of this on Ali. She'd brought all this on herself.

"Mike, I'm sorry," she murmured, feeling the tears roll down her cheeks. "Please, let me explain."

Mike hitched his bag higher on his shoulder. "I have

to go," he muttered, heading toward the auxiliary lot. For the second time that day, Hanna watched as someone she cared about walked away from her in angry silence.

26

ARIA'S ANGEL—OR DEVIL—INVESTOR

The boning on the emerald-green strapless dress Aria was wearing to Rosewood Rallies dug into her boobs, and she was wearing uncomfortable heels, but when she glanced at herself in the long mirror in the lobby of the country club, she had to admit she looked pretty damn good. So did her dad, who had on a dark suit, and Meredith, who wore a structured red dress with a gardenia tucked behind her ear.

But it was Harrison who looked truly amazing. He'd shown up in Rosewood earlier that day wearing a crisp, slim-fit black suit with a huge bouquet of flowers for Aria. Now, as he regarded the two of them in the mirror, he slung his arm around her waist. "I am, without a doubt, with the prettiest girl in the room."

Aria ducked her head bashfully and said something that came out like, "Oh, you." She wanted to feel something for Harrison—she really did. He was *perfect* for her: He said sweet things, he fawned over her, and they had the same interests. But a nagging feeling told her she should have felt *more* flattered than she did, *more* fluttery, *more* turned on by how gorgeous he looked in that suit. Right now it was hard to muster up any feeling at all beyond generalized nervousness at being back in the Rosewood Country Club among all her peers.

She looked around. Even though she hadn't been there since the party Mona Vanderwaal had thrown for Hanna after she was hit by a car—the very night, in fact, they'd discovered Mona was A—the place hadn't changed a bit. The same plaid wallpaper and heavy mahogany paneling covered the walls, the same ornate carpet lined the floors, and it still smelled like a mixture of cigars, red wine, and cream sauce. There were tons of people milling about in the main ballroom already, looking perfect in their gowns and suits with drinks in hand. A gaggle of kids in their country-club best were running up the dramatic double staircase past the lobby. A large ROSEWOOD RALLIES sign was propped up on a table, complete with photos and a description of the charity they were supporting. People barely looked at it, though, more interested in finding their place cards to see which room their family was seated in. Aria couldn't help but notice that no one here particularly looked like a troubled or disadvantaged youth, either.

"The girl of the hour!" a woman with heavily sprayed blond hair and in a tweed Chanel suit crowed. She gripped her arm hard and said, "My name is Sharon Winters, and I'm the head of the committee who arranged this party.

It's so *wonderful* for you to come, Aria. Now, come with me! I've seated you at the front!"

Aria grabbed Harrison's hand, and Sharon pulled them through a throng of people, past a large room where a buffet had been set up, and into a dining area that featured an enormous bar and at least twenty stools. At the end of the room was a stage, and before that was a long table with four place settings. Hanna, dressed in a sparkly gown Aria didn't recognize, was already sitting on one end, biting her red-painted fingernails.

Aria slumped down next to Hanna, and her friend rolled her eyes at Sharon, who'd crossed the room to speak to more guests. "Sharon told me that I should give a speech tonight. Yeah, *right*."

"Well, you *are* the movie star," Aria couldn't help teasing. Then she motioned to Harrison. "This is Harrison. He writes *Fire and Funnel*, the art blog."

"You're a movie star?" Harrison asked, shaking Hanna's hand.

"Not exactly." Hanna's gaze flickered to Aria. "Do you know if Mike's coming tonight?"

Aria shook her head regretfully. She'd known that Mike was taking the train home to see Hanna, but then her dad had told her he'd changed his mind and was hanging out with some lacrosse buddies tonight. She didn't want to pry, but by the look on Hanna's face, she wondered if they'd had some sort of fight.

"Whatever it is, it will blow over. I know how Mike

feels about you," she said quietly. Hanna just looked away, seeming unconvinced.

They settled into their seats, Harrison sitting to Aria's left. The crowd in the dining room was thick; almost every table was filled. "A *lot* of people from school are here," she murmured. There were James Freed and Lanie Iler, laughing over a plate of ravioli. Kirsten Cullen and Scott Chin were in line for the caricature artist. Then she saw Mason Byers, looking sporty in a shirt and tie, and a bunch of other kids from the lacrosse team flop down at a table near the emergency exit at the left.

"Not because they want to support troubled youth," Hanna said sourly. "It's probably because they can sneak free cocktails." Then her face paled at something across the room.

Aria tried to follow her gaze, but Hanna leapt up and stood in her way. "Um, we should mingle. Introduce Harrison around, don't you think?"

Aria frowned. Hanna's voice was so squeaky all of a sudden. She craned her neck around her friend's skinny frame and stared at the lacrosse table. Then she saw what Hanna was trying to block. Noel was sitting at the lacrosse table, too. With Scarlett.

You're not supposed to be here! Aria wanted to scream. Hadn't Noel told her he was busy tonight? Then again, *busy* could have meant "I already have a date."

She peeked at Scarlett. The little blonde was wearing a black dress that fit her lean frame perfectly, and her hair was twisted into a complicated updo. Noel leaned forward and whispered something in her ear. Scarlett tilted her head back and laughed, touching Noel's hand.

Then Noel glanced up. His gaze found Aria instantly, and his eyes narrowed. His lips parted. He didn't drop Scarlett's hand. Aria turned quickly to Harrison, who was leafing through the program that described the Rosewood Rallies charity. She grabbed his hand tightly, squeezing it hard, then slid even closer to him and pretended to hang on every word of the story he was telling Hanna about the private high school he'd attended in Montgomery County.

After a decent amount of time, she peeked at the lacrosse table again; to her frustration, Noel's attention was on Scarlett and the pasta she'd gotten from the buffet. All of a sudden, Aria felt overheated. There was no way she could take another moment in this room. She shot up and fumbled into the hall. "I have to . . . ," she mumbled to Harrison and Hanna, but then darted toward the door without finishing her sentence.

There was no line for the women's room, and the little dressing area at the front was empty, too. Aria flung herself on the paisley-printed couch and rubbed her temples hard. *Don't be mad about stupid Scarlett*, she told herself sternly. But it was beyond painful to see Noel with someone else. Someone so different. Someone so much prettier.

The door whooshed open, and Aria lifted her head. At

first, she thought she was seeing things.

Noel was standing in the doorway.

He gaped at her, arms at his sides. He looked out of breath, his cheeks flushed.

Aria shot up from the couch. "You can't be in here!"

Before Aria knew what was happening, Noel had stepped forward and taken her by the shoulders, pressing his lips to hers. Aria shut her eyes, the familiar sensation washing over her as she kissed him back.

Then she pushed him away, her eyes wide. "What are you *doing*?" she snapped.

Noel was too out of breath to answer. He kept staring at her lips.

"We're *over*," Aria added. "You said so yourself. And what about that girl?"

Noel looked tormented. "I don't know what I want," he blurted, and darted for the door. Then, with a swoosh, he was gone.

Aria sank back onto the couch, her pulse hammering in her throat. She could still taste Noel's lips on hers. Her whole body felt invigorated and flushed. Part of her wanted to run after him, but another part of her held back. Noel was probably already with Scarlett, regretting their kiss. And somehow, that made her feel even worse.

The door swished open again, and Aria half rose, hoping it was Noel . . . and hating herself for hoping. But Spencer walked in, dressed in a twenties-style, fringed black dress, looking down into her oversize envelope clutch. She stopped when she saw Aria, and her expression turned to worry. "Are you okay?"

Aria blinked. There was no way she could explain what had happened. "Where have you been?" she asked instead.

Spencer squirted some lotion on her palms. "I've spent all morning trying to figure out who Dominick is. I called about fifty private investigators to see if they'd help, but they actually need a full name before they can do anything. I even called the bullying organization who made that video to see if they got everyone's names from the audience. But no one's gotten back to me yet."

"That sucks," Aria said faintly. But her mind was still on Noel. He'd followed her in here and *kissed* her. Had he been thinking about her all this time? Or had seeing her across the room, in a dress she'd worn once on a date with him, brought back memories and longings?

"Aria?"

She snapped back to attention. Spencer pointed at Aria's purse. "Your phone's ringing."

The screen was lit up; she'd been so lost in her thoughts she'd completely tuned it out. A 212 number was on the screen. Aria swallowed hard, then answered.

"Aria Montgomery?" came an unfamiliar voice. "My name is Frank Brenner. I'm calling from the *New York Post*."

Aria ran her hand over the top of her head. "I'm sorry, I'm not really in the position to do an interview right now."

"Oh, I'm not calling for an interview, per se." There

was a smarmy tone to Mr. Brenner's gravelly voice. "I'm calling for a quote from you about the stunt Mr. John Carruthers is claiming you pulled."

Aria blinked. For a moment, she forgot who Mr. Carruthers was. Then she remembered: *the Ali portrait.* "I'm sorry?" she said. "What stunt?"

"He's saying he didn't buy your painting." Mr. Brenner sounded amused.

"What?"

"He was in Africa when that painting sold. Apparently, someone posing as his assistant bought it. But it wasn't his *real* assistant."

Aria paced around the little room. "But I was paid. Presumably from Carruthers's account."

"Nope. Carruthers checked his books. There's no transaction for it. He claims that someone else paid for it and just used his name. He said he'd never buy a portrait like that—I believe his exact words were 'garish and disturbing.'"

Aria's stomach twisted. "He *said* that?"

"Indeed he did!"

It bothered Aria how gleeful the reporter sounded. She struggled to put all the pieces together, her mind still confused over everything that had happened with Noel, and now this. What was going on? "But . . . why would someone *else* pay all that money for that painting and claim that Mr. Carruthers had bought it?" she asked slowly. "Why didn't they give their own name?"

Mr. Brenner's laugh was sharp and a little nasty. "I was hoping *you* could tell *me*, Aria. Is it true you placed the call and the order yourself, posing as Mr. Carruthers's assistant? And you paid for it out of a private account?"

"Of course not!" Aria cried. "I don't have that kind of money. And anyway, my mom took that call from the assistant. I had no idea until she told me about it later."

The reporter chuckled. "I guess this is why they call you a Pretty Little Liar. So can I put down here that you orchestrated the whole thing?"

"No!" Aria gripped the phone hard. Her mind was doing somersaults. "Wait. Start from the beginning. What was the name of the assistant who ordered the transaction? What account was supposedly used to pay for the painting?"

Mr. Brenner clucked his tongue. "I think *I* should be asking *you* the questions, not the other way around."

"Please tell me!" Aria cried, a hot, fizzy feeling bubbling up inside her. "Let's just say I *don't* know about this account. What's the name on it? Do you know?" She had a feeling she knew where this was going. But she needed to know for sure, right now.

The reporter sighed. Then came the sound of papers flipping. "It's Maxine Preptwill," he read, stumbling over the syllables. "That ringing any bells?"

Aria's knees went weak. "Say that again?"

Mr. Brenner repeated it. A thin, low buzz took over Aria's thoughts, and she hung up the phone without saying anything else. She sank to the ground, staring dazedly at the huge, slightly psychedelic roses on the carpet.

Spencer dropped down beside her. "Aria!" she hissed. "What the hell is going on?"

"Maxine Preptwill," Aria repeated in a whisper as the room started to spin. She knew that name. It was the secret code name Noel and Ali had used to communicate when Ali was in The Preserve.

Ali had been behind Aria's success all along. And now she was behind her downfall.

27

MEOW MEOW MEOW!

Spencer picked Aria up off the floor and helped her out of the bathroom. For a few minutes, Aria was unable to talk, so they sat on a bench away from the noise while Spencer rubbed her back. Finally, Aria told her everything.

"It was Ali," she whispered, her eyes wide. "She was the assistant on the line with my mom that day in the gallery—well, either her or an Ali Cat, in case she thought Ella would recognize her voice. And the money came from *her* account. Nick has so much money. He must have left her some."

Spencer swallowed hard. It didn't seem fair that Ali had a hundred thousand dollars to throw around willy-nilly. "Maybe we could trace the bank account," she said. "That could lead us back to her, right?"

"Or it will lead us to another Ali Cat who won't talk," Aria grumbled.

Spencer thought about Dominick again. Maybe *he'd*

been the assistant on the line.

"Hey."

Greg stood above them, dressed in a crisp blue oxford and dark khakis. "Hi!" Spencer cried, jumping up. "Y-you're here!"

His gaze fell to Aria, who now was bent over, head in her hands. "Am I interrupting?" he asked softly.

Spencer smoothed down her skirt. "Greg, this is my friend Aria. Aria, Greg. We met at the anti-bullying taping."

Aria raised her head and shook his hand limply. Then she slumped back on the seat, saying nothing. An awkward few seconds passed, and then Spencer said, "Aria, why don't we get food."

"No," Aria answered in monotone, staring straight ahead. "Go. Have fun. Enjoy life while you can."

Spencer pulled her bottom lip into her mouth. After a moment, she turned to Greg. "I'll be right back."

She took Aria by the arm and walked her through the crowd toward the girls-of-honor table at the front—Hanna was still there, talking to a tall guy in an expensive-looking blazer who must have been Aria's blogger date. But Aria shook her head. "Do you know where my dad is?" she asked in a small voice.

"Of course," Spencer said, putting an arm around Aria's shoulder and guiding her to Byron and Meredith's table at the back. Meredith looked worried when she saw Aria's stricken face. "Are you okay?" she asked.

"Boy troubles," Spencer said, patting Aria on the

shoulder and gently sitting her down. It was the perfect excuse.

Once Aria was safely surrounded by her family, Spencer returned to Greg, who was still waiting in the hall. "Let's grab something to eat," she said, leading him toward the buffet room. The line for food was about twenty people long. At the front, a woman dripping in diamonds sloppily spooned pasta sauce on her plate. One of her mom's friends, heavily Botoxed and looking rigid in a Chanel suit, plucked a canapé from a silver tray with her fingers. Sometimes, Spencer thought, rich people could be awfully uncivilized.

Greg took his place behind Spencer, but his gaze quickly found Aria at her dad's table. "Is she really okay?"

"Sure," Spencer answered hurriedly, grabbing a plate and silverware from the stack. She didn't want to go into any more Ali stuff right now. "So how was traffic? You have any trouble finding the place?"

"I had GPS." Greg craned his neck, seemingly still searching for Aria in the hall. "Does she think Ali's after you guys, too?"

Spencer winced at the mention of Ali's name. She pointed at a large tureen, desperate to change the subject. "Ooh, their French onion soup is amazing. You have to try some."

She handed Greg a bowl, but he kept his arms at his sides. "I'm not an idiot, Spencer. Something happened, didn't it?" He moved closer. "What is it? I want to help."

Spencer shut her eyes. It felt so good to hear someone else offer their help, but she didn't want to involve Greg more than she had to. What if Ali came after *him*? "It's nothing," she whispered.

"It's not nothing. It's something with Ali, right?"

Spencer looked around carefully, but all the glammed-up moms and golfer dads were too busy loading their plates with honey-glazed ham and salmon to notice the conversation she was having. All she'd wanted were a few Ali-free hours. But she could tell by the way Greg was looking at her that he wasn't going to let this drop.

She placed the empty soup bowl back on the stack and took his hand. "I can't talk here."

She led Greg down a maze of halls and into a quiet bar with a fireplace, where she and Ali used to come after long summer days at the pool. There was an old bartender named Bert who'd leave his post for long stretches of time to use the bathroom across the hall; they would sneak themselves secret nips of vodka or white wine while he was gone. Today, not a single soul was inside except for an unfamiliar, younger bartender toweling off some martini glasses. He nodded at Spencer and Greg, then returned his gaze to the baseball game on the TV screen.

She sat on the leather couch in front of a roaring fire—a little unnecessary, given how warm it was outside—and Greg sat, too. Spencer looked at him for a long time. "Ali is closing in on us," she finally admitted in a low voice.

Greg blinked. "What do you mean?"

She told him about the prison murder and Aria's painting scandal. "Maxine Preptwill was a secret name Ali used to use," she said. "She knew that we'd recognize it but no one else would. It's, like, a code."

Greg nodded, the worried creases on his forehead growing deeper. "Maybe you can trace the account?"

"That's what I suggested." Spencer shrugged. "I guess we could try."

Greg took her hand and held it tight. "That's not all, though. Is it?"

Outside the room, a bunch of kids thundered past, balloons that said ROSEWOOD RALLIES! trailing behind them. The chlorine smell of the indoor pool at the very end of the building suddenly wafted into her nostrils. Spencer sighed deeply. "It's about Dominick," she whispered. "He's an Ali Cat. I'm sure of it."

"How do you know?"

"Because . . . I just do."

He set his jaw and stared into the fire. "This isn't going to work unless you actually *talk* to me, Spencer."

She stared at her palms. "We tracked Ali down to a property about an hour from here. She was definitely there—the inside smelled like vanilla soap, which is so utterly *her*. It was more than that, too. We just felt . . . a presence."

Greg's eyes widened. "She's living in a house?"

"In a pool house in the back of Nick's family's property in Ashland. We went inside, but Ali wasn't there. So we decided to monitor the place with cameras connected to a wireless feed. We made sure to hide them really carefully, so she wouldn't know."

Greg's head shot up.

"There are . . . *cameras*?"

Spencer wasn't sure what to make of his horrified reaction—placing the cameras hadn't seemed *that* dangerous. "I camouflaged them with leaves. You can't see them from the ground at all. And there are no wires—they run on solar batteries. There's really no way for anyone to tell they're there unless they're really looking."

Greg ran his hand over the top of his head. "I can't believe you got that past her."

She hugged her arms to her chest. "Well, I *think* we did. We've been watching it day and night, and so far, Ali hasn't taken them down or come back. But . . . *someone* was there." There was a lump in her throat. "Dominick. I'm almost positive."

She told him about chasing Dominick down the other night. Greg sat back. His eyes were kind of glazed. "And what do you think Dominick was doing there?"

"I watched the tape again. It looked like he was waiting for someone." Her mouth twitched. "Maybe Ali."

Greg nodded faintly, then stared at his phone in his lap. It pinged, and he tapped on it, answering a text as casually as if they'd been talking about the weather. But a muscle twitched in his jaw. Spencer wondered if he was really upset. Maybe he was really angry that she'd taken such crazy risks. Or maybe he was upset she hadn't told him before.

"Look, I know you don't want me to handle this on my own, but I have no choice," she said. "No one is listening to us. No one wants to help. We have to catch her." She shook her head. "But now with this whole Ali Cat wrinkle, I'm starting to wonder. What if the Ali Cats are the people we need to worry about? What if they're behind everything, and Ali really *is* dead?"

"Oh, she's not dead."

Spencer flinched. Greg's face was in profile, lit orange by the fire. "Pardon?" she asked.

He turned to face her. His expression was oddly placid, no longer freaked or worried. "I said, she's not dead," he repeated, cracking a smile. "And she's definitely coming for you."

Spencer's heart jumped. She pulled her hand away from Greg's and shifted back on the couch. "W-what?"

Greg smiled blandly. "I have to thank you, Spencer. I wondered if there were cameras. I was thinking about that when I was there yesterday."

Spencer blinked hard. Her mind scrambled for a foothold. "What do you mean, *yesterday*?"

He draped his arm over the back of the couch. "That wasn't Dominick you saw at the pool house. Dominick doesn't even exist."

Spencer shot to her feet, feeling sick. "O-of course Dominick exists. He's been sending me emails. I *saw* him, at the panel discussion in New York."

Greg just smiled. "That was a friend I asked to help me out for the night. And those emails? I wrote them." He cast his gaze to the sky. "*You think you're so awesome, but you're not. You're nothing but a poser, and pretty soon, people are going to figure you out.*"

Her heart was pounding fast. She took a step away from him. "*You're* Dominick? Why?"

"Because I needed you to trust me, to create a threat so that you would let me in." He crossed his arms over his chest proudly. "And it totally worked. You've told me what I need to know."

Spencer felt her stomach drop, just like it had the time her car hydroplaned during a rainstorm and she'd nearly crashed into a guardrail. "*You're* the Ali Cat," she whispered.

He grinned. "She'll love me so much for this."

She. Spencer knew it was coming, but she clapped her hand over her mouth all the same.

Greg rose from the couch and stepped toward her, the same weird smile on his face. Spencer darted back, almost bumping into the fireplace. She moved to the right, narrowly avoiding a wooden credenza. Greg followed her, his shoulders squared and his eyes cold. With one lunge, he could tackle her to the ground. What was he capable of? What had Ali ordered him to do?

"You *know* Ali," she whispered, her voice trembling. "You've actually *talked* to her."

Greg shook his head. "Never directly. But yes. And I love her."

"*Why?*" Spencer almost shrieked.

"Because she's fascinating. And elusive. And beautiful."

It was the craziest thing Spencer had ever heard. "And all this time . . . *that's* why you wanted to get to know me?" Tears filled her eyes. "Because she *asked* you to?"

Greg snorted. "She told me you'd get attached like this. She said you were emotional."

She told me. She said. As if Ali really knew what Spencer was like. But it hurt—because Ali was right. She *had* gotten attached. All her promises not to trust anyone again, all her vows to be careful, and she'd stepped right into Ali's wide-open jaws. Ali had known Spencer was lonely. She'd known she was looking for someone to bolster her ego. It was like she'd engineered Greg herself, programmed him so that he'd hit Spencer in all her soft spots.

Then something else hit her. Finally, here was someone who actually knew something. Slowly, carefully, she felt in her pocket for her phone. She had to call the police. Her fingers fumbled. She tried her hardest to dial 911.

The phone rang. Then she heard someone say, "What's your emergency?"

Spencer looked at Greg. "Tell me how you contacted Alison DiLaurentis. And tell me where she is now."

Greg burst out laughing. "Spencer, I'm not a fool." With lightning-quick reflexes, he grabbed her phone from her pocket, ran into the hall, and tossed it into a large fountain. There was a loud *splash*, and then it sank to the bottom.

"Hey!" Spencer shrieked, plunging her hands into the cold water. Water dripped off the phone as she pulled it to the surface. The screen was dead, the 911 call disconnected.

Someone gasped behind her, and she whipped around. A little boy with a blue balloon that said ROSEWOOD RAL-LIES! stood in the hall, his eyes wide. "Is your phone dead?"

Spencer looked down the hall, her heart racing. Greg was *gone*.

"Where did the guy I was talking to go?" she asked the little boy. He just looked at her blankly, then went back to batting his balloon in the air.

This couldn't be happening. Spencer sprinted down the hall wildly, tripping in her heels. "Greg!" she called out. She ran to the long windows that looked out on the golf course, thinking she'd see him disappearing over a hill.

But he had vanished completely. And taken her secrets with him.

28

LOOP-DE-LOOP

"There's our final girl of the hour!" a woman in a tweed suit crowed, taking Emily's hand and leading her farther into the country club's lobby. "Emily Fields, I'm Sharon Winters! What a pleasure! Come in, my dear! Have some punch!"

Emily glanced nervously over her shoulder at her parents, who'd walked her in, but they were already talking to someone from her mother's welcome wagon committee. Some support *they* were.

She peeked surreptitiously at her cell phone in her purse. The surveillance feed was up on her screen, the same four shots of the house unchanged except for an occasional leaf pressing up against the windows. It would be just her luck, though, that something would happen there the second she looked away. Spencer had seen someone on the cameras. That same person—or someone else—could come back.

Sharon continued to drag her into the ballroom. Emily

looked around. A DJ table had been set up at the far end, and dance music pumped out of gigantic speakers. Tons of kids Emily recognized from high school were waving their arms in the air and grinding on one another. Just looking at their carefree faces made Emily want to turn around and never come back.

But Sharon's grip was too forceful. "Here's Hanna!" she chirped, pointing to a long table at the other side of the ballroom. Hanna was the only one sitting at it, punching desperately at her phone's keyboard.

Emily broke away from the woman and walked over to her friend. Hanna looked up at her miserably, then pushed a plate of cookies toward her. "Sharon brought these for us. But there's no way *I* can eat." She gazed forlornly around the room, then at her hands. "Mike's not speaking to me. Everything is a mess."

Emily couldn't think about eating right then, either. "How long have you been here?" she asked Hanna.

"About an hour. I don't know where Aria went—her date went to look for her." She sighed. "I tried texting Spencer, but I haven't heard from her, either."

Emily checked the surveillance images once more—nothing. Then she looked around the room. She didn't see any signs of the other two girls anywhere. Her gaze locked on a large banner near the DJ that said WE LOVE EVERY-THING AND EVERYONE IN ROSEWOOD! There were pictures of places around the town: the shops on Lancaster Avenue, the covered bridge, the fall foliage, the Hollis spire. As

Emily looked at the images, she realized she had a negative association with each one of them. She'd received texts from A by the Hollis spire and outside the shops. She remembered kicking through a pile of fallen leaves last fall, still trying to process that Ali, her old friend, had tried to kill them. And she'd tried to *kill herself* by jumping off the covered bridge.

"I *hate* everything and everyone in Rosewood," she whispered, realizing she pretty much meant it. Aside from her friendships with Spencer, Aria, and Hanna, she would have no warm and fuzzy memories to take with her when she left. Living here, experiencing what she had with A, had ripped away years of her life.

She stared around at all the dancing kids in their Marc Jacobs dresses and Jimmy Choo heels. They didn't understand what Emily had gone through—not at all. And they probably never would. Why did *they* get to have happy lives? Why did *they* get to love and laugh and enjoy themselves, when all she faced was painful experience after painful experience?

Ali *so* deserved to pay for this.

"Emily!" Mrs. Fields was racing toward her, her cheeks flushed pink. She held a short-haired girl by the wrist. "This is Melodie. Melodie, Emily! I know her mother! And Melodie's working at the country club this summer as the junior women's golf coach and the assistant groundskeeper!" Emily's mom turned to Melodie and smiled hopefully. "I think you guys have some, um, common interests."

"H-hi?" Emily said uncertainly, annoyed that her mom was forcing her to make a friend right now. Why on earth would her mom think she'd want to meet this girl? But then she noticed how Melodie was checking her out, her eyes grazing the neckline of her dress. Emily's whole body flushed hot. *Common interests.* Was her mother actually *trying to set her up?*

Emily couldn't think of anything she'd rather do less. She stood up awkwardly and backed away. "It's really nice to meet you, Melodie, but I have to do something right now."

Melodie's face drooped. "Emily!" Mrs. Fields called out. But Emily didn't turn back. She whipped blindly past kids in her class, fumbling for an exit. Across the room, she noticed Spencer in the doorway, a panicked, nervous look on her face. But Emily couldn't go to her right then. She needed a few minutes alone.

She found a dark hall at the back of the country club and turned down it. Then she leaned against the wall and took heaving breaths. *Get a grip*, she told herself, but her mind felt like it was careening down a long, steep hill into a deep ravine. Even glancing at Melodie's expectant expression had just made her think, *Why bother? Ali would ruin that, too.*

Then Ali's red furious face looming above her in the natatorium flooded her thoughts, pumping her with so much anger she whipped around and smacked the wall hard. Why couldn't they *find* her? Why wouldn't she just *die?*

Spikes of laughter drifted down the hall, along with the beginning notes of Lorde's "Royals." Emily slid to the floor and looked hard at the surveillance feed. There *had* to be something there. But it was the same birds landing on the same branches brushing across the window. The same flicker-and-pop in the fourth-quadrant image, the one that showed the only view of the main room. The same fluttering of leaves.

Until she realized.

The leaves kept fluttering against the window in *exactly* the same way. It was uncanny: One maple leaf would flatten completely against the window for a second, then droop. Was it that windy up there? Did the wind keep gusting in the same direction?

Then she noticed the same fizzle and pop from that same camera angle. There seemed to be a pattern: fizzle-pop, then gust of wind, then flattened leaf, then a long stretch of nothing. Emily looked at her watch. Five minutes passed, but the sequence repeated. She counted off another five minutes again. There was the fizzle-pop and flattened leaf again.

Her hands started to shake. It seemed like the video was on a loop. She'd seen it in movies: Burglars would use loops to fool security guards so they could sneak in unseen and steal the jewels. Had Ali done the same thing? That camera angle showed the *inside* of the house, unlike the others. When had this started?

"Emily!" Spencer ran down the hall, her hair streaming behind her and her breathing hard. "I don't even

know how to say this. The guy I've been seeing? He's an
Ali Cat. And I told him everything. About the cameras.
About how we know where Ali is." She winced. "So now
he knows. Which means Ali knows, too."

Emily held up the phone. "I know," she said shakily.
"And I think Ali's already done something about it."

29

A LIGHT IN THE ATTIC

Ten minutes later, Hanna had swung into the driver's seat of the Prius and started the engine. Her friends piled in next to her, looking bare in their skimpy party dresses. Their faces glowed in the dim, greenish interior lights.

"Okay, *what* does all this mean?" Hanna demanded.

"Isn't it obvious?" Spencer asked, her eyes wild. "When I told Greg about the camera, he was totally surprised. He must have told Ali, and she must have *just* made the loop to throw us off. Which means she had to be at the pool house to access the camera to *make* the loop. And the only reason she might *want* to make the loop is if she's there, right now, doing something *in* the pool house. We have to get her before she leaves again!"

Hanna glanced over her shoulder at the bunch of balloons and the ROSEWOOD RALLIES banner across the front entrance. She felt a guilty pang. It felt weird to leave the party, even if it sucked. What if Mike showed up? She'd texted him a thousand times, apologizing again and again

and begging him to come to the party so they could rec-
oncile. Mike hadn't replied, but Hanna hated to think that
he might change his mind and she wouldn't even be here.

"What if it's a trap?" she said quietly. "What if Ali's
not there at all? Maybe she just made that loop to get us
up there."

Spencer's brow furrowed. She looked at Aria worriedly. But Emily shook her head. "We won't know until
we actually check it out. We're going to get her tonight,
you guys. I can *feel* it."

"But there's only one camera on a loop, right?" Hanna
asked. "Wouldn't the other cameras show Ali on the
porch? Coming through the door?"

"She could have come in a back window," Emily said.
"For all we know, she could have scaled a wall and climbed
in through the second floor."

"Shouldn't we call the police?" Hanna asked, her last-
ditch effort.

Everyone was silent for a moment. Spencer licked her
lips. "And tell them . . . what?"

"We could have them come to the pool house," Hanna
suggested, feeling desperate. "Or we could tell them about
Greg—that he knows Ali."

Aria spun a silver ring on her finger around and
around. "If they drive up to the property, Ali will see the
cop cars and bolt. She'll probably never go to that place
again. *And* the police will be furious that we trespassed
and put up cameras."

"And I don't know what we could say about Greg," Spencer said. "Even if they found him and asked him questions, he'd lie. He'd say he'd never talked to Ali. I doubt he's kept any evidence that he's been in touch with her."

"That's why we have to go ourselves," Emily said determinedly.

Hanna ran her fingers on the surface of her clutch. "I just hate that we're doing this alone," she said in a small voice.

Spencer grabbed her hand. "We're not alone—we're together. And this time, we're really going to finish this."

Hanna didn't know what else to do except drive to Ashland. No one spoke as she steered up the silent suburban streets. Huge houses on the golf course whisked past, shimmering majestically in the setting sun. Then she turned past the studio lot where *Burn It Down* was being filmed. She felt another regretful twinge. She *should* be euphoric today—she'd scored a huge role in a movie. But without Mike to celebrate with, the whole thing felt . . . hollow.

The sky darkened as she turned onto the highway to Ashland. The drive felt strangely calm and peaceful, like a cloudless sky before a storm. Before long, the familiar Turkey Hill mini-mart swam into view. Hanna took the left that led to a smaller, twisty road. The dusk cast long shadows across the pavement. She spotted the red mailbox and signaled.

"Wait!" Emily cried, grabbing the wheel. "Maybe we should park on the street. We'll attract less attention."

"Good idea." Hanna pulled about a quarter-mile down the road to a large spot on the shoulder. When she cut the engine, darkness enveloped them. It was a new moon, too; Hanna could hardly see a few inches in front of her face. She grabbed her phone and turned on the flashlight app. Aria did the same. Emily was still using hers to look at the cameras.

"Okay," Hanna whispered, taking a deep breath. "Let's go."

The only sounds were their heels crunching unsteadily on the gravel and an occasional owl's hoot from the woods. They reached the red mailbox and made the turn up the steep hill. Hanna cursed under her breath as her ankle twisted in a pothole. The Maxwells' estate rose above them, its porch light lit.

"Come on," Spencer said, forging ahead.

Hanna's phone made a zigzagging beam across the side yard. The light bounced on the plastic pool cover, then reflected against the walls of the pool house. Emily held her arm across Hanna's body to halt her. "That light wasn't on before, was it?"

Sure enough, a single bulb burned on the second floor. Hanna's heart pounded faster. Ali could be here. This could really be the end of it.

Holding hands, they made their way slowly toward the pool house. When they were about ten feet away, everyone hesitated. Spencer swallowed hard. "So do we go in, or what?"

Aria shifted her weight. Hanna was too afraid to move. Then Emily broke her grip and tiptoed onto the porch. She shifted her weight, a floorboard squeaking. Hanna winced, frightened that the loud sound might attract attention.

Emily eyes were wide as she peered through the window. Hanna's heart banged hard. "What do you *see*?" she hissed. "Is someone in there?"

Emily looked at the others, a haunted expression on her face. "It's not Ali," she said in a wobbly voice that terrified Hanna. "But it's *something*."

30

CLEANUP JOB

Aria rushed to the window and peered through. At first, all she saw were long, dark shadows in an empty room. But as her eyes adjusted, she realized that the room was very different from when she'd last seen it—and not at all what was on the looped footage of the surveillance camera. There was another table inside. And a second chair, upturned. Newspapers scattered on the floor. A mop was propped against the wall, and a bucket sat next to it. And there was something *on* the floorboards. Something thick and viscous, seeping into the wood.

"I'm going in," Emily insisted.

"No!" Hanna grabbed her sleeve. "What if she's still in there?"

"I'm ready for her," Emily said, pulling away. "And if she's not, there still might be evidence inside. Something the cops could really use. All we need to do is find a hair or a fingerprint. Then we call them."

Aria let out a note of protest. This felt *really* wrong. All she wanted, suddenly, was to be back at the Rosewood Rallies party. She hadn't even told her dad she was leaving. And Harrison? After her kiss with Noel, she hadn't been able to find him in the banquet room. She'd even asked Hanna, but Hanna had said she hadn't noticed him leaving. Had Harrison somehow known about Noel? Had he heard the news about her fraudulent painting sale and bolted?

Spencer touched her arm. "Em's right," she said. "We're here. We might as well go in."

Emily turned the knob. It gave way easily, and the door swung open with a loud groan. The same pungent vanilla scent washed into her nostrils, turning Aria's stomach. Did Ali *bathe* in the stuff?

They walked inside. Spencer felt around the wall and found a light switch, but none of the bulbs brightened. Aria teetered toward the table and stared at its wooden surface. It was covered with the same thick substance as the floor. Her nose twitched, filling with the smell of something sour and familiar. All at once, she knew what it was. She glanced at the others, seeing the horror of the realization reflected on their faces.

"Is that *blood*?" Aria cried.

"Oh my God." Emily curled her hands into her chest as though afraid to touch it.

Hanna tiptoed into the small kitchen area. "There's more blood here."

"And here," Spencer called out from a back closet.

"Whose blood *is* it?" Emily cried.

An ominous silence followed. It was clear everyone was thinking the same thing. Maybe a murder had happened here.

Maybe Ali had killed someone.

Aria peered up the stairs to the second level, then took a deep breath and began to climb them. She gripped the rail hard, feeling unsteady. As she reached the top of the stairs, she noticed another light shining from the back room. Her heart stopped. Was Ali still *here*, hiding?

She pushed forward, ignoring the frenzied fear pulsing through her. More floorboards creaked as she peeked around the corner. When she saw lumpy shapes in the middle of the room, she let out a tiny scream—but as she moved closer, she realized that it was only a dead rat . . . and a crumpled-up dress.

She ran to the dress and picked it up, holding it away from her body. The fabric smelled powerfully of vanilla, and it, too, was covered in blood. Parts of it were still damp, maybe with blood.

"Guys," she called, holding the dress by two fingers. "Come here."

Everyone thundered up the steps and gathered in the room. "Look," Aria whispered, shaking the dress side to side.

Emily clapped a hand over her mouth. "Was that Ali's?"

"That's what I'm thinking," Aria said. "Maybe she had

it on while she . . . you know . . . did whatever she did down there." She pointed to the floor. "This could have all kinds of DNA on it. Hair, skin cells, maybe even Ali's blood, too. Everything the cops need, right?"

"Great," Hanna whispered excitedly. "Let's take it to the cops and get the hell out of here."

Creak.

Aria's heart jumped into her throat, and she reached for Emily's hand. It sounded like a window opening. *Please let it be the wind,* she willed. But then she heard footsteps across the floor.

Everyone skittered to the back of the room and huddled together. Aria fumbled for her phone in her pocket. The surveillance cameras were on the screen, but the images showed nothing on the porch and no figures in the yard. The last view, the one that *would* show whoever was downstairs, still displayed that maddening loop.

A *glugging* sound followed. Aria stared at the others. *Gasoline?* she mouthed. Was Ali going to torch this place with them in it, like she'd meant to do in the Poconos? But then a scent filled her nostrils. It smelled nothing like gasoline at all.

It smelled like *bleach*.

Another *creak* sounded, then a small *pffft* of a window closing. Everyone remained very still for what seemed like hours. Finally, Aria tiptoed to the doorway and peered over the railing. The room was empty, but the stench of bleach was overpowering.

Someone had moved around the furniture in the

room. The blood on the floor and the table had disappeared. The mop and the bucket were gone, too. It looked like someone had come in, dumped a bunch of bleach everywhere, and tried to clean up.

But clean up *what*?

She turned back to her friends, her instincts urging her to run, *now*. "We have to get out of here."

Everyone scrambled into action. Aria grabbed the soggy dress, sidestepped the rat, and thundered down the stairs as quickly as she could. Emily lunged for the front door, pulling it open and tumbling outside. As Aria and the others followed, no explosions sounded behind them. No figures shot out from the trees to attack them.

They sprinted toward the road as fast as they could. Aria had never been so grateful to see Hanna's car on the shoulder. They hurried inside, and Hanna locked the doors and started the engine. When Aria breathed in, all she could smell was bleach. It had soaked into their skin and clothes. She could taste it, even, on her tongue.

As they pulled away, Aria swiveled around and stared out the back window. The road was dark and desolate. Even if someone was there, she wouldn't be able to see who it might be.

Beep. Aria looked at her phone. Byron was calling, but she let it go to voice mail. How could she answer and not sound completely freaked?

Then she looked at her texts. There were four from Byron. Several from Harrison, too, replying that he was going to leave the party since he couldn't find her any-where. Then one from Ella, who hadn't even attended the party: *Your father called me. Where are you? Call me as soon as you get this.*

When she looked around, the other girls were look-ing at their phones, too. "Shit," Spencer whispered. "My mom's *pissed*." Hanna chewed on her bottom lip, glanc-ing at her screen as she drove. Only Emily stared straight ahead, her hands folded in her lap. Tears were rolling silently down her cheeks.

"What just *happened*?" she whispered. "Was that Ali? Why didn't we ambush her? I should have *done* something."

Aria patted her hand. "No, you shouldn't have. We had no idea what she was doing down there. And she could have had a gun, Em. We did the right thing by stay-ing put."

"But what was she doing?" Emily cried. "What was with all the bleach?" She looked around at the others. "Did she kill someone in that house?"

"*Someone* killed someone," Aria said slowly. She stared at the dress in her hands. Maybe she was imagining things, but it still seemed sort of warm, as if the heat from Ali's body hadn't left it yet.

She swallowed hard, suddenly realizing what they needed to do. She pulled out her phone and unlocked the screen. Emily watched her carefully, then breathed in. "What are you doing?"

"I think we need to call the police," Aria said.

Emily held Aria's gaze, but she didn't protest. It was the right thing to do. Whatever they'd witnessed was beyond their control. And even if it *wasn't* Ali who'd killed someone in there—which Aria highly doubted—*someone* had.

31

THE WAITING GAME

Emily suggested the girls all sleep together at her place, since no one wanted to go home alone. They scampered into her garage as Emily opened the door to the house. The room was silent and dark, the lights and the TV off. The faint scent of a blown-out candle lingered in the air.

"You have some explaining to do."

Everyone screamed. A light flicked on. Emily's parents sat in the loveseat in the corner. Her dad was still in a suit, her mom still in her flowered dress and heels from the Rosewood Rallies party. Mrs. Fields's nose and eyes were red, like she'd been crying.

Emily lowered her eyes. Her friends had all handled their situations with their families on the drive home. Emily knew that calling her parents would have been the right thing to do, too, but somehow she couldn't will her finger muscles to dial their number. Her mind was too distracted, her thoughts still on Ali and the pool house and whatever had happened.

Mrs. Fields rushed over to her and took Emily by the shoulders. "Where have you *been*?"

"We . . ." Emily shrugged and shook her head. She had no idea what to say. "I'm sorry. I shouldn't have just left the party without telling you."

"Sorry?" Mrs. Fields's eyes boggled. "You disappear, and all you can say is you're sorry? You weren't picking up your phone, you weren't here. . . . We feared the worst."

Emily's father frowned deeply. "We were considering calling the police."

"It's my fault," Spencer piped up, her voice cracking. "I gathered everyone together and asked that we get away for a few moments. We all felt kind of traumatized being at that front table, everyone looking at us—it brought back some tough memories. We grabbed a bite to eat. That's it."

Emily lookd at Spencer gratefully. It was the same story the other girls had told their parents, but she was astonished at how Spencer could lie so expertly to her mom's face. It *was* kind of the truth, except for the eating part. They *had* been traumatized. Just for different reasons.

Mr. and Mrs. Fields exchanged a glance. Mrs. Fields looked like she was going to start crying again. "We're just so concerned," she scolded Emily. "You've been so . . . *troubled* lately. All those things you said about causing those bruises on your neck yourself. And you've been spending so much time in your room. I *know* you've been sleeping in your closet instead of your bed.

And I've *heard* you crying. . . ."

Emily could feel her friends shifting uncomfortably. She kept her eyes on the ground. Maybe she should have told her mom about Jordan a long time ago. Maybe now her mom would understand . . . and get off her case.

"If you didn't want to go to the party, you should have said something," Mr. Fields added gruffly.

"I didn't know I had a choice," Emily mumbled, the words coming out a bit harsher than she'd intended.

Mrs. Fields sighed. Emily didn't know if it was a sign of confusion or disappointment—maybe both. She was too numb to really care. "We're going to have to ground you," Mrs. Fields said. "Two weeks. No more going out. Anytime you leave the house, one of us is going with you."

Emily could barely react. Why did she care if she was grounded? There was nothing for her on the outside anymore.

She looked up at her mom. "Can my punishment start tomorrow? Can they at least stay here tonight?" She gestured to her friends. There was no way any of them were sleeping alone.

Mrs. Fields tapped her lips, then looked at the others. "Have you called your parents? Do they know where you are?" Everyone nodded, and Emily's mom shut her eyes. "Fine. It's late, so you can sleep here. But no TV. And if I hear you girls up much later, I'm sending you all home."

Then she and Emily's dad padded out of the room.

The stairs creaked as they retired to their bedroom.

Spencer looked at Emily, one eyebrow raised. "Sleeping in your closet?"

"It's a long story," Emily mumbled.

"Why did you tell your parents you gave yourself those bruises?" Hanna asked.

Emily looked at her exasperatedly. "What was I *supposed* to tell them?"

Her friends exchanged a glance. It was that look again, that *Emily's lost it* look. But she was too worn out to care. So they were worried about her. So her parents were worried about her. Why couldn't they all just leave her alone?

Aria flopped on the couch and hugged an embroidered pillow to her chest. "What do you think the police are doing right now? Do you think they're at the house?"

It was a question they hadn't dared to ask. When Aria had been connected to the police station, she'd told an Ashland officer that they'd been hiking around in the woods, it had gotten dark on them quickly, and they'd stumbled upon a pool house whose floors were covered in blood. The police officer said they'd send someone to the address immediately, but when he asked for Aria's name, she'd hung up. The police didn't need to know it was them. They'd go there, they'd find Ali's prints—for there *had* to be some. And once Fuji was involved, she'd form that conclusion on her own.

Emily walked over to the closet near the den and pulled out blankets and pillows the family kept there for sleepovers. "I hope they're surrounding the pool house right now. Maybe they even caught Ali in the woods."

Aria helped her spread the blankets on the floor. "Do you really think it's that easy?"

Hanna dug her phone from her clutch. "Let's check surveillance." They'd periodically looked at the camera feed on the drive back; the loop was still playing on camera four, and the other angles showed no movement. They'd even rewound the tapes to see if there were any flashes of someone getting into the house, but there weren't. Ali must have gotten into the house through a way the cameras didn't see.

But now, surely, the cameras would show something different. Police investigating the space. Forensic teams testing the traces of blood.

Hanna tapped the screen and logged on to the site. Her mouth dropped open. "Uh-oh."

"What?" Emily rushed over and looked at the screen. Every one of the camera feeds said *No Signal*. The video images were gone.

Spencer's eyes widened. "Ali shut them down?"

"Maybe that's good," Emily said. "Maybe she was disabling the cameras as the police rolled up."

Aria twisted her mouth. "Or maybe she got away."

A lump formed in Emily's throat. If Ali got away, that meant she could be coming for them. She looked at the blankets and pillows strewn on the floor. They were right in front of a huge window. The lock on the garage door was flimsy at best.

Straightening up, she rolled an armchair in front of the door. Then she moved the couch to block the windows. Her friends seemed to sense what she was doing because Aria ran into the kitchen and barricaded chairs against the sliding doors to the back. Hanna checked and rechecked the bolts of the front door, too.

There was nothing to do after that except change into T-shirts and pajama pants Emily lent everyone and huddle under the covers together. For a long time, they were very quiet, listening to the sounds of one another's breaths. Emily considered turning on the TV, but she knew none of them would watch. She didn't even know what to *talk* about. She kept refreshing her phone, thinking something would be listed about a murder at the Ashland property. But there was no news. Hanna brought up the surveillance site again and again. The lines were still cut, the images of the house gone.

Knock.

Emily shot up. The hair on the back of her neck rose.

Knock.

"What was that?" Hanna whispered.

Emily thought she might throw up. It sounded like it was coming from the kitchen. She listened hard. Then, a barrage of banging sounds followed, and the girls screamed and held one another even tighter. But then Emily realized what the sounds were.

"It's the ice maker," she whispered, rising and pointing

to the fridge through the kitchen doorway. The appliance was older; sometimes the ice hit the bucket in one big, loud clump. Feeling brave, she peered into the dark room. The kitchen chairs were still against the sliding doors. The clutch her mother had brought to the party sat on the island, its silver clasp glimmering in the single beam of light from over the sink.

"Ali's not here," Emily said as she turned back to her friends.

Aria twitched. "Not *yet*."

They returned to the blankets. Emily stared into the darkness, her mind frantic and alert. The hours crept past. Every noise, every tiny click, sent her into a panic. She felt herself drifting off every once in a while, jumping back to consciousness after only minutes of sleep. The final time, when she awoke, the smell of vanilla hung heavily in the room. A figure stood over her. Emily blinked hard. Ali's blond hair hung in knotted tendrils down her chest. Her eyes were hollow, her posture stooped.

Emily sat up hurriedly, her heart leaping into her throat. She'd been anticipating this, but it was still horrifying. "Please," she said, scuttling backward. She glanced at her friends. Astonishingly, they were all still sleeping. "Please don't hurt us."

Ali tilted her head and offered Emily a smile. "Oh, Em. I didn't hurt you. You hurt *me*."

"What?" Emily whispered. She looked at her friends, but still none of them stirred. "What do you mean?"

Ali's smile didn't waver. "You'll see." Then she climbed over the chair Emily had pushed in front of the garage door and slipped through. A faint giggle trailed behind her. She slammed the door loudly with a *bang*.

Emily shot up and looked around. Pale light streamed through the windows. The room no longer smelled like vanilla. She ran her hands along the back of her sweaty neck. Had she *dreamed* that?

There was another *bang*, but this time it was her father opening and closing cabinets in the kitchen. Hanna stirred next to Emily. Aria rolled onto her side. Spencer shot up, her eyes wide. "What time is it?" she whispered. "What's going on?"

"It's morning," Emily said groggily, staring at the empty room again. Ali had seemed so *real*. "And nothing happened."

Everyone looked at one another, blinking hard. *Nothing happened.* It was actually more shocking than Ali breaking in.

"Maybe they got her," Spencer whispered.

Aria's mouth dropped open. "Maybe this is over."

"Maybe," Emily said shakily. But she couldn't stop thinking of what Ali—or dream-Ali—had said. *I didn't hurt you. You hurt me.*

It meant something. Emily just didn't know what.

32

ALL'S WELL THAT ENDS WELL

Hanna had never been so tired in her life. Staying up last night, one eye on the door, certain Ali was going to burst through at any moment, was more exhausting than any all-nighter she'd ever pulled. Worse than the night when they'd thought they'd accidentally blinded Jenna Cavanaugh with a firework. Worse than the night of Mona's death, when she'd lain awake all night, wondering how her best friend could have been A. Worse than the night they'd seen Ian Thomas's dead body—Hanna couldn't get the sight or the smell out of her mind. Today, her limbs felt like she'd run back-to-back marathons. It took everything in her to drive home, change her clothes, and make her early call-time for her new role as Hanna Marin.

There were knots in her stomach as she drove to the set. Why was she even *doing* this? She got to be Hanna, but the victory had come at too high a cost—she'd lost Hailey and Mike, and who knew how many other people on the set would hate her, too, seeing her only as a backstabbing, overly ambitious bitch? Plus, she looked like hell today, and she certainly wasn't up to performing–Hank was probably going to fire her on the spot. Should she quit and save him the trouble?

She pulled to a red traffic light and looked at her phone. A local news feed for Ashland was on her screen, but there was still nothing on the police investigation at the pool house. But that had to be a good thing, right? She and the others had talked about it before they left Emily's this morning. News that Alison DiLaurentis was still alive–and had killed someone *else*–was a huge deal. An FBI screwup, actually. Of course the cops would keep the press at bay for as long as they could until their PR people figured out how to positively spin things.

The light turned green, and she rolled through it and made the turn to the set. The parking lot was mostly empty, and as she drove past the soundstages, she peeked into the alley where *BreAk a leg, Hanna* had been written on the ground in chalk.

She found a spot right in front of her trailer. Sighing, she got out of the car and started toward the steps, trying to figure out how she was going to tell Hank she didn't want the job after all. Then she noticed someone standing on the steps already, blocking her way in.

Hailey.

Hanna's heart dropped. Hailey looked tired and frazzled, her dark hair in a messy knot on her head and her makeup a little smudged. When she regarded Hanna, her eyes were narrowed and her lips were taut. Hanna wished she could whirl around and pretend she hadn't seen her. She *so* couldn't do a confrontation right now.

But Hailey was right there, staring at her. After a moment, she nodded at Hanna in greeting. "So my agent sent me dailies for the film yesterday," she began. "I got to see my performance as Hanna Marin up close and personal."

"Oh," Hanna said uncertainly, wondering where this conversation was going.

"And I was *awful*."

Hanna's head shot up. Hailey's eyes were wide and she looked distraught, but not at Hanna. "I was *dreadful*, Hanna. I used this stupid voice, and I was chewing *gum* all the time—I'm not even sure why I did that. My movements were all over the place. My agent was, like, *Thank God you got out of* that *thing. You were a train wreck*."

"No, you weren't!" Hanna cried automatically.

Hailey lowered her chin. "Don't lie to me *again*, Hanna. I was terrible. Hank was right to get rid of me. And you know what? I kind of knew I was terrible, deep down. I never felt right playing you."

Hanna awkwardly twisted her hands. "Well, I'm sorry to hear that." It was all she could think to say.

"Oh, whatever." Hailey waved her hand. "You know who I *do* think would be good at playing Hanna Marin? *You*."

Hanna laughed nervously. Hailey didn't look like she

was kidding, though. In fact, she was kind of . . . smiling.

"Actually, I don't think I want the part," Hanna said. "Not anymore."

"Are you kidding?" Hailey burst out. "You'll be *amazing* in this movie, Hanna—in a way that I wasn't. So do it for me. *Please.*"

Hanna blinked hard, astonished this was happening. "I'm sorry I went behind your back and asked Hank. But I really thought you didn't want the part anymore. I wasn't trying to be mean, or—"

"I know." Hailey leaned against Hanna's trailer. "We're all good." She looked contemplative for a moment, then added, "And *I'm* sorry I sent in that photo to TMZ. That was pretty bitchy of me. I hope Mike isn't too upset."

Hanna looked away, tears prickling at the corners of her eyes. "Actually . . . I think it ruined my relationship with Mike forever."

One corner of Hailey's mouth inched up slightly. "Don't be so sure about that."

Then she turned. The trailer door opened. Mike stood in the doorway, dressed in a lacrosse sweatshirt and jeans and with a sheepish look on his face. Hanna's mouth dropped open.

"Hey," he said shyly to Hanna.

"H-hey," she stammered just as shyly back.

Hailey beamed at both of them. "I called Mike this morning and explained everything, especially about how that kiss with Jared was completely initiated by him *and* totally harmless." She smiled broadly. "You've got yourself a keeper, Hanna. I wish *I* were so lucky."

"Thanks," Hanna said tentatively. Then she peeked at Mike. He was still smiling. "I'm sorry I didn't tell you about that kiss."

"I'm sorry *I* didn't give you the chance to explain," Mike said. Then he grinned mischievously. "Although, now that you're a big-shot movie star, do you think you can maybe get that Jared guy fired? I mean, not only do I not want him thinking he can go around kissing you on the reg, but he really doesn't have my vibe at *all*."

Hanna burst out laughing. "Only if *you* volunteer to play yourself."

"Done," Mike said. "Now, come here and hug me so we can make up for the few hours I have until I have to catch a train back to soccer camp."

Hanna ran up to him and fell into his arms, squeezing him as tightly as she could. It was incredible. In one fell swoop, everything was right again. Wouldn't it be wonderful if things would just . . . *stay* this way?

A new sensation blossomed inside her. Hanna basked in the unfamiliar feeling. It was so unknown that at first she couldn't even put a name to it.

But then she realized what it was. *Hope.*

33

NO PRESS IS BAD PRESS

Aria parked on a side street in Old Hollis and looked around. The same beat-up Mercedes, vintage Jaguar, and bright orange VW bus surrounded her at the curb. The same potted plants sat on the front stoop of the large Victorian across from the gallery, and the same rainbow gay pride flag waved over the front porch of the Tudor-style house next door. The neighborhood was unchanged. . . . It was only *Aria* who was different.

An older couple walked out of the gallery hand in hand. Aria crouched down behind a bush, not quite wanting anyone inside to see her yet. She wasn't ready to do this.

She looked at her phone again. PRETTY LITTLE FRAUD, read the front page of the *New York Post*. Frank Brenner, the reporter who had called her yesterday, had written about the fake transaction using John Carruthers's name as a publicity stunt of Aria's. "'My mother took the call, so I had to disguise my voice,'" Brenner quoted Aria as saying. He'd also said that Aria had seemed very "distraught" on the phone when he'd called her, clearly because "she was horrified that she'd actually gotten caught."

The story also said that a banking institution was tracking down the source of those funds, implying that Aria had randomly used someone's account. In a normal world, that would be a good thing—the account would lead back to Maxine Preptwill. But Aria knew Ali was too smart to be sloppy; she'd probably used Aria's name and Social Security number at the bank. Because she was *just that devious.*

Everything was such a mess. Patricia, Aria's agent, had called her a zillion times, but Aria hadn't picked up, way too embarrassed to have the inevitable conversation. She couldn't even bring herself to listen to Patricia's messages. There were other ramifications, too. How would this affect Ella? Her mom had facilitated the sale; what if the press thought she was involved in Aria's get-famous-quick scheme? What if Carruthers sued her? Would Ella's boss fire her mom? What if she was blacklisted from the art world? What if the whole *gallery* shut down because of this stupid—and untrue—scandal?

And then there were the texts from Harrison. Last night's were full of concern; he'd wondered where Aria had disappeared to. The ones this morning were a bit more circumspect: *Saw the post. Is that why you ran off last night? Can we talk? I like you no matter what the truth is.*

She stared at the latest one from him. It was sweet for Harrison to say he'd stand by her, but the thing was,

Aria didn't want him to be her boyfriend. Not-very-deep-down, Aria knew she felt nothing for him. She *wished* she did. It would be so much easier. But her feelings were her feelings.

Sighing, she composed a reply. *"It's not the truth, but I can't get into it right now. To be honest, I kind of need my space. I'm sorry. Good luck with everything."* Then she hit SEND. It was ironic, she realized, how much her text sounded like what Noel had said to her only two weeks before. But she sent it off anyway, just needing it to be done.

Taking a deep breath, Aria started up the sidewalk. Every step to the gallery was painful. She pushed the door open, wincing at the cheerful bell chimes. Her mother was standing at the desk, looking at some papers. She looked up, straight into Aria's eyes. Heat filled Aria's cheeks. *Here goes.*

Ella swept up to her. "Guess who had two more sales today?" she chirped happily. She waved some faxed papers in Aria's face. "A buyer from Maine and someone in California. Not for as much as the Ali painting sold for, but still—congratulations!"

Aria blinked. Her mother's excited demeanor was heartbreaking. This was even worse: She didn't *know* yet.

Wordlessly, Aria passed over the phone and pushed the icon for Safari. The *Post* article was still up. "You should see this."

Ella glanced at it, then shrugged. "I already have." She straightened Aria's hair behind her shoulders. "Your agent told me. I hope that's okay—she was trying to reach you, but you weren't picking up, and your voice mail was full. Is this the real reason you ran off last night? You should have just *told* me, Aria."

Aria blinked, then nodded. She *had* found out last night. It seemed like as good an excuse as any to explain her mysterious absence.

Ella looked at the phone again. "Your first *Post* article—and front page, too! I'm so proud."

"Mom!" Aria cried. She couldn't believe how oblique her mom was being. "The story is awful. And untrue. I didn't pose as Carruthers's assistant or get anyone else to. I had nothing to do with that sale at all—to be honest, I'm horrified that Ali painting sold. I was going to burn it."

Ella looked at her intently. "Aria, of course I know you didn't have anything to do with it." She placed the papers back on the desk. "Are you truly *worried* about that article? If you're serious about being an artist, you're going to have all kinds of crazy things written about you, a lot of it negative criticism, much of it lies. My guess? Someone used Carruthers's name because he or she didn't want to admit who they were. Maybe it's someone notorious. Or maybe it's a celebrity!"

Aria stared at her mother. Well, Ali was both those things. "S-so you're not mad?" she finally eked out.

Ella walked to the corner of the gallery and straightened a crooked landscape of the Brandywine River. "The transaction has nothing to do with you, honey. We all know that. Besides, your agent told me that this scandal has actually drummed up *more* interest in your paintings. The buyer in Maine specifically bought something after that *Post* article came out. Sasha was there when he came in—said he was a youngish guy, mid-thirties, super-artsy. His name was Gerald French."

Aria blinked hard. So Ali's plans to ruin her actually *hadn't* worked? She almost couldn't swallow it. She looked around, waiting for the gallery to explode or Ella to drop to her knees, severely food-poisoned. *Something.* But Ella just smiled at her warmly, then moved into the back room, where they kept the inventory.

The bells on the door chimed again, and Aria turned. "Oh my God," she blurted, her mouth moving before her brain. Standing in the doorway, hands shoved in his pockets, was Noel.

A nervous expression flashed across Noel's face. Aria felt the blood rushing to her cheeks once more. The memory of their kiss in the bathroom pulsed in her mind. With all of the Ali and art stuff, she'd pushed it to the back burner.

"Uh, hey," Noel said. He licked his lips. "I wanted to see if you were, like, okay. They were looking for you at the party last night. No one could find you."

"I'm fine," Aria said. She stared at the floor. "Thanks for checking in."

"Of course I was going to check in."

Aria whipped her head up, filled with a sudden confusion—and anger. "What do you mean, *of course*? I've been pretty much dead to you."

"Yeah, well, I think that was a mistake." His eyes were crinkled and filled with remorse. He seemed serious. A crack opened inside her. Did he want her *back*?

Aria wanted that to be enough, but suddenly she felt so exhausted. "Noel, you've put me on a roller coaster the last few weeks," she said. "I've been up, then down, then *miserable*. I was just starting to feel better about things when last night happened."

"I know."

"I mean, first you want to be apart, then you're with Scarlett, then you *kiss* me, then you run away, and—"

"I *know*," Noel interrupted. He took a tentative step forward. "Not to mention what I did to you *before* all that."

"You basically . . . dropped me," Aria said, feeling choked up.

"I never *really* dropped you," Noel said gently. "And I'm sorry—for everything."

"But what about Scarlett?"

"We broke up. She's just . . . not you." He ran his hand through his hair. "Look, I thought putting some distance between us would give us time to . . . think, maybe. Process. But I can't stop thinking about you. I've followed your art success, you know. It's *so* amazing. And then that story that came out today—I know what that's about, too."

Aria looked at him sharply. "What do you mean, you *know*?"

Noel's mouth twitched. "I think I know who's behind it. Am I right?"

Aria glanced over her shoulder, but Ella was still in the back.

She gave Noel the tiniest nod. "She has a lot of fans," was all she said.

Noel nodded back. "Well, I hope you know *I'm* not one of them."

Aria drew in a breath. That hadn't even occurred to her . . . but maybe it should have. He had been manipulated by Ali once before. Then she sighed. "Well, just because you know about it doesn't mean you're getting involved."

"I hope you're not getting involved, either."

Aria shrugged. It wasn't worth explaining to him right now. Hopefully it was over.

Noel shuffled his feet. "But aside from that, I *miss* you. I can't stop thinking about you."

Aria felt a lump in her throat. "I can't stop thinking about you, either. But, I mean—"

Noel cut her off. With the tip of his finger, he tilted her chin up so she was looking at him. "Isn't that enough for us to try again?" he asked.

Aria pulled her bottom lip into her mouth. Noel's skin smelled like the oatmeal soap his mom always put in the family's powder room. And when she looked at his fingers, still on her chin, she realized she knew every inch of his hands by heart—the scar on the side of his thumb from the time he'd cut himself carving a Halloween pumpkin, how his palms got chapped in the winter, the raised bump on the back of his hand from an old burn he didn't remember getting. She thought she knew *him* by heart, too—but he had surprised her lately. And they weren't good surprises, either. How would he surprise her in the future?

If only she lived in a world with no surprises—no Ali coming back to life, no evil A notes, no horrible secrets that a boyfriend kept from her for years. But would that also mean she'd miss out on good surprises, too? Like Typical Rosewood Noel Kahn turning out to be not Typical Rosewood at all. Like the art world accepting her anyway, despite Ali's best efforts.

Like Noel coming to his senses and wanting the space between them to close.

Aria lifted his fingers from her chin. After a breath, she leaned forward, as she'd done so many times before.

Yes, her mind said as they kissed. This was right. This was home.

34

SPENCER BOOKS IT

Ping. Ping. Ping.

Spencer's email in-box was chiming nonstop. She picked up her phone for the sixth time that minute and glanced at the screen, anxious that it might have something to do with whatever the police had found at the pool house. She'd set up Google Alerts for "Alison DiLaurentis," "Nicholas Maxwell," even the property's address. But over and over, it was another email from people who'd contributed to the bullying site, congratulating her for being part of the anti-bullying group's video. Last night, the organization had sent out a press release talking about the film. Spencer's name and credentials had been mentioned.

She clicked over to the press release, which linked to a YouTube video. *Stand Up: Youths Speak Out Sneak Peek*, read the title. Spencer pressed PLAY, watching clips of herself and the others answering questions. The camera panned on the audience, pausing on Greg. Her heart jumped in her chest. Imagine what the organizers would do if they knew he was the ultimate bully, an Ali Cat.

She typed his name, *Greg Messner*, into Google. The Facebook page she'd looked at plenty of times appeared; it said he lived in Delaware, but it didn't list a high school and certainly didn't mention an address. Spencer culled through kids he was friends with; he'd known people from New York, Massachusetts, Maine, Indiana, California, and New Mexico. Not a single person on his friends list was from Delaware—did he live there at all? Then Spencer thought about his story about his stepmother berating and bullying him. Had that been a lie, too?

It was possible his whole persona was a lie, just like he'd made up Dominick. She could just imagine Greg and Ali plotting the whole thing out together, chuckling about how Spencer would most definitely fall for it. But here was the million-dollar question: Why had Greg turned to Ali in the first place? Because of some twisted, psychotic affliction? Had Ali promised him something?

The church bell chime she'd set as her ringtone began to blare, and she lunged for her phone, eager for answers. The caller ID listed a 212 number. Spencer picked up.

"Spencer!" a familiar voice rang out through the receiver. "It's Alyssa Bloom! How are you?"

Spencer blinked. It took her a moment to remember that Alyssa was the editor from HarperCollins. "I-I'm fine," she said, sitting up straighter. "How are *you*?"

"I'm doing really well." Ms. Bloom sounded like she

was smiling. "And it seems like you are, too. I saw that you were part of an anti-bullying video. And your blog is doing incredibly well."

"Thanks," Spencer said shakily. "I'm really glad you think so."

"That's not all I think," Bloom said. "Listen, I've spoken to some other people at the office, and we really think the concept you created in your blog could be turned into a book. If you're interested, I'd like to offer you a two-book contract."

"*What?*" Spencer's legs felt shaky. "Are you serious?"

"I'm not one to joke around about these sorts of things. It's the right time to come out with something like this, Spencer. And you're the right person to tell these stories. Now, as for an advance . . ."

She rattled off an astonishing sum of money, so surprising that Spencer plopped down on her butt and stared blankly across the room. It was happening. *Really* happening. She was going to get to write a book—*two* books, actually. Hopefully they would be meaningful and helpful, and something good could come out of all of A's abuse.

But suddenly, the images of the other kids on the stage for the anti-bullying video swam into her mind. And then she thought of the kids who'd emailed their tales. Some of them were in such horrible living situations. A lot of them were lower-class. A lot of them wanted the right clothes or shoes or accessories to fit in but couldn't afford them—and *that* was the stupid reason why bullies targeted them.

The trust they'd put into her. The honest, earnest support they'd given her when they found out she was in that video. They didn't have to. They could have felt jealous that *they* hadn't gotten the attention instead. Which made her think of Dominick's—or, really, *Greg's*—words: *You're just doing this to capitalize off of what happened to you.*

Was she?

"Spencer? Are you there?"

Spencer cleared her throat and pressed the phone to her ear. "This all sounds wonderful," she said. "B-but I'm wondering. Maybe everyone who contributes could be coauthors, too. I can't accept all that advance money for myself."

Alyssa Bloom chuckled. "You can split up the money however you like."

She gave Spencer some more details, mostly about deadlines and on-sale dates and possible book tours. Spencer barely heard her, her heart was pounding so hard. She probably said "thank you" a hundred times before she hung up. Then she sat quietly on her bed, taking even breaths. She was already thinking of the stories she wanted to include on the pages. She couldn't wait to tell the contributors that they'd profit from this, too. After all they'd been through, they deserved it.

Take that, Ali, she thought with satisfaction. She thought she was so smart with her minions and her video loops and her quick-escape tricks. But here was something wonderful that had happened, and Ali hadn't squelched it. Maybe she *was* losing her touch.

Ping.

She glanced at her phone again, wondering if it was from Ms. Bloom—she'd said she was going to follow up with an email. But it was a Google Alert for "Ashland, PA."

She shot up and looked closer. Google didn't link to the pool house story. Instead, a headline read YOUNG MAN FOUND DEAD BEHIND ASHLAND'S TURKEY HILL MINI-MART.

With shaking hands, Spencer opened the link to a website for the *Ashland Herald*: OFFICIALS FOUND THE BODY OF A YOUNG MAN FACEDOWN AT THE CREEK BED BEHIND THE TURKEY HILL MINI-MART IN SOUTHWEST ASHLAND EARLY THIS MORNING AFTER GETTING A 911 CALL FROM A MAN WALKING HIS DOG. POLICE DESCRIBED THE MAN AS DARK-HAIRED AND DRESSED IN A JACKET, A SHIRT AND TIE, AND WINGTIP SHOES, AND WITH A TATTOO OF A BIRD ON THE BACK OF HIS HAND. A DRIVER'S LICENSE WAS FOUND ON HIM, BUT FAMILY MEMBERS HAVE NOT BEEN REACHED TO IDENTIFY THE BODY. CAUSE OF DEATH IS UNCLEAR.

Spencer was so horrified she threw the phone across the room. A shirt and tie. Wingtips. *A tattoo of a bird on the back of his hand.* It was Greg.

She stood and paced around the room.

What had happened after he left Spencer? Maybe he'd wanted to see Ali in person, finally—and he knew where she'd be. After all, he'd said he was in love with her.

Spencer stopped in her tracks, realizing something huge. Maybe it was *Greg's* blood all over that pool house. It totally made sense. Ali had killed him because Greg had broken a cardinal Ali Cat rule.

Never kiss and tell.

35

THE MASTER PLAN

That morning, Emily sat in her bedroom, the box of Jordan's possessions in front of her on the mattress. She ran her hands over its smooth cardboard sides, then thought about what she was about to do. After she looked at whatever was inside, she was going to tape the box back up and bury it in the backyard. It was just like how she and her friends had buried things that reminded them of Their Ali.

It wasn't that Emily wanted to forget Jordan—not at all. There would be a real funeral for Jordan next week, in New Jersey, and Emily planned on attending. But the funeral would be strange and impersonal: Other people would be at the pulpit, giving speeches about who they thought Jordan was. None of Jordan's family would know Emily; none of them had any idea what Emily and Jordan meant to each other. Emily would merely be another mourner, a stranger. She needed a way to honor Jordan in her own way, right here, all alone, just her. Burying the box just seemed right.

Taking a deep breath, she lifted the lid and removed the Bubble Wrap. A carefully folded T-shirt was on top, followed by a pair of jeans. Emily pulled them out and felt a whoosh of pain, for they still *smelled* like Jordan, even though it was clear they'd been washed. She pressed them to her nose, inhaling again and again. The fabric felt so soft against her skin, as soft as Jordan had been. She ran her fingers along the hem of the jeans, the button at the waist. It was almost too much to handle.

But she kept going. Underneath the jeans, she found the earrings she feared she'd see, little diamond studs Jordan had worn since the first day Emily met her. They were in a plastic Baggie, and Emily was too choked up to even take them out. Below that was a small pouch containing some money, a key card to a Marriott hotel, and a receipt from McDonald's for a six-piece chicken nugget meal and a small Diet Coke.

But it was what was at the very bottom of the box that made her heart stop. There, folded several times, the creases worn, the paper wrinkled as though it had been through the washer a few times, was a drawing Emily had given to Jordan when they were on the cruise. She'd done it on cruise ship stationery, penning a picture of herself and Jordan as stick figures, standing on a boat and holding hands. *Our trip*, she'd written, and then she'd described, in words and pictures, their adventures on the zip line, and the long walk they'd taken on the secluded beach, and the time they'd stolen the boat in Puerto Rico for a joyride around the harbor. Emily had drawn herself and Jordan kissing—their first kiss—adding *Amazing!* and drawing a little heart around the two of them in red pen.

Emily's eyes welled. The little drawing had survived the dive into the harbor. It had survived Jordan's travels south and all her hiding spots. And there was something else, too: a second heart around the red one, a newer one drawn in blue. Jordan must have drawn it after she'd escaped off the boat—the ink didn't seem as faded. Which meant that even after Jordan thought Emily had betrayed her, she'd drawn the heart and carried the drawing with her anyway, not throwing it out. Maybe she, like Emily, knew that someday they'd work everything out.

The tears ran hot down Emily's cheeks, blurring her vision. She cried for a long time, the sobs convulsive but also cathartic. Finally, once she felt drained, she placed everything back in the box except for the drawing Jordan had saved. She taped up the top, then hefted it into her arms and started downstairs.

A pang hit her halfway down. *How* could she say good-bye? How did you let someone like this go? She hated that Ali had done this. But she hoped with all her heart that the cops had actually found some evidence—or Ali herself. And that soon enough, Ali would be behind bars. Somewhere dark. And miserable. And totally hopeless.

Something out the window caught her attention. Aria had pulled up to the curb. Spencer's car was behind hers, and Hanna drove up in her Prius and parked in the driveway. Slowly, the girls got out and stepped toward Emily's front door with all the sobriety of government officials coming to a family's door to tell them that their child had died in an overseas battle.

Emily swallowed hard. None of them had announced they were coming. Had they found out something she hadn't? Was there news about *Ali*?

She placed Jordan's box on the steps and opened the front door before they could ring the bell. "What's going on?" she hissed, stepping onto the porch and shutting the door behind her. Her parents were in the den; the last thing she needed was for them to listen in. They'd already asked her a ton of questions about all the stuff barricading the doors this morning. "What happened? It's the pool house, isn't it? Did they find Ali?"

"Slow down." Spencer caught Emily's arm. "We haven't heard anything. We thought you might have."

Emily stopped and peered at them. *"Nothing?"*

"Aside from Greg turning up dead at a creek," Spencer said. "Which was probably Ali's doing. He told me he knew her, and that was a big mistake. So she killed him."

Emily's stomach swooped. "Do you think it was his blood in the house?"

"I don't know. Maybe." Spencer stared down the street. Emily's next-door neighbors, an older couple named the Gauls, were hard at work setting up sprinklers on their front lawn. When they saw the girls, they waved. Everyone waved back, though not nearly as enthusiastically.

"But we haven't heard anything about the pool house investigation," Aria continued. "I even tried calling the local police station, but when someone asked my name, I hung up." Then she looked at the plastic bag in her hands. "I don't know what to do with this." She opened it a little; Emily could see the crumpled dress they'd pulled out of the house the night before. "Drop it off anonymously at the police station? Burn it?"

"Do you think we should go up there?" Emily asked. "What if they have Ali under arrest? What if she's caught and they haven't even told us?" *That would be just like Fuji*, she thought bitterly.

Spencer shook her head. "The place is probably crawling with cops—us being there would complicate things. We'll know soon enough. But I feel really positive, you know? I feel like this could be it. And now we can go on with our lives for real."

Emily bit her lip. Tears rushed to her eyes. She had been about to *bury* her life. She couldn't imagine blithely moving forward.

A siren wailed down the street, and everyone looked up. Seconds later, a police car appeared from around the corner and began to roll toward them. It was followed by a second police car, then a third. Emily took a quivering step back, momentarily frozen in the lights. Then she realized who was in the front seat of the first car.

Fuji.

The cop cars rolled up to the curb in front of Emily's house and came to a stop. Agent Fuji, dressed in a crisp black suit and sunglasses, stepped out of the vehicle and strode toward them. The agent's face was stern and hard as she approached the girls. She came to a stop and looked around at all of them. A few beats passed. Behind her, Emily heard her front door open. She knew without looking that her mom was standing there, staring.

"We need to speak to you," Fuji said in a gruff voice.

"Of course," Spencer said quickly. "Whatever we can do to help."

"This is about the pool house, right?" Hanna asked excitedly. "What did you find?"

Fuji winced. She reached into her pocket and whipped out a ziplock bag marked EVIDENCE and shoved it in the girls' faces. "We found this."

The bag shook before Emily's eyes. Slowly, her vision adjusted. Something pearly and white and tipped in blood was caught in the bag's corner. Emily frowned, then backed up. A *tooth*.

"Whose is that?" Aria cried.

Fuji removed her sunglasses and stared at them hard. There was no kindness in her eyes, which surprised Emily. Fuji should be grateful, shouldn't she? "I think you know whose it is, girls. What *I* want to know is: Where's the rest of the body?"

Everyone flinched. Emily's heart began to pound.

"The rest of *what* body?" Hanna asked.

"Isn't Greg's body by the creek bed?" Spencer piped up.

Fuji pressed her hand to her brow. "We know what you've been doing in Ashland, girls. We have witnesses attesting to you skulking around up there. Testimonies about the questions you've been asking neighbors and people at the mini-mart. And then we found your surveillance equipment. Saw your shoddy cleanup job for ourselves. Found your prints all over the house."

Fuji's words made sense to Emily individually, but not as a whole. She couldn't even comprehend what the agent was saying. "Wait," she blurted. "Our *cleanup job*? What do you mean?"

"You obviously did something last night, and then tried to clean it up. Badly, I might add." Fuji scowled. "Throwing bleach haphazardly on the floor doesn't eradicate blood, ladies."

Bleach? Emily's heart stopped.

"*We* didn't clean that up!" Spencer cried, getting it, too. "Someone else did! We were there, in the house, on the second floor. We heard everything, but we were too afraid to look and see who it was."

"It's true," Emily said. "It was our surveillance equipment—we were spying, but it was in hopes of catching Ali. But we didn't do *anything* in that house. We didn't hurt anyone; we didn't clean anything. We just happened to *be* there."

"Are you sure about that, Emily?" Fuji's gaze was

unblinking. "So then you didn't go up there yourself and trash the place a few days before, and then make a threat that you were going to *kill* someone if she ever returned?"

Emily could feel her friends staring at her. Her cheeks started to burn.

"What's she talking about?" Spencer demanded.

"When did you say that?" Aria hissed.

"Emily, what's going on?" Emily's mother said behind her.

"The surveillance cameras store the last seven days of data," Fuji said, a whisper of a smile on her face. "Three of them we found were smashed, but the fourth—the one that showed the inside of the house—was still intact, though no longer recording. We watched that video of you, Emily. Watched you tear things off the wall, smash anything in sight. Your prints were all over the cameras, too. We knew they were yours before you told us."

"I . . ." Emily trailed off. She had no idea what to say. She *had* trashed the house. That awful day, after Jordan died, when she'd gone up there—she'd said all *kinds* of things. But . . .

She shook her head. "Okay. *Okay*. But we didn't . . . *kill* anyone. It was *Alison*. I swear."

"That's impossible!" Fuji fumed. Her face was bright red. "The neighbors say they heard screams. Then came that call—from *you*. And what's this about the boy at the creek bed?" She narrowed her eyes. "How did you know about that?"

Spencer's chin wobbled. "I—I saw it on the news site."

But Fuji looked furious. Emily's mind continued to unfurl. What the hell was happening? Why did she suddenly feel so . . . accused?

"And then, girls, we found the diary," Fuji went on. "Of all the things you did to her. All the *torture*. We found everything listed there. The knives. The chains. The ropes. The pliers and other tools." She shook her head, disgusted. "And you thought you were going to get away with this?"

"What are you talking about?" Hanna cried.

Fuji gnashed her teeth together. "Yes, you were right about one thing—Alison *was* alive. She must have survived the fire in the Poconos, just like you said. But don't play dumb about everything else. I am *sick* of it, okay?"

"What do you mean, *was* alive?" Aria asked in a quavering voice, tears running down her cheeks. And then, slowly, she looked down at the plastic bag she was holding. Fuji followed her gaze. The bag was open just slightly, blood smeared on the plastic. Fuji's eyes widened.

Aria shut the bag tight, but it was already too late. Fuji had seen. And now, Emily knew, the agent was assuming all kinds of things. Things that weren't true.

Veins popped out on Fuji's neck. She glanced over her shoulder, indicating that the other waiting agents close in. "Because that's *her* blood all over that pool house. And this is her tooth. And we know you are responsible."

"Us?" Emily's jaw trembled. "F-for what?"

She already knew the answer a split second before it came. The methods were clear, the strategy so precise and cunning and subtle it left her breathless. The pool house. The camera loop. Getting them all up to Ashland at that exact moment, waiting until they were upstairs and terrified. Messily cleaning up with the bleach, the bucket, the mop. And then that *tooth*.

Ali had set them up. *Spectacularly.*

Fuji rolled her eyes and said just what Emily feared. "You *know*, Miss Fields. For Alison's murder."

ACKNOWLEDGMENTS

Many thanks, as usual, to my stellar team at Alloy, including Josh Bank, Les Morgenstein, Sara Shandler, Lanie Davis, and Katie McGee—without you this book wouldn't be nearly as compelling (nor would I know what it means to "White Fang" someone). Thanks to Kristin Marang and Theodora Guliadis in Alloy Digital for all their smart ideas to garner even more PLL fans. A huge thank-you to Kari Sutherland, Sarah Landis, and Alice Jerman at Harper for their smart insights and never-ending support. My usual gratitude to the amazing writers, producers, and actors on *Pretty Little Liars* on ABC Family: I draw inspiration from you guys, and sometimes it is incredibly frustrating NOT to use your plot lines in the books!

Thanks as well to my parents, Bob and Mindy Shepard; to Ali and Caron, who opened their lovely Upper East Side home to us several times during the brainstorming process for this book (and who wrangled a certain Bumby during meetings!); and love to Michael, for many things including being patient and understanding about ice cream. Thanks to the many fans on Twitter and to all those who answer my random questions when I throw them into the Twitterverse. And of course a big hug to Kristian, who is the best little man ever. *Choo choo!*

Also, this book is dedicated to Volvo, my loyal friend. For drooling on me through a cross-country move, a cross-town move, and then a cross-state move; for being my longtime running partner, a reliable vacuum cleaner, and a steady guardian. Always smelly, always sneaking onto a bed, and always the most-loved at parties, you're the best dog anyone could ask for. Now go outside and catch some squirrels.

Vicious

Have you ever dreamed about starting a new life? Running away from your school, your town, your home, even your family and friends, and starting over somewhere else. Changing how you look, what you like, who you *are*. In a new place, you'd have no baggage. Your past and your future would be a blank canvas. Of course, you'd also no longer be *you*, and that might mess with your head. And it would suck to have the people back home *worry* about you, going so far as to, say, put your face on a milk carton. Which is why it's just a fantasy.

But for one manipulative girl from Rosewood, it isn't a fantasy. It's survival. And to her four enemies, it might mean the end of their pretty little lives–*forever*.

YOU DON'T HAVE TO BE GOOD TO BE PERFECT.

Read on for a sneak peek at Sara Shephard's next series

The Perfectionists

IN MANY WAYS, BEACON HEIGHTS, Washington, looks like any affluent suburb: Porch swings creak gently in the evening breeze, the lawns are green and well kept, and all the neighbors know one another. But this satellite of Seattle is anything but average. In Beacon, it's not enough to be good; you have to be the *best*.

With perfection comes pressure. Students here are some of the best in the country, and sometimes, they have to let off a little steam. What five girls don't know, though, is that steam can scald just as badly as an open flame.

And someone's about to get burned.

On Friday night, just as the sun was setting, cars began to pull up to Nolan Hotchkiss's huge, faux-Italian villa on a peninsula overlooking Lake Washington. The house had wrought iron gates, a circular driveway with a marble fountain, multiple balconies, and a three-tiered, crystal chandelier visible through the front two-story window. All the lights were on, loud bass thumped from inside, a cheer rose up from the backyard. Kids with liquor spirited from their parents' cabinets or bottles of wine shoved into their purses sauntered up to the front steps and walked right inside. No need to ring the bell—Mr. and Mrs. Hotchkiss weren't home.

Too bad. They were missing the biggest party of the year.

Caitlin Martell-Lewis, dressed in her best pair of straight-leg jeans, a green polo that brought out the amber flecks in her eyes, and TOMS houndstooth sneakers, climbed out of an Escalade with her boyfriend, Josh Friday, and his soccer friends Asher Collins and Timothy Burgess. Josh, whose breath already smelled yeasty from the beer he'd drunk at the pregame party, shaded his brown eyes and gaped at the mansion. "This place is freaking sick."

Ursula Winters, who desperately wanted to be Timothy's girlfriend—she was also Caitlin's biggest soccer rival—stepped out of the backseat and adjusted her oversize, dolman-sleeve shirt. "The kid has it all."

"Except a soul," Caitlin muttered, limping up the lawn on her still-sore-from-a-soccer-injury ankle. Silence fell over the group as they stepped inside the grand foyer, with its checkerboard floor and a sweeping double staircase. Josh cast her a sideways glance. "What? I was kidding," Caitlin said with a laugh.

Because if you spoke out against Nolan—if you so much as boycotted his party—you'd be off the Beacon Heights High A-list. But Nolan had as many enemies as friends, and Caitlin hated him most of all. Her heart pounded, thinking about the secret thing she was about to do. She wondered whether the others were there yet.

The den was filled with candles and fat red cushions. Julie Redding held court in the middle of the room. Her auburn hair hung straight and shiny down her back. She wore a strapless Kate Spade dress and bone-colored high heels that showed off her long, lithe legs. One after another, classmates walked up to her and complimented her outfit, her white teeth, her amazing jewelry, that funny thing she'd said in English class the other day. It was par for the course, naturally—everyone *always* loved Julie. She was the most popular girl in school.

Then Ashley Ferguson, a junior who'd just dyed her hair the same auburn shade as Julie's, stopped and gave a reverent smile. "You look amazing," she gushed, same as the others.

"Thank you," Julie said modestly.

"Where'd you get the dress?" Ashley asked.

Julie's friend Nyssa Frankel inserted herself between the

two. "Why, Ashley?" she snapped. "Are you going to buy the exact same one?"

Julie laughed as Nyssa and Natalie Houma, another of Julie's friends, high-fived. Ashley set her jaw and stomped away. Julie bit her lip, wondering if she'd been too mean. There was only one person she wanted to be mean to deliberately tonight.

And that was Nolan.

Meanwhile, Ava Jalali stood with her boyfriend, Alex Cohen, in the Hotchkisses' reclaimed oak and marble kitchen, nibbling on a carrot stick. She eyed a tower of cupcakes next to the veggie tray longingly. "Remind me why I decided to do a cleanse again?"

"Because you're insane?" Alex raised his eyebrows mischievously.

Ava gave him an *uh-duh* look and pushed her smooth, straight, perfect dark hair out of her eyes. She was the type of girl who hated even looking at cross sections of the human body in biology class; she couldn't stand the idea that *she* was that ugly and messy inside.

Alex swiped his thumb on the icing and brought his hand toward Ava's face. "Yummy . . ."

Ava drew back. "Get that away!" But then she giggled. Alex had moved here in ninth grade. He wasn't as popular or as rich as some of the other guys, but he always made her laugh. But then the sight of someone in the doorway wiped the smile off her face. Nolan Hotchkiss, the party's host, stared at her with an almost territorial grin.

He deserves what he's going to get, she thought darkly.

In the backyard—which had high, swooping arcades that connected one patio to another; huge potted plants; and a long slate walkway that practically ended in the water— Mackenzie Wright rolled up her jeans, removed her toe rings, and plunked her feet into the infinity-edge pool. A lot of people were swimming, including her best friend, Claire Coldwell, and Claire's boyfriend, Blake Strustek.

Blake spun Claire around and laced his fingers through hers. "Hey, watch the digits," Claire warned. "They're my ticket to Juilliard."

Blake glanced at Mac and rolled his eyes. Mac looked away, almost as if she didn't like Blake at all.

Or perhaps because she liked him *too* much.

Then the patio door opened, and Nolan Hotchkiss, the man of the hour, sauntered onto the lawn with a smug, *I'm-the-lord-of-this-party* look on his face. He strolled to two boys and bumped fists. After a beat, they glanced Mac's way and started whispering.

Mac sucked in her stomach, feeling their gazes canvass her snub nose, her glasses with their dark hipster frames, and her large, chunky knit scarf. She knew what they were talking about. Her hatred for Nolan flared up all over again.

Beep.

Her phone, which sat next to her on the tiled ground, lit up. Mac glanced at the text from her new friend Caitlin Martell-Lewis.

It's time.

Julie and Ava received the same missives. Like robots, they all stood, excused themselves, and walked to the rendezvous point. Empty cups lay on the ground in the hall. There was a cupcake smashed on the kitchen wall, and the den smelled distinctly of pot. The girls convened by the stairs and exchanged long, nervous glances.

Caitlin cleared her throat. "So."

Ava pursed her full lips and glanced at her reflection in the enormous mirror. Caitlin rolled back her shoulders and felt for something in her purse. It rattled slightly. Mac checked her own bag to make sure the camera she'd swiped from her mom's desk was still inside.

Then Julie's gaze fixed on a figure hovering in the doorway. It was Parker Duvall, her best friend in the world. She'd *come*, just as Julie hoped she would. As usual, Parker wore a short denim skirt, black lace tights, and an oversize black sweatshirt. When she saw Julie, she poked her face out from the hood, a wide grin spreading across her cheeks and illuminating her scars. Julie tried not to gasp, but it was so rare that Parker allowed anyone to see her face.

Parker rushed up to the girls, pulling the hoodie around her face once more.

All five of them glanced around to see if anyone was watching. "I can't believe we're doing this," Mackenzie admitted.

Caitlin's eyebrows made a V. "You're not backing out, are you?"

Mac shook her head quickly. "Of course not."

"Good." Caitlin glanced at the others. "Are we all still in?"

Parker nodded. After a moment, Julie said yes, too. And Ava, who was touching up her lip gloss, gave a single, decisive nod.

Their gazes turned to Nolan as he wove through the living room. He greeted kids heartily. Slapped friends on the back. Shot a winning smile to a girl who looked like a freshman, and the girl's eyes widened with shock. Whispered something to a different girl, and her face fell just as quickly.

That was the kind of power Nolan Hotchkiss had over people. He was *the* most popular guy at school—handsome, athletic, charming, the head of every committee and club he joined. His family was the wealthiest, too—you couldn't go a mile without seeing the name *Hotchkiss* on one of the new developments popping up or turn a page in the news-paper without seeing Nolan's state senator mother cutting a ribbon at a new bakery, day care facility, community park,

7

or library. More than that, there was something about him that basically . . . *hypnotized* you. One look, one suggestion, one command, one snarky remark, one blow-off, one public embarrassment, and you were under his thumb for life. Nolan controlled Beacon, whether you liked it or not. But what's that saying? "Absolute power corrupts absolutely." And for all the people who worshipped Nolan, there were those who couldn't stand him, too. Who wanted him . . . *gone*, in fact.

The girls looked at one another and smiled. "All right, then," Ava said, stepping out into the crowd, toward Nolan. "Let's do this."

Like any good party, the bash at the Hotchkiss house lingered into the wee hours of the morning. Leave it to Nolan to have an in with the cops, because no one raided the place for booze or even told them to cut the noise. Shortly after midnight, some party pics were posted online: two girls kissing in the powder room; the school's biggest prude doing a body shot off the star running back's chest; one of the stoners grinning sloppily, holding several cupcakes aloft; and the party's host passed out on a Lovesac beanbag upstairs with something Sharpied on his face. Partying hard was Nolan's specialty, after all.

Revelers passed out on the outdoor couch, on the hammock that hung between two big birch trees at the back of the property, and in zigzag shapes on the floor. For several hours, the house was still, the cupcake icing slowly hardening, a tipped-over bottle of wine pooling in the sink, a raccoon digging through some of the trash bags that had been left out in the backyard. Not everyone awoke when the boy screamed. Not even when that same someone—a junior named Miro—ran down the stairs and screamed what had happened to the 911 dispatcher did all the kids stir.

It was only when the ambulances screeched into the driveway, sirens blaring, lights flashing, walkie-talkies crackling, that all eyes opened. The first thing everyone saw were EMT workers in their reflective jackets busting inside. Miro pointed them to the upper floor. There were boots on the stairs, and then . . . those same EMT people carrying someone back down. Someone who had Sharpie marker on his face. Someone who was limp and gray.

The EMT worker spoke into his radio. "We have an eighteen-year-old male DOA."

Was that Nolan? everyone would whisper in horror as they staggered out of the house, horrifically hungover. *And . . . DOA? Dead on arrival?*

By Saturday afternoon, the news was everywhere. The Hotchkiss parents returned from their business meeting in Los Angeles that evening to do damage control, but it was too late—the whole town knew that Nolan Hotchkiss had dropped dead at his party, probably from too much fun. Darker rumors posited that perhaps he'd *meant* to do it.

Beacon was notoriously hard on its offspring, after all, and maybe even golden boy Nolan Hotchkiss had felt the heat.

When Julie woke up Saturday morning and heard the news, her throat closed. Ava picked up the phone three times before talking herself down. Mac stared into space for a long, long time, then burst into hot, quiet tears. And Caitlin, who'd wanted Nolan dead for so long, couldn't help but feel sorry for his family, even though he had destroyed hers. And Parker? She went to the dock and stared at the water, her face hidden under her hoodie. Her head pounded with an oncoming migraine.

They called one another and spoke in heated whispers. They felt terrible, but they were smart girls. Logical girls. Nolan Hotchkiss was gone; the dictator of Beacon Heights High was no more. That meant no more tears. No more bullying. No more living in fear that he'd expose everyone's awful secrets—somehow, he'd known so many. And anyway, not a single person had seen them go upstairs with Nolan that night—they'd made sure of it. No one would ever connect them to him.

The problem, though, was that someone had seen. Someone knew what they'd done that night, and so much more.

And someone was going to make them pay.

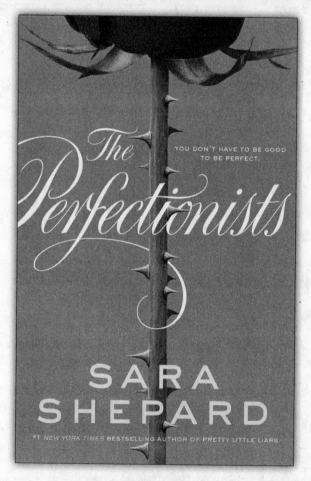

Don't miss a single scandal!

EVERYONE IN ULTRA-EXCLUSIVE ROSEWOOD,
PENNSYLVANIA, HAS SOMETHING TO HIDE . . .

   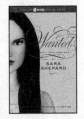

DISCUSS THE BOOKS AND THE HIT TV SHOW AT
WWW.PRETTYLITTLELIARS.COM.

An Imprint of HarperCollinsPublishers